# THE PUCKABLE PLAYBOOK

WARNER UNIVERSITY BULLDOGS
BOOK 3

E. M. MOORE

*For my husband, Tommy, who always supports me. As of the publication of this book, we will have been married for 17 years and 1 day and not one day has gone by that you were not my biggest fan. No words could thank you enough.*

Manufactured in the United States of America
First Edition July 2024

Edited by Chinah Mercer of The Editor & the Quill, LLC

Cover by 2nd Life Designs

Huge thanks to my beta readers, Jennifer, Sam, and Jorden!

Foul Line

At the Buzzer

## Rockstars of Hollywood Hill

Rock On

## Spring Hill Blue Series

Free Fall

Catch Me

## Ravana Clan Vampires Series

Chosen By Darkness

Into the Darkness

Falling For Darkness

Surrender To Darkness

## Coveted by the Dark

Thirst For Her

Ache For Her

## Order of the Akasha Series

Stripped (Prequel)

Summoned By Magic

Tempted By Magic

Ravished By Magic

Indulged By Magic

Enraged By Magic

**Safe Haven Academy Series**

A Sky So Dark

A Dawn So Quiet

# CHAPTER ONE

## Len

THE WARNER NEWSROOM BUZZES WITH electricity, alive with ideas, creativity, and the spark of the next best thing. The muted sounds of barely audible typing mix with low conversations about different stories, and my skin's about to jump off my bones because I'm sitting next to Clark Davis...and our knees are touching.

*Go to press...our knees are freaking touching.*

His mouth moves while I stare at his profile: the adorable black ink smudge on his cheek that he probably doesn't even know is there calls to me like a lighthouse beacon; the day-old stubble haphazardly growing in different directions; the way his black-frame glasses slip down his nose. He uses his pointer finger to push them back up, then peers over at me...and I nearly have a heart attack. He is *so* perfect.

Quickly changing the direction of my stare, I focus on the layout he's started for the next edition of the Warner Gazette.

*This is important*, I remind myself. The adorable ink smudge can wait. My unrequited crush on him can wait. The way he looks like Clark Kent—literally— right before he turns into Superman will still be there while we hammer out this layout. I am a professional, for crying out loud.

"What do you think?" he asks.

I blink. Of its own accord, my mouth moves, but not a single sound comes out. My brain works, trying to think of one thing he showed me while I drooled over him, but I have nothing. The fact that I'm such a spaz in moments like this is mind-bogglingly embarrassing, and honestly, the story of my life.

Ninety-nine point eight percent of the time, I am a level-headed, abysmally normal person. The moment he walks into the room, I act like a Netflix junkie on a fluff binge who spends her free time staring at walls.

I give him a grin that I hope appears cute, but more than likely struggles to be this side of passably sane. "Sorry, Clark. Would you mind explaining again?"

His jaw twitches, and my gaze focuses there like a love-seeking missile. What does that mean? Is he mad? Does he think I'm an imbecile? Heck, I'd take frustrat- ingly endearing right now.

Fixing my glasses back to their rightful position, I turn toward the screen while Clark talks me through his thought process again. I listen to his layout choices, and I'm glad I paid attention this time because there are minor tweaks he should take into account before finalizing. Gesturing at the layout, I point them out, then shrug. At least my words come out intelligent enough.

He stands, squeezing my shoulder. "You're a godsend, Lenore. I've been..."

*Staring at this all day.* Yeah, I know.

An internal, contented sigh accompanies the glazing over of my eyes. I could repeat his spiel back to him—I've heard it so many times—but I'm too busy studying his perfectly pink lips. What would he do if I kissed him? Right here, right now. Stood up with him and sealed my lips to that flawless cupid's bow.

He pats my back, jarring me out of my reverie, and then hurries off to his workspace on the opposite end of the room. Since we work with each other a lot, I've always wondered why he doesn't move closer. The resounding thought is that he wants to kiss me too and sitting so close would only tease him. We are at work, after all. Both über-professional newspeople, so staying away is for our own benefit.

When I'm having a bad day, though, it's because I have stinky cheese breath that roils his stomach every time he's near.

I'll never know which it is because, besides the possible cheese breath, I'm also a certified chicken. No way on this Earth would I ever approach Clark with my fantasies.

Moving my attention to my own laptop, I stare at

my Word doc for a bit before getting back into the groove of the article I'm writing about the Warner clock tower. The clock hasn't worked in years, yet it's a Warner staple. Upperclassmen use the never-moving hands to trick younger classmen into being late to classes. Stately pictures of it stand out among clouds and a blue sky on all the Warner University brochures. Symbolically, it's right up there with our Bulldog statue in the quad.

Recently, however, the college board has proposed to actually fix the clock in a massive undertaking. The student body instantly divided into two camps: one that wants the repairs, and one that is very vocal about keeping the nostalgic, broken timepiece what it always has been.

Rumors abound as to why it stopped working in the first place. One particularly macabre story has lived on longer than most. In a fit of jealous rage, an under-grad climbed to the top of the tower on a dark and stormy night. With thunder rolling all around her, she called out one last time for her unfaithful love before diving to her death.

There are also less tragic stories, like it was hit by a single bolt of lightning on a clear day. Though, I tend to think that theory took hold in the 80s when *Back to the Future* released.

Since no one on the board can tell me why it stopped working, I need to research the exact reason. A significant historical fact might help sway the interested parties one way or the other—keep the wistful marker as is or fix the "embarrassment."

Their words, not mine.

Like any other quality reporter, I'm only here to record the facts. A good story backed by truth can at least give everyone the same knowledge to base their decisions off of with confidence.

Unfortunately, the story of this clock tower is slippery at best. Nailing down the actual reason it ceased to tell time is proving to test my research skills, and I need this information before going to print on this article.

"You look better."

I peer up from my screen. Kitty-corner from me, across the white table that spans the length of the newsroom, sits Flora, my work buddy. Her curious gaze traces over my face.

Warmth creeps up my cheeks. "Finally. The roommate from hell moved out, so I can sleep."

She opens her slim, silver laptop. "Any word about a new one?"

I roll my eyes. "You know, being a senior should come with perks, and one of them should be that I'm not utilized as a test subject for the TV pilot of *My Crazy Roommate*."

Flora lifts her brows while still clicking away at her keyboard. Me and roommates never seem to work out, and I'm praying Housing will take pity on me and let me live out the rest of my senior year in peace. Unfortunately, that probably won't be the case since I live in a highly sought-after dorm on campus. A two-person suite, attached, private bathrooms, with the living room and kitchen the lone communal spaces.

My last roommate turned our shared spaces into a hippie haven, which prompted me to write an extensive article on cannabis use on campus. Needless to say, we didn't jive at all. Luckily, she got kicked from the dorm because she stopped going to classes altogether.

If my roommate history is any indication, I'm a magnet for eccentric personalities who think college is a hobby at best.

"I can't wait to hear the next chapter in *Roommate Woes*." Flora drops the name she coined my roommate horror stories and smiles. Woes is too romantic for the shit shows I've been dealing with, but she's had the same roommate since her freshman year, so it's likely she'll never have to experience the true depth of what I've had to endure. I'm glad for her. Despite being my only confidant, the raven-haired junior with the penchant for dark clothing has been my ally in the newsroom on more than one occasion. She's smart, crafty, and she doesn't type too loud, so I like her.

After another few minutes of staring at the blinking cursor on my screen, I close my laptop and shove it in my bag. It's evident I'll have to have another go at the campus library, and if I can't find my answer there, I'll move on to Warner's town library, and then the county library if I have to. I'm wasting precious time by not having this one fact.

"Going so—" Flora cuts herself off, her stare landing behind me. "Man crush, nine o'clock," she singsongs.

"What?" I push my glasses up again, peering at her.

Clark's voice sounds behind me. "Oh, are you leaving?"

My heart immediately takes off. I fist the straps of my bag before turning. "L-library," I stammer. Closing my eyes briefly, I take a deep breath to attempt to calm my crazy, out-of-control heartbeat. "Why? Did you...need me?"

For a split second, my brain switches to full-on porno territory.

*"Did you...need me?"*

*He did. He absolutely needed her. The pulsing of his engorged cock hammered out a rhythm of need only she could satisfy.*

*He stepped close, forcing her back against the desk while he rolled her pencil skirt up, finding her pantie-less and wet.*

*"Are you my dirty little reporter? Is all this for me?"*

*"Y-yes."*

*In a slow, methodical way that intensified her anticipation, he lowered the zipper on his jeans and—*

I shake my head, my skin flushing with heat. I hate when I go 80s erotica. I can imagine the red painting my cheeks right now as I push away thoughts of his *engorged cock.*

7

Clark has a nice cock, I'm sure. A perfectly adequate penis for lovemaking.

"Are you okay, Len?" Flora's voice filters through my lust-filled brain. "Clark asked how you were doing on your assignment."

"Fine," I force out between two buzzing lips. "Great, actually. Just trying to nail down a fact, and it'll be good. Perfect. Really, really perfect."

My gaze lands on his ink smudge, and my heart flutters. Perfections in the imperfections.

*I could lick that ink smudge off his cheek right now—*

*Pull yourself together, woman. You are a professional.*

Clark taps a pen onto the notepad he's holding. "Do you know when your piece will be done?"

"Um, next week." The answer comes out of my mouth as a statement rather than a question. Next week? *Next week?* What the fuck am I thinking?

"That would be perfect," he exclaims, and for a split second, I don't care that I've put a ridiculous time-line on myself if I've caused him to smile like that. "I look forward to seeing it."

"Great. Good. I look forward to you reading it...in the near future." The *too* near future.

Clark nods, taking his ink smudge and cupid's bow with him.

Before I can even break down what happened, Flora snickers. I turn to her, cringing.

"You've got it bad. It's a shame he takes advantage of you."

I recoil. "What? No." My brain flicks to my erotic image, but I force it away. *That's not the kind of scenario she's talking about.*

Flora gives me a look, her fingers still moving over the keyboard. It's a trick of all reporters to be able to type while carrying on detailed conversations, yet Flora has also added a pointed look that says "*Sure, you keep thinking that.*"

My entire being balks. "Clark is smart and talented. Plus, he's the editor."

She continues to work but lowers her voice. "Clark wouldn't be so smart or so talented if he wasn't over here asking what you would do all the time."

"We bounce ideas off each other."

"If by 'bounce ideas off each other,' you mean you give him the ideas that make him look good, then sure, that's exactly what you do."

I roll my eyes. She doesn't know what she's talking about. She hasn't worked as closely with Clark as I have. He's a genius. His words are like crack. In a time when people could get all their news from television or a Google search, our college-run newspaper is thriving. It's amazing, and no one will be able to convince me that it's not in part due to Clark Davis. My pre-Superman.

*Sigh.*

Flora shrugs, as if she can hear the inner workings of my mind and is brushing them off. I like the girl, but yeesh. She'll see next year when some other editor takes over and this place isn't run nearly as well. I've worked side by side with Clark for four years. I think I know.

"See you tomorrow?"

"I'll be here," she says, gaze focusing on her screen.

I give her a wave that she doesn't see, and then I skirt around the long table and exit out the glass double doors. While walking away, I stare inside the newsroom for one last glance at Clark. It's easy to do since the entire wall of the hallway is glass so the student body walking by can see us working inside.

Being on display was a little unnerving at first, but I don't even notice it now. Plus, it's smart. As reporters, we have to be in the midst of things. We can't sequester ourselves away from the world with our narrow focus on the blinking cursor mocking us. No, we have to go out there, *be* out there.

Also, it's nice to sneak glances at Clark.

His brow furrows while he stares at his screen. That look of concentration is sexy as hell. He's—

I slam into something large and solid. My feet freeze in place, and I peer up at a towering body, an apology on the tip of my tongue. However, it dies in my throat when I meet familiar eyes. Isaiah. Isaiah James. I swallow the sudden dryness, a whirlwind of memories washing over me.

Even though I haven't seen him in a while, his smile still disarms me. "Hey, Nor."

He's still broad shouldered and effortlessly good

looking with soft-brown eyes and caramel-colored hair. Plus, the charm. It oozes off him even when he doesn't talk.

For a moment, I get caught up in him, but then his words chisel past the initial shock and right into my brain. No one has called me Nor since *her*—and only ever her...and by extension, him. She thought Len sounded too masculine, and I despise my full name, so we compromised on Nor.

Well, actually, the one doing the compromising was me. I understand that now.

But the worst part is the memories that claw to the surface from the hollow dip in my stomach that I tried so hard to forget. He opens his mouth to say something again, but I cut him off. "Hi, I'm actually going somewhere." I maneuver around him and start walking once more, trying to steady my feet underneath me.

Instead of leaving it at that, he steps in line with me, keeping pace. "I was hoping to talk to you about something."

Yes, and I'm sure that *something* is a five-foot-seven, leggy blonde who I used to call a best friend. "Listen, I don't know where Trish is, okay?"

Images flit through my mind, and every one of them makes me feel small. Like my world is turning in on itself.

"Trish?"

Oh, please. Why the feigned shock? What else would he want to talk to me about except his ex-girlfriend who's also my ex-best friend?

Isaiah James and I are not friends. We're barely acquaintances. We were tethered together by an unfortunate excuse for a human being, and we have the scars to prove it.

I pick up the pace, and it takes me a few moments to realize he's not walking next to me anymore. A sigh punctuates the relief that brings me. The last thing I need to worry about when I just told my editor I'd have my article done by next week is old feelings popping up.

No, my ex-best friend's ex-boyfriend needs to stay wherever he's been hiding for the last several months because I can't take the reminders of them.

# CHAPTER TWO

Zaiah

M<small>Y SHOULDERS DEFLATE AS</small> N<small>OR WALKS AWAY</small>, hiking her purple laptop bag up, her blonde hair swinging behind her.

The reminder of Trish was a quick blow, rotting the contents of my stomach. Memories of her are like an anchor snagged on a boulder that's bolted to the bottom of an unforgiving ocean. Some days, I think I've cut the tether. Others, the line tightens stronger than ever.

That feeling, coupled with the one lifeline I had walking away, sends a surge of frustration the size of a gnarly defenseman through my limbs. Nor has never been anything but nice to me. Always had a smile on her face. But that right there? I don't know what that was.

Nothing is going my way lately.

"Z," my friend calls out.

Turning, I spy Adam, the other winger, over the heads of several students who pass between us while they head to class. He stands underneath a huge Warner football banner, putting an exclamation point on my dark mood.

I glower in his direction.

He lifts a brow. "Who was that and why does she hate you?"

Making my way back toward him, I slow so he can fall in step beside me. "Nor."

"Never heard of her."

"Yes, you have," I grumble.

"Is she some puck bunny?"

I nearly choke. As I recall, Nor was far from a rink girl. She's not the type. In fact, I don't remember her liking hockey at all, but that aside, what world is he living in? "You're delusional."

"Oh, I forgot." He rolls his eyes. "Girls are dead to you."

"Have you also forgotten we don't have puck bunnies? We have a smattering of jailbait, senior-citizen groupies, and family members."

"Aw, don't sell yourself short." Adam peers up and catches the attention of a brunette passing by. "Hey, do you know who he is?"

He hikes his thumb at me, and the girl looks me over, gaze narrowing. "Should I?"

I glare at him, then turn toward her. "Who's your favorite athlete on campus?"

She blushes, the pink reaching all the way into her hairline. "The Hulk."

The Hulk, a.k.a. West Brooks, celebrated *football player*.

I push Adam forward, and he chuckles, calling back, "You know he has a girlfriend."

"Don't remind me," she huffs.

"If you ever want to watch a real sport, you—"

I hit him in the chest with the back of my hand, and he coughs, unable to finish his sentence. "Cut your losses," I advise.

He rubs his chest. "I was doing promo."

"By starting a war with the football team?"

He grins. "Everyone knows hockey is the superior sport." Gazing around, he latches onto another female student. "Hey, do you know who he is?"

I push him forward before she can answer. "Don't mind him. Hit in the head too many times."

Adam laughs, drawing the attention of those nearby. "All those years playing goalie in peewee."

"You were supposed to block the puck, not eat it."

"I was defending the net by any means necessary, even taking shots to the helmet. Which, by the way, hurt like a bitch, and that's why I moved to winger."

"Yeah, yeah."

"They used to call me 'The Adam Bomb.' Get it?"

I wipe a hand down my face. When I peer over at him again, he's peering forward with a slight smile. Discreetly, I take my phone out of my pocket and snap a pic before sending it to the teammate group chat with the caption: **The Adam Bomb.**

The first ping comes before I can even get my phone back in my pocket. Then another and another. Adam pulls out his cell while I try to keep a straight face.

"Breach of trust," he chuckles out, then turns his phone to me, showing off all the bomb GIFs coming through. Sweeney even texts a pic with the infamous mushroom cloud with an arrow labeled The Adam Bomb that points to a tiny cartoon explosive in the corner.

I turn Adam's phone back toward him so he can see it. He clutches his chest, laughing, and quickly types a reply into the chat.

The hockey team might play the least popular sport on campus, but at least we've got each other.

"So..."

I peer over at Adam, who's looking at me expectantly. "So?"

He shakes his head. "The girl. You're not going to tell me who she is?"

I shrug, mind working on how I can approach her again.

"Come on. Am I supposed to believe you stopped dead in the middle of the hallway, watched a random girl appear out of those glass doors, and took off after her if you have no interest?"

"Getting with girls isn't the only reason you run after them."

"In my experience, that's completely false."

Chuckling, I shake my head. His words serve to remind me that I'm in a vastly different space than my teammates right now. Hell, most college guys. "Nor and I are more like friends."

Adam pushes the exit doors open. The rush of cool winter air zaps at my lungs. Years of hanging out in chilly ice arenas has made me immune to the cold, though.

"I know all your friends," Adam scoffs. "They're big, tall, and skate around on the ice. Some of them are assholes."

"Fine," I admit. "She's Trish's friend."

Adam smacks me in the chest, a cloudy look taking his face hostage.

"Who just so happens to have a room at Knightley," I explain.

"The roommate debacle *again*?"

"Dude, I can't stand it. Ever since Button transferred out and I had to move into the dorms, these underclassmen they pair me with are complete dicks. Girls knocking on doors at all hours of the night. No courtesy or consideration whatsoever. Plus, they're disgusting fucking pigs."

"Okay, but do you really want to live with *Trish's* friend? What's that about?"

"I wanted the option, but she blew me off." I peer over my shoulder in case she's come back to apologize, but all I see are the closed doors of the classroom building. "Trish probably made up some shit like *I* cheated on *her*. Or worse." That, more than anything, pisses me off.

"Zaiah..." Adam starts. He's not the type to hesitate, and as expected, he forges on. "This is a bad idea. Do I have to remind you of the hell you went through last year because of *her*?"

No, he doesn't. I try not to let my mind go there.

"It's actually the perfect idea because she's the exact opposite of Trish. Nor is chill. She studies and goes to class. I don't remember her ever having a boyfriend. She's a girl, so by default, she's going to be cleaner than most dudes. Plus, Knightley Hall? I'd get my own room. I'm a senior, for fuck's sake. I need my own room."

"Don't take this the wrong way, but you're coming off as super high maintenance right now."

Every one of the stupid underclassmen roommates who didn't work out noted the same thing, but I can't help it. Living with these assholes is too much. It's impacting my sleep, and more than anything, student athletes need sleep. "Fine. When should I stop by your place with all my shit? We'll be cuddle buddies."

"Fuck no."

Then I better get Nor on my side and fast.

---

I PULL my beanie around my ears. Sweat clings to my skin from my afternoon workout, the cold air drying it on my face while I stare up at Knightley Hall. *Man, this place is fantastic.* No loud music blares from the windows. There isn't a constant stream of screaming and laughing underclassmen spilling out the front doors or milling out on the quad.

One deep, hopeful breath later, I open up the main entrance to the possible solution to my nagging problem. One step inside the quiet, calm place and I already feel rested.

The truth is, I could've put my name down for the available spot without talking with Nor first. By all rights, the room is mine. I just need to claim it before another eligible senior snatches it up, and since I got the call from Karen at Student Housing this morning, time is slipping away.

I didn't want to start off our roommate relationship like that, though.

Taking the stairs two at a time, my feet move quickly until I'm standing in front of suite five and knocking. Shifting from foot to foot, several long seconds pass. Movement sounds from inside, but no one answers. She's probably on the other side of the door, waiting for me to go away.

I try again, knocking a bit harder and saying, "Nor, it's me. It's Zaiah. Or Isaiah. Whichever." I can't remember which she called me or if she ever said my name at all, to be honest. She was always so quiet.

"What are you doing here?"

I try to keep my cool, tapping my foot against the carpeted floor. The *carpeted* floor. Just the idea of not having footsteps echo off tile and concrete at all hours of the night spurs me on. "I'm not here to talk about Trish. I promise. Come on, open up."

There's another pause until the sound of metal sliding across metal meets my ears and the door cracks. She steps back, the available space to peer inside widening in her absence.

The smell of cleaning products wafts toward me. From what I can see, the suite is neat and tidy, and Nor is as she ever was. Clear glasses frames sit on the bridge of her nose. Her dark blonde hair, now up in a messy bun, sticks out above the crown of her head, and two-sizes-too-big clothes that look suspiciously like pajamas hang from her body.

Ah, yes. I remember now. Trish's shy friend was very much into lounging and being extremely comfortable. Baggy sweatshirts. Loose pants. Hair tied back— or up—basically styled in any way where it was out of her face.

"Hey."

"Hey," she says, distrust lacing her tone. She even takes a step back and crosses her arms in front of her chest.

"Sorry I accosted you in the middle of the hallway earlier. I need to talk to you." She stands there, not quite letting me in, so I tack on, "May I?"

She peers behind her. "I...guess."

I don't wait for her to change her mind. I push past her, scoping the place out. As expected, Nor is organized. Peering over at the open door of what must be her room, I spot a made bed with a teal comforter and throw pillows. There's nothing on the floor anywhere, and it doesn't smell like stale beer.

I'm in love.

"So, what have you been up to?" I ask as I take the liberty of sitting on the gray couch. It's pretty comfy. A little springy, but who knows how many students it's supported over the years. I can live with it.

Nor stares at me through the lens of her glasses. "This is weird. Are you okay?"

I chuckle, feeling a little off myself. The desperation clinging to me is making me force this, but I'm not going to say that. "What about it is weird? We were friends."

She scrunches up her face, and I'm with her on that one. I'm taking liberties with the word *friend*. We were acquaintances at best. She was just around when I was with Trish. The third wheel. The girl who tagged along to some dates. In fact, on occasion, I found her presence annoying, but Trish felt bad leaving her behind.

Or so she'd said.

"I haven't spoken to Trish, so if that's why you're here..."

"It's not," I grind out. If I never hear another word about her, I'll be happy. "That's not it at all."

Nor tentatively takes a seat on the other end of the couch before folding her legs up underneath her. "Help me understand, then. I haven't seen you since..."

Uneasiness creeps in. I don't see her or talk to her because the one thing that ever tied us together was my ex-girlfriend. "Listen, I'm sorry for showing up like this. You actually have the power to help me out, and I'm hoping you'll say yes."

"I have a lot of work to do," she says, peering longingly over my shoulder into her bedroom.

"Nor..."

"Don't." She sighs. "Don't call me that, okay? I prefer Len."

"Len?"

"Yes, it's my name."

The gruffness in her voice takes me aback. "I thought your name was Norah?"

"Actually, it's Lenore."

I almost face-palm myself. Of course it is. I knew that. The lady in Student Housing told me, and it's why I didn't know who she meant at first until I put two and two together.

Peering away, she picks at a loose string on her sock. The printed design creeps up and under her multicolored gummy bear pajama bottoms, but I can't quite tell what it is.

"Sorry, I...forgot." Though, *never knew* is more appropriate. "Your name is pretty."

"Thanks, I hate it."

Her defeated tone sparks my caring side. She clearly doesn't want anything to do with me, and in different circumstances, I would drop this whole thing. However, the image from earlier this morning of my roommate picking up one of his dirty socks, smelling it, then sliding it onto his foot pushes me forward. "Listen...Len. I hear you're having roommate problems. I'm also having problems, and the Housing lady called me this morning to say this room was available, and I really want it."

"This...room? *My* extra room?"

"You wouldn't believe the losers they've stuck me with. I can't sleep. I—"

"But you're a guy."

The outrage in her voice makes me laugh. She looks away, and I clear my throat. "Sorry. Yes, I am. I didn't think that would be a problem, what with the separate rooms and all. Knightley is co-ed. We're both adults." With history, I could add. I wouldn't be a total stranger.

"No, no," she says, standing before I can say anything more. She flails her arms around. "You'll have your teammates over here all the time, eating my food and breaking things. You'll leave the toilet seat up and the milk on the counter. And a stream of girls coming from your room. I swear to God, I cannot deal with another nightmare roommate right now. I will lose it."

She pushes her glasses up her nose, her hands in tiny fists. She's kind of cute when she's all worked up. The urge to tease her rises, but I stop myself. Instead, I press my lips together to think about the best way forward. "Trust me, I've also had some nightmare roommates, so I know exactly how not to act."

She nibbles on her lip. "I thought you had a room-mate? Your friend..." She snaps her fingers, like she's trying to recall his name.

"Sarge. Sarge Button. He transferred out." I peer away. Sarge was too good to play here, what with the lack of notoriety Warner hockey gets. We're having a winning season and absolutely no one cares. He was the smart one.

"Oh, I'm sorry. He was always nice."

For the first time, she looks like the Nor—Len—I remember. "Yeah, he was the best. We had a place off campus, but I couldn't afford it on my own, so I had to move back to the athletic dorms. Ever since then, it's been one nightmare after another. Student Housing called me this morning because the nice lady over there thought this might be the perfect fit."

Nor— Len worries over her lip before focusing on me. "Are you seeing someone?"

I shake my head. She doesn't want a "string of girls" in and out of the suite. Neither do I. "You?"

"No." Her answer comes quickly but morphs into shocked anger. "Who are you to even ask?"

I place my hands up in protest. "You asked me."

"I wanted to know if I was going to have to hear you have sex all the time because let me tell you, these walls are good, really good, but they're not perfect. Far from it. There must be dead spots with no insulation because—"

"If you want me to say no girls, I will. I'll sign a freaking contract."

Her brows pull down, studying me. "You'll sign a contract? Outside of the Student Housing one?"

Now it's my turn to appear concerned. A few locks

24

of hair have fallen out of her bun, mimicking the appearance of an overworked, underappreciated housewife like you see depicted on TV. "What would be in said contract?"

She shrugs. "I would have to think on that."

"Would I have the chance to add my own stipulations?"

Her gaze narrows even further. "Perhaps. A few."

"A few, huh?" Oddly, I have to stop myself from grinning. I haven't smiled in weeks, but this conversation is amusing. *She's* amusing.

She taps her chin. "It sounds like we've both had some terrible experiences." She sympathizes for a brief moment, but then her gaze moves into distrusting territory again. "But how do I know you weren't actually the problem? I need to gather my thoughts. Plus, Knightley Hall is a needle in a haystack situation. The holy grail."

"Why do you think I'm here? I'll get down on my hands and knees."

Her eyes flash, and I suddenly regret those last words. She wouldn't really make me...

"I'll have a contract for you by email in two hours."

"You—" *Wait.* I peer from her to my surroundings, then back to her. A contract in two hours. Okay. I was prepared to keep fighting.

"You'll have thirty minutes to add any stipulations of your own. Send it back to me to agree. Once it's signed, you can go to Housing."

Man, she's...*something*. Thorough might be one

word. High-strung could be another, but I've been called that recently, so I'll reserve judgment.

I stand. She doesn't seem the least bit intimidated that I tower over her by at least a foot. I hold out my hand, and she shakes it, her grip firm.

By the time I'm walking down the carpeted hallway back to my shithole of an underclassmen dorm, I already know there isn't a lot she could put into that contract that would prompt me to let this go.

I'll stay out of her way, and Nor— Len is the type of roommate to stay out of mine.

Match made in heaven.

# CHAPTER THREE

## Len

*NO GIRLY SHIT IN COMMUNAL SPACES.*

That's what he wants to add? I put real issues into the contract and he wants to tack on that I can't put any *girly shit* in the communal spaces? I don't even know what constitutes as girly shit, nor do I know if I own any.

I pull up the school app on my phone, my heart fluttering in my chest like a raging hummingbird. Is this a joke? He wrote down something just to be an ass, didn't he? I search his name in the message directory, and when I click on it, I find an old message thread from back when he and Trish were together. From the sound of the thread, Trish had left her phone, and he'd messaged me to find out where we were.

I remember this night and I don't want to.

*This is all a terrible idea.*

I hesitate, tapping my foot on the floor. Isaiah James and I should not be roommates. For one, he plays hockey. Dear God, why?

My only consolation is that the hockey team here is nothing. It's not constantly thrown in my face like back home, but *ugh*. I've already written in the contract that he can't have his equipment all over the place. I wanted to put in a clause that he couldn't talk about hockey either, but I can't censor someone's words. That would go against everything I believe in. If he talks about hockey, I'll leave the room.

My thumbs hover over the on-screen keyboard, poised to ask for examples of girly shit, but will it change my mind? I'm not the girliest person ever, anyway. I can't think of one thing I own that would be labeled girly shit, so there's no chance of it being left in the communal space.

If he wants to add this in, he can sit with his own anti-feminist verbiage and be the quintessential jock he is.

*Girly shit. Ugh.*

I bite my lip. If this one statement has me annoyed, what will having a jock—full-time, in my space—be like? Horrifying. It'll top the cannabis lover or the girl who spoke loudly on the phone at all hours of the night.

However, he's doing this contract for my benefit, and we both know it. He has the points racked up to live in Knightley. That's obvious. If the Housing lady called him, it's him. I don't have a say. He's being nice by talking to me first.

Instead of calling him out for his anti-feminist words, I pull my laptop toward me, sign the contract, and send it back. I don't even have time to berate myself for my life's choices when my laptop dings with a new email, and it's his signed contract back with "Calling Housing now. Thanks, Len."

At least he remembered to call me Len. I peer around the suite, specifically looking for...what? Pink glitter? Then I do a second scan to make sure none of my personal items are out. The place is bare compared to the dorm room I shared with Trish that had art and inspirational quotes on the walls. Our shared space was like everything else with us. On the surface, it had a full face of makeup, but when you wiped that away, what was underneath wasn't always something nice to look at, let alone live through.

I open up the picture app on my phone and scroll until I get to some of the last pictures of Trish and me. She was so fun, so quirky. But she had a venomous bite like a King Cobra, and when she struck, she struck hard.

The picture on my phone vanishes, switching to an incoming call. I stare down at the word *Dad*, my body deflating. I can't with this right now. I don't want to talk about his future plans for my degree or coming back home or anything else he wants me to do that I don't.

Tossing the phone aside, I decide to work in the

living room to soak up as much alone time as I can before Isaiah moves in tomorrow.

*God, my dad would find my living with a hockey player super ironic, wouldn't he? He would laugh and laugh...*

---

THE DOOR to the suite bounces off its hinges, and I'm startled awake. My heart hammers, and I shoot to my feet only to see a wide-shouldered body walking backward down the hall, followed by two more wide-shouldered bodies. The first two carry a TV, while the third carries a large tote.

I don't recognize them, and when they stop to ask where Zaiah's room is, I point in that direction on autopilot. Finally, the man himself strides through the door holding a small box.

"What is this?" I nearly shriek.

He grins. "I contacted Housing before they closed. Actually," he appears smug for a second, "Karen and I have become good friends, and she kept the office open for a few minutes until I could get there. I signed the *real* contract, was handed the key, and I'm here."

"Tonight?"

He shrugs. "Nothing specified I couldn't, and it is my room now." He peers around, grinning. "This is fucking awesome."

The wide-shouldered guys come walking out of the

room, and I point at them like they're on display. "And who are they?"

"Freshmen."

I blink at him. "You grabbed any old freshman on campus to help you move in?"

"No, freshman hockey players doing their lowly duty." He shoves one of the guys playfully, who flips him off, and then he follows them to the door and locks it behind them.

A bout of stubbornness rears up, but what am I going to say? He can't actually move into his room? It's *his*. We have two contracts that have established that.

He saunters back, this time standing nearer. He's taller than me by about a foot, and this close, it's easy to see the cut of his jaw and wide shoulders. "Hey, Roomie. I want you to know how much this is saving my ass. I really appreciate it."

*Oh*... "O-kay," I stammer out, not expecting that.

He leans in, and my heartbeat skyrockets. His brown-eyed gaze narrows. "You have some crusty stuff on the corner of your lips."

My face heats. Immediately, I reach my hand up and rub it away, mumbling how I fell asleep. *Oh my God, it's dried-on drool.* This clock tower article is really taking it out of me. I'm exhausted.

The corners of his eyes crinkle. "You drool? If you're going to take a nap on the communal couch, you should use your own pillow."

"I don't— *Ugh*. How are you here for only a minute and already annoying?"

31

"You're the one drooling on shit. What if I had guests over and they sat on our drool pillows?"

*Oh, fuck me.* He already had guests over, and they looked straight at me. I peer down, still wearing my dancing gummy bear pj's, and my hair is probably a freaking mess. Plus, he's now had more visitors than I've ever had. Within seconds!

"I'm messing with you, Len." He drops his enormous athlete hand onto my shoulder, making me jump. "It's your place. You can look however you want."

I frown even more at my choice of attire. "I don't usually have drool on my face. I didn't know you were coming or...or—"

"None of that matters." He shakes me by the shoulders. "We're about to get super close, Lenore... Wait, what's your last name?"

"Um, Robert...son. Robertson." I close my eyes briefly as dread rears its head. The urge to lie is strong, but no way he would put two and two together of who my dad is, anyway.

"We're about to get super close, Lenore Robertson. Just you wait."

I kind of want to opt out of the closeness right now. An awkward buzz creeps over my skin. Shrugging away from his large hand, I tell him I have work to do because already I feel the weight of the two issues I was worried about: hockey and Trish. And something tells me this eager beaver attitude of his means he feels it, too, but he's intent on sweeping it under the rug.

He checks his watch. "Yeah, and I should get my

room together." Turning, he walks toward the spare bedroom like he's been living here for months instead of a few minutes. I stand in place for a moment, wondering if I should ask him if he needs help. I did with everyone else. Start things off on a good foot and all that. Quickly, I run to my bathroom, redo my hair, and double-check there are no crusties on my lips before I head to his room.

I reach out to knock on his open door to let him know I'm here, but I pause as he takes out a couple of framed pictures. The first he puts back immediately, and I'm almost one hundred percent sure I spotted Trish, but the other, he places on the stand near the bed. A picture of his family—a smiling older couple with their arms around a younger version of Isaiah and an even younger girl.

The floor creaks underneath my feet, and he whips his head around. *Damn.* I didn't even have time to knock. "J-just wanted to know if you needed help unpacking."

The olive branch has been extended. When he says no, I can go work on my article.

"Actually, do you mind helping with the fitted sheet? I don't know what wizard came up with the idea, but its usage eludes me."

"Oh. Yeah." I take a hesitant step forward. "Sure."

Seems a little strange to touch his sheets, but okay. He points to a tote on the floor labeled *bedding*. At least they don't look gross.

"They're clean," he says. "I see you over there

33

eyeing them. I wouldn't shove used sheets in your face on the first day."

"Oh, is that a second day kind of thing?"

He thinks for a moment. "Maybe like a second month kind of thing."

I smile, though it comes slowly to my face. He was always funny. That I remember. Trish would look at him with contempt every time he cracked a joke, like she was exasperated that he even talked. God, she'd be so pissed to know he was moving in here...with me.

That thought brings an even bigger smile to my face.

After getting the tote open, I bring his pale-gray sheets over to the bed and start to make it when I frown. It doesn't fit. On a hunch, I peer down at the label. "Well..." I turn toward him, "I've found your problem. These mattresses are twin XLs. Not twins."

"Wait, are you serious?"

"As a heart attack."

He stares from the mattress to the sheet hanging from my fingers and back again. Then he starts to laugh. "I haven't figured that out this whole semester."

"How have you been sleeping?"

"I drape it across the mattress the best I can. Sometimes I use two of the other sheets."

"Sounds like you're in desperate need of a fitted sheet. It will change your life."

"I'll order one, thanks."

"You know, I might have an extra. Let me look."

"Really? Yeah."

I walk from the room, shaking my head. He's a senior and didn't realize the beds were twin XLs. Like, *what*?

I rifle through my closet and smirk when I pull out my spare sheets. It was the first sheet set that I came here with.

Pink polka dots.

He'll love it.

Walking back with a pep in my step, I flourish the sheets. "Ta-da."

His face drops. "Are you serious?"

I shrug. "Those with incorrectly sized sheets shouldn't complain."

His lips thin. "I can't. This is ridiculous."

"Oh, come on. You can use your own comforter and no one will even know."

I start to make the bed while he sighs next to me. A smile pulls at my lips when I tug on the fitted sheet, waving like Vanna White when I'm finished.

"Looks girly," he grumbles.

I bark out a laugh. "What was the rule about having girly shit out?"

He beams. "I thought you might like that."

I study his smirk. Conniving. Teasing. "I knew you did it on purpose, you jackass. I'll stack up all the pink and purple shit I have wherever I want."

His chest rumbles with a laugh, his shoulders moving up and down like his body can't contain it.

Being this close to him again, I remember how in awe I was that his body dwarfed mine. Well, more like Trish's because he was only ever close to her. He was a marble statue among normal men. As if an artist took his time chiseling at his face to make his perfect features.

The memory of the first moment I saw him shoots through me, but I quell it. It can't be good to think these things about my new roommate and my ex-best friend's ex-boyfriend.

Plus, none of what initially happened mattered. He ended up being a stupid hockey player, anyway.

Without another word, I pull the flat sheet on, then throw his pillow on the bed along with his steel-gray comforter, turning down the corner. "That actually looks good," I muse, admiring how the pink and gray play off each other.

"It looks like I'm having an identity crisis."

"It looks like you're embracing your feminine side, which is hot as fuck." I smooth a wrinkle out of his sheets, then freeze. *Did I say that out loud?* I press my lips together and peer up at his waiting gaze. "I didn't mean *you* were hot as fuck. I meant that for a man to embrace that part of himself is super sexy. Any man. No one in particular. He could be, you know, a mad scientist intent on blowing up the world, but if he sleeps in sheets like these, at least he has a sexy side going for him."

"All I heard was that you think I'm hot as fuck *and* sexy, and I have to tell you, Len, if we're going to be roommates, you can't let your deep, dark feelings for me interfere. This is strictly a platonic relationship."

My face burns.

His lips twitch, then he bursts into a laugh. When I don't join in, he abruptly stops. "Don't look like I kicked your puppy, I was joking."

"I knew— I know that." Defiance laces my words, and I wish I'd taken the time to strain the vinegar out of them because now I sound like I care more than I actually do.

It's silent between us for a moment while he continues to place his things around the room. I stand there, running my fingertips along his comforter. It's going to be weird sleeping in the other room knowing he's in here. I hope he doesn't snore. Or invite girls over and be loud. Or—

"What are you writing your article about?"

I settle my nerves with a deep breath. "The clock tower."

"Oh yeah? Interesting."

"Yeah..." I hover there for a second longer before a familiar, uncomfortable feeling fills me. "I'll leave you to it, then. I'll be working in my room and will head to bed after."

"Okay. I have an early workout in the morning, so I might not see you, so see you...whenever."

"Whenever," I echo, then walk from the room as fast as I can, tension suddenly sliding off me once I hit the living room.

That wasn't so bad. Weird and uneasy at times, but

that's to be expected with any new person moving in. We'll get into a routine and it'll be fine.

I hope.

I mean, I sincerely wish this won't turn out to be a huge mistake, but because I know Zaiah, it feels like there's so much more on the line.

# CHAPTER FOUR

Zaiah

MY SKATES GLIDE EASILY OVER THE ICE WHILE Coach runs us through drills. He keeps barking out encouragements like he sits on a fortune cookie committee, except his quips are laced with f-bombs.

"Our winningest season in fucking decades!"

"Get your fucking asses in gear!"

"Do you know why we fucking win? Because we're fucking good."

A sliver of annoyance digs into me. Not at Coach per se, but at the feelings his words bring to the surface. We're having a damn good season, yet no one cares. Attendance is down. I don't need anyone to tell me the actual numbers, I see it every time I skate out onto the ice to an abysmal number of people. The trash talk from the opposing team is fucking embarrassing. Plus, when we go to away games, their arenas are always brimming with spectators.

Warner does not care about hockey. That much is clear.

Football is their obsession. The town flocks to their games in blue and white despite the bad publicity they received last year from their involvement in that prank.

Adam skates next to me, leaning on his outside edges as we practice footwork. "The Fresh say your roommate is, um... How should I say this? Mousy? Boring? Forgettable?"

For the first time in months, I actually slept well. I didn't want to leave my bed, waiting until the last possible second to get ready for practice. The air smelled normal. There wasn't some asshole snoring off alcohol. My new place is the picture of peace and tranquility...and this makes me oddly defensive of my roommate. "Len? So?"

"I thought you said her name was something else?"

"It is. Was. She said she prefers Len, so obviously, I'm calling her Len."

We both stop fast, spraying ice against the boards, then spin around and start again. He chuckles. "I thought a talk with you would be necessary, considering your history together, but the Fresh assured me you'd be fine living with her. Zero temptation."

"I told you not to worry. Len isn't Trish, and you know I'm not interested in dating right now."

"Says every man until a girl traipses around in lace

panties and bras and booty shorts and crop tops in a confined, private space. The struggle is real." He laughs again. "But the guys say she's more the type to wear Grandma's nightgown than any of those things."

Truthfully, I barely looked at Len before. She was always just there. I had eyes for Trish from the beginning. It was a ridiculous way to meet, really—walking around campus, slightly inebriated, and looking up to find a girl dancing on a table. The curtains were wide open, and there she was. I was struck.

Before I even knew what I was doing, I'd picked up a pebble and threw it at the window to get her attention, then my drunk ass gestured to come up. Who opened the door but a freaking bombshell.

My blades cut through the ice, and I don't even realize I'm going faster than normal until I have to turn quick to avoid hitting the boards, making Adam sprawl so he doesn't barrel into me. "You dick!" he calls out as he slides into the wall with a *thunk*.

I chuckle under my breath, then circle back around. "My bad, bro. I was distracted."

"Yeah, I can only imagine what had you unfocused."

"You're the one who brought her up."

I grasp his hand and pull him upright as Coach calls it. The team and I walk into the locker room, energized from the morning skate-around. Adam throws his gloves into his locker. "You should watch out anyway."

*Jesus, are we still talking about this?*

"I know, I know, quit bringing it up," he mimics, still eyeing me. "But you moved in with the wrong girl. She's going to get attached."

"She was Trish's best friend."

"So? Trish is out of the picture, and this shy girl just got this handsome new roommate."

"Aww, you think I'm handsome?"

He ignores my banter. "With your luck, you'll have a stalker next."

I roll my eyes. "You couldn't be further off. Len is... What's that word when you don't like sex at all. Asexual? It's possible she's asexual. I've never seen her look at anyone before."

"Maybe she's a closet lesbian?"

"If she is, I wouldn't have to worry, right? I'm telling you, this is the best thing that could've happened. She'll be the perfect suitemate. She's clean. She keeps to herself. She went to bed early last night to work on her article, and I didn't even see her this morning. I've stumbled upon gold here."

"Well—"

I cut him off because when Adam starts down the "sky is falling" path, sometimes you have to do that, or he'll go on and on. First, it was because Len was Trish's best friend. Then it was because Len's going to fall for me. Next, it'll be that she'll introduce me to weird reporter sex parties or something he saw on Dateline reruns five years ago. "Well, nothing. I'm good. She's good. You're not in this equation, so you don't need to worry about it."

He lifts his hands in surrender and grins. "Alright, alright. I'll let you make your own bad decisions."

I groan before heading into the showers to wash up. He means well, but his ability to conjure up worst-case scenarios in every possible situation is exhausting. When I get back out there, most of the guys are gone, so I quickly gather my things and walk toward the cafeteria. The crisp morning air bites at my skin while I trek across campus.

The state-of-the-art football stadium looms above everything in the distance, but when I pass by the new football facility, jealousy washes over me. They don't even try to hide the discrepancy between how they treat football players versus other Warner athletes. Our practice rink needs major updates, and instead of getting our own beautiful arena on campus like the football team, we have to go to the closest city and use the triple-A team's facility. The public doesn't care, and the students who might watch us don't have transportation. It's a sorry situation all the way around.

A few members of the football team spill out of the side door, and I watch them before making myself turn away. I thought I was coming to Warner to play hockey for people who cared. They promised so many things. I should've entered the transfer portal with my roommate, then maybe I'd be living it up somewhere else, playing for actual fans and crowds in nice arenas with teams who have a support system.

And the only fucking reason I didn't enter the

transfer portal cheated on me. Fuck my life. Since I'm a senior, there's nothing I can do about it now. I'm stuck.

A few underclassmen scurry out of my way as I walk into the building that holds the cafeteria. I can imagine the scowl I'm carrying right now; however, I can't help but be mad about the injustice of it all. Coach says he lobbies for us with Warner Athletics, but whatever he's doing isn't enough.

If things were different...

I spot Len out of the corner of my eye and stop in my tracks. People steer around me in the hall, but I'm transfixed. Through the large newsroom window, I spy her smiling. Her face is flush. She swipes her hair around her ear. She's...pretty. Her blue eyes sparkling. I walk toward the glass, watching her the whole time until I realize she's staring up at some guy.

So, she's definitely not asexual. Maybe she's just shy...and awkward.

I know she's smart. Trish used to say all the time how Len was studying or writing an article or had her nose in a book. We went out to dinner to celebrate her article exposing the football team's antics. The local news even picked it up and ran it. I don't know how much media attention she received, but I could tell how proud she was of it. Plus, I was selfishly loving it since it made the football team look like assholes. Not that it did any lasting damage to their reputations.

One of the players is even dating the girl who got caught up in their rivalry. Like, how the hell does that happen?

If only the hockey team had more press...

I blink as the guy leans over her, peering at something on her computer. She tenses, like she doesn't know what to do, and a smile peels my lips apart. She's cute like this. Her shyness is endearing, but I also feel for her. It doesn't take long to figure out that she's crushing on this guy and he has no idea. Or if he does, he doesn't care.

Someone walks by them, and he asks, "Hey, are you finished with that piece on the football team?"

It's probably some glowing play-by-play of their latest win. If only someone would write a piece—

*Holy shit.* My new roommate is literally a reporter. She could— Well, I could ask her to write an article about the hockey team. I don't know why I didn't think of this earlier.

My feet start moving before I even consciously know what I'm doing, and within a few seconds, I'm pushing open the glass doors. Several people peer up at me and stop what they're doing, eyes rounding.

"Zaiah?"

I follow the sound of Len's voice. She's standing, her eyebrows arched as she takes me in.

"Hey," I say, walking toward her.

She gives me an even more incredulous look. "Is there something wrong? Did you forget your key?"

The guy she has a crush on peers back and forth between the two of us, but it's merely confusion, nothing more. "No, I was hoping I could talk to you."

"Right...now?"

I nod.

Her face flushes pink. "I'm in the middle of something with my editor." She hikes her thumb over her shoulder at the male version of herself. Glasses. Studious. Maybe doesn't have the best taste in clothes.

"Oh, hey, man." I hold out my hand.

He shakes it, and it's weak as hell.

This *is the guy she likes?*

I toss that thought aside because it's none of my business. I'm pretty sure staying out of each other's personal lives was implied in the contract. Hell, she may have even put that stipulation in there, but I barely skimmed through it before signing. I would've agreed to anything.

When I stay where I am, Len's shoulders deflate. She turns toward her "editor," though I'm pretty sure he's still a student and not some trained guy the school hired. "Sorry, could I have a minute?" she asks him.

"Yeah, sure."

He steps back, and I give him a polite wave.

Immediately, Len grabs my shirt and drags me all the way down the length of the white table and into a corner. Unlike her crush, she's surprisingly strong.

"What are you doing?" she hisses. "I didn't think I needed to explain in the contract that work is work and you're not to bother me at it." She pushes her glasses up her nose and crosses her arms in front of her chest.

I smile, leaning against the wall. "You're mad I interrupted that moment with your boy toy."

The color drains from her face.

"If you're a reporter and he's your editor, isn't he, like, your superior? I didn't peg you as that kind of... Well, isn't that kind of risqué?"

"I don't like him," she rushes out, glancing up to make sure no one is close enough to hear us talking. Her eyes catch on him all the way across the room.

I watch the whole thing with a knowing grin. "You're a lying liar."

"What are you? Five?"

I shrug. "Sometimes, and this moment calls for it because you're also acting like you're five. You're an adult. Own up to a crush."

"Zaiah, I'm going to need you to— Wait, is this the reason you came in here? To ask me about Clark?"

I grimace. "His name's Clark? He's trying too hard."

"Oh yeah, because I'm sure he came up with his own name."

"People do," I tell her. "You'd be surprised." She rolls her eyes, and I can't help but watch with fascination. Teasing her is fun. "If it's any consolation, I'm pretty sure he has no idea you like him."

She drops her façade. "Really?" As soon as the question pops out of her mouth, she shakes her head. "I could care less because it's not about that. So, now that we're clear about," she waves her hands, "that, is this really what you wanted to come in here to talk to me about?"

She's adorable when she's annoyed, just like my little sister. I love to get her all wound up and then set her loose like an Energizer bunny with hormones. "No, I came in here to ask you a favor."

She smiles. "Oh, good. No."

"I haven't even said what it is yet."

"Still no. Now, can I go back to work?"

She taps her foot against the floor, her gaze darting to Clark across the room. I doubt I'm actually getting her in trouble, but invading her space wasn't the best idea. "Look, I'm sorry, okay? I didn't mean to bother you at work. I was walking by and saw you, and I had an idea. My mistake about you having a crush on Clark." *It's not a mistake at all. I'd bet on it.*

She peers away. "It's none of your business."

"Plus, it's none of my business," I echo.

She's quiet for a few moments. "Fine, okay. What, then?"

"I was watching you in here and I had a thought. The hockey team is having a great season, but no one knows about it. I thought maybe you could write an article detailing how awesome we are."

The dead stare she gives me catches me off guard. Her once sparkling eyes are now cold. "Wow, you really don't know me at all. No, I won't. Final answer."

She spins on her heel and walks right back to her laptop. I blink at her rapid exit. O-kay. I hit a nerve. Guess she's not a hockey fan. Or maybe a sports fan in general. Or it's possible she's just not a *me* fan...

Dejected, I walk past, and when she doesn't even look up, I realize I've stepped in it big time.

That's the last thing I wanted to do.

*Fuck.*

*Way to go, James. Well played.*

# CHAPTER FIVE

Len

My body flushes with inferno-level heat, embarrassment pricking at my skin. Zaiah knows no boundaries. Showing up at my work, shaking Clark's hand, and asking me to write an article for him? What the hell?

I'm glued to the seat, making sure my eyes don't stray from my laptop to do something stupid like glare at him walking his jock ass out the door.

The entrance door finally snicks closed. My shoulders relax but tighten again when quick footsteps approach. Judging by the way the person leans into my chair and the smell of Bath & Body Works enveloping me in a cloud of fruity perfume, it's Candice. "Who was that? I don't recognize him."

Knowing her, I won't need to answer. She has more thoughts to share than anyone I know. Like those clickbait articles on the internet, she spits out useless information repeatedly.

"Is he your boyfriend?"

I nearly choke.

It must echo in here with my own thoughts because two distinct voices answer at the same time with a resounding "No." Peering up, I spot Flora first. She's not looking at me, she's eyeing up someone else over my shoulder. I hesitate to glance that way because I'm pretty sure I know who it is, and I'm already mortified enough if he overheard anything Zaiah said to me.

My brain tells me to get it over with—like ripping off a Band-Aid—so I meet Clark's horrified stare.

My heart starts to beat faster. His nose scrunches up. Another "No" flies out of his mouth like Zaiah and I dating is the worst possible scenario.

*He likes me. I knew it.*

I practice my calm breathing exercises to quit freaking out, but my brain still works in overdrive. How do I tell him I like him too? Should I say it now? Perhaps *Hell no, I don't like Zaiah James because I'm already crushing on someone else.* Then, I could peer deep into his eyes until his analytical brain figures it out.

"No?" Candice continues. "You two looked cozy."

Some sort of weird noise escapes my throat, but again, another voice answers. I stare at Clark, and I swear literal hearts come out of my eyes. He's making sure everyone knows there's no way I could date someone else. Staking his claim like Clark Kent would, only slyly. He's not showy or dramatic.

Except...

He laughs. "Len? Date? She's not really..." He pauses as if he's someone who doesn't work with words all day. "I mean, Len doesn't date. Look at her. She's the type of girl who's not worried about stuff like that. No makeup. Hair thrown on top of her head every day. She's married to the job. Everything about her says she doesn't care about the opposite sex. She cares about the stories. Really, Candice, if you're going to be a reporter, you should work on your observation skills."

My gut twists. Horror fills me. A Godzilla-sized footprint tramples my heart. He doesn't think I date. Or care about my appearance. Or—

Flora nudges me under the table, but I can't look at her. Shame washes over me. Of course I would never be able to attract a guy like Clark. Or Zaiah. Or anyone. I'm nothing like Trish. I'm the sidekick. The hanger on. The—.

"Clark," Flora calls out to get his attention, and I can only count it as a blessing because he's continued his analytical tirade over me like I'm a specimen under a microscope. "I have a question about my article."

The smell of Bath & Body Works dissipates, and Clark walks to the other side of the table, leaving me with my tiny thoughts. I'm about the size of an ant. Even pebbles and dirt and discarded trash outshine me.

Slowly, I pack up my things, throw my bag over my

shoulder, and walk from the newsroom. When the glass door closes behind me, I run. All those feelings I thought I overcame six months ago slam into me once more. Shame. Being an outcast. Being not good enough. I had no idea the old wound remained, festering, waiting at the surface to be ripped open again.

Once I step outside, I stop for a second, peering around wildly. The first tear falls, and red-hot anger fills me. I take off for Knightley, cutting through the quad. I thought I could fit in around people who don't know who I am or where I came from. That was the beauty of college. No one knows your story, and you can remake yourself. I—

My legs buckle beneath me, and I sprawl. I land in the frost-laden grass, embarrassment adding to my shame. Worse yet, whispers rise up, and when I glare that way, I realize I'm right outside the cafeteria.

I pull myself to a seated position, keeping my gaze on the grass while I work up the courage to block everyone out, stand, and run. I'm never coming out of my dorm room again.

A bag drops next to me, and then someone sits. I peek up to find Zaiah, and I immediately look away again.

"Hey, you okay?"

The tears come faster now. What is it about my stupid body that reacts to people asking if I'm okay? I have enough strength to hold back until someone utters that ridiculous question and then the waterworks are inevitable.

"Len, are you hurt?"

I wipe at my tears and sniffle. "That's a difficult question to answer." My high-pitched voice cracks, like it's at its breaking point. "Physically, I'm fine. Just fell."

He reaches for my chin, and I twist it out of his grasp. He drops his hand to my knee, rubbing it. "You want to go back to the room? I can take you."

I scramble to my feet, indignation sweeping through me with a healthy helping of distrust. "I don't need your sympathy...boy I could never date." I cringe. That was only supposed to be inside my head.

His brows knit together. "What?"

My face crumples. "Nothing. I need a moment. I'm going back to the room."

Like a ninja, he rises to his feet and snatches my arm as I'm about to make my escape. "If this is about me showing up while you're working, I'm really sorry. I didn't know you would react this way. I won't do it again. Promise."

I yank my hand from his grasp. "It's not about you." I wipe furiously at my face while tears still fall.

"Then what is it?"

"Don't you have a class to get to?" I snap, walking away.

I make a beeline for Knightley, power walking like I can escape Clark's words swirling through my head. My bed calls to me. Throwing myself under the covers and sobbing the rest of the day sounds like the perfect plan. I'll put on *The Notebook* so I can really feel like shit.

Finally, I arrive at Knightley and trudge up the main steps while taking out my student ID. I swipe it, but it doesn't read. Furious, I press the ID into the reader. Nothing happens again. I groan out in frustration, and suddenly, another card pushes mine out of the way and swipes instead.

Isaiah James's picture stares back at me. He even looks good in his ID photo. Caramel-brown hair styled short, the sides shaved with longer hair on top, flopping over. Those sparkling brown eyes. I can imagine him charming the pants off whoever took the photo at the DMV.

Some people have it all.

His look is so effortless, yet ridiculously handsome at the same time. A bit of hair product and it's as if he stepped off a magazine cover. Plus, hockey keeps his body toned and muscular. Add to that his tall frame, and he's basically a god.

With the way Clark talks about me, Zaiah can't even stand to look in my vicinity. "Thanks," I mutter, then run for our suite to hide.

Luckily, his footsteps don't follow.

After I shove the key into our main door, I don't stop until I'm safely in my room. Dropping my bag in the middle of the floor, I go straight to my bed and face-plant the mattress.

Clark said those things with utter conviction.

*"Len doesn't date. Look at her."*

*"Everything about her says she doesn't care about the opposite sex."*

He doesn't see me like I see him. Clearly. Not by a long shot. Rejection ripples through me with the aftermath of a tsunami. He practically described me as a troll. Maybe I should find a bridge to live under to spare everyone the burden of looking at me.

Shifting my mouth away from the sheets so I can breathe, I stay there until I convince myself to move again. Even then, I only exert myself enough to start *The Notebook* on the TV I bought after one of my roommates commandeered the communal space, and then prop myself up against the headboard with the sheets pulled up to my chin. I'm not that far into it when the main door to the suite opens and closes. Muting the movie, I pray Zaiah goes to his room, but I have the luck of a bad penny today because his footsteps grow louder and there's a knock on my door.

I swallow before answering, trying to appear unfazed. "I'm fine. I want to be alone."

He doesn't listen. He opens the door and strides inside, carrying a grocery bag with him. "Sorry, no can do." He points to the clear plastic. "I need to know what flavor you like before they all melt."

"What is it?" I ask as he moves closer. I glance into the bag and take in several pints of Ben & Jerry's ice cream.

"I wasn't sure which you preferred. My sister is a Half Baked kind of girl, but I didn't want to presume."

I fish through the offerings. Half Baked is good, but I find myself pulling out the—

"Wait, let me guess." Zaiah turns away, his eyes closed. "The cheesecake one?"

"No."

"The Tonight Dough?"

"No again. You're missing an important ingredient."

"Chocolate Fudge Brownie?"

"Getting warmer," I say, taking off the top.

He peers over, eyes widening. "I should've guessed. Chocolate Therapy. That bad, huh?"

I stifle the comment I want to make and instead ask, "You buy your sister Ben & Jerry's?"

"I know the way to a female heart."

I tug off the plastic covering and look up at him. "Right now, you're only teasing me."

His brows pull together, then he realizes I don't have a spoon and zips off to the kitchen with the ice cream, returning with a utensil in record time.

"Thank you." I take it from him and dig in. The chocolate goodness practically melts on my tongue. I don't care that all I had for breakfast was half a bagel before I decided to go to the newsroom and that this will probably wreck my stomach. Worth it.

My phone dings, and I leave the spoon in my mouth to reach for my bag. Zaiah picks it up and throws it on the bed while I take out the device. It lights up with a message from Flora.

Are you okay? He was out of line.

I roll my eyes, throwing it onto the bed next to me without responding.

"You want to talk about it?"

"Not really."

Especially not with perfect Isaiah James. What would he know about being below average and having people look over or through you as if you're not even there? It's embarrassing.

Instead of leaving, Zaiah physically pushes me toward the wall and gets into bed next to me, pulling the comforter back up over my waist. I eye him. *He doesn't listen very well, does he?* But despite my thoughts, his presence feels better than being alone. His large body blocks out some of the numb that would be very easy to catch with this pint of Ben & Jerry's in my hand.

"*The Notebook*, huh?"

"Don't like it?"

"Didn't say that."

I shove a whole spoonful of ice cream into my mouth, letting the chocolate work its magic while the movie plays. It's at the part where they're in the ocean and Rachel McAdams is asking Ryan Gosling to say she's a bird.

As soon as he says, "If you're a bird, I'm a bird," my tears run over again.

Why is that line everything? It packs so much meaning.

"My sister cries at that part, too. I don't get it."

I blink at him, my vision blurred. He stares at the

TV, forehead cinched in confusion, and I sit up straighter, gesturing toward the scene with my ice cream spoon. "He wants to be what she is. If she wants to be a bird, he'll be a bird too. It's so romantic."

"Being a bird is romantic?"

"No! *Ugh*," I groan. "It means he'll follow her. He'll be next to her through all her craziness, even her wanting to be a bird, and he'll do that forever and ever. Meanwhile, I can't even get a guy to look at me. It's like that part in *Pride and Prejudice* when Lizzie's father says: 'Mr. Darcy, who never looks at any woman but to see a blemish, and who probably never looked at you in his life.'"

My eyes widen. *I'm a blemish.* Is there anything worse than to be a blemish?

"You're not a blemish," Zaiah states.

"*Ugh*, why do I keep saying things out loud that I mean to say inside my head?"

"Because you're sad?"

"You know, not everything I say needs an answer."

He nods. "Okay."

I have to admit, he's taking all of this well. He's only been my roommate for about twelve hours and I'm already having a meltdown.

"It's admirable that you take care of your sister this way, but you know you don't have to watch me blubber over *The Notebook* and gorge myself on ice cream. Thank you for this, by the way."

"What are roomies for?"

"I don't know," I say honestly, voice cracking.

59

Another tear falling over. I thought I had the best roommate. The singular best friend someone could ever ask for, but all of that was a façade too. Why does everything in life suck?

"Hey," Zaiah says comfortingly. He slides his arm around my shoulders, and I snuggle into his chest, still scooping ice cream in between trying not to cry. "Tell me what happened. It'll be good to talk about it."

A few minutes ago, he was the last person I wanted to divulge my problems to...

"Come on," he encourages. "I promise I'll just listen. Get things off your chest."

I swallow, setting my ice cream on my leg, my fingers cupping the cold carton. "When you left the newsroom, this girl Candice came over and asked if you were my boyfriend. She seems interested, just so you know."

"I don't give a flying fuck about Candice." He squeezes my shoulders, his gaze intent. "Then what happened?"

"Well, I said no, but the worst part was, so did Clark. Except, he didn't only say no. He went on a long spiel about how I'm basically incompatible with dating and that I put no effort into my appearance, and then berated Candice for asking because she should have a better analytical mind to observe that about me."

"He...said that? All of that?"

I nod into his chest.

"What a dick."

I shrug my troll shoulders. "What about it isn't

true, though? I don't put makeup on. I don't dress like I'm trying to impress people. I'm really only trying to be a reporter because that's the one thing I want most in this whole world... I thought he would respect that."

"He shouldn't have said anything about your appearance. He's a douchebag."

"But he's such a cute douchebag. We have the same interests. If he would *see* me."

"I knew it," he remarks. "You like him. But listen, I'm not sure this dickh—"

I bolt upright. "You could help me."

"What?"

Excitement peaks when the plan starts to unfold in my head, and I smile. How many times have I thought that whatever Zaiah does is so effortless? I want that. I want attention without even trying. I want charm to ooze out of my pores. "What if you showed me how to get Clark to notice me?"

"Len, he doesn't—"

My eyes round as I come up with the perfect bartering token. "I'll write an article about your hockey team. I'll make sure they publish it."

He sits up straight. "You're serious about this?"

I nod enthusiastically. Strictly speaking, this is the best idea I've ever had. Look at Zaiah. He's perfect. If he teaches me one ounce of the charisma he holds, Clark won't be able to look away from me.

He sighs, running a hand through his floppy hair. "Despite this working out in my favor, I feel I should tell you that this asshole isn't the one you should be seeking attention from. He sounds like a jerk, Len."

My mind automatically refutes that. Clark isn't an ass. He's far from it. He was being observant, and had I really been paying attention instead of looking at him with heart eyes, I might have understood that I wasn't what he was looking for. This doesn't have to be the end of the story, though. "Right now, I want him to eat his words. I can be all those things he said I couldn't. He said I'm not the type to date because I don't put in the effort, but I could."

"You don't need my help, though." Zaiah hesitates. "Look it up on the internet."

"Well, you're a guy. Your feedback will be invaluable. Plus, it's not only about putting effort into my appearance. There are intangibles. Like charm. Flirting."

"Wait, you think I'm charming?" His lip twitches, and it's ridiculous that he doesn't know what he has. His personality comes so naturally. It makes me think of the night I first met him.

Even from two floors up and standing on a table staring down at the figure below asking to come up, I knew he was gorgeous. He was swathed in shadows, but you could tell by the cut of his clothes and his angular jawline that he was built. I started freaking out, asking Trish what I should do. She had only let me borrow the dress I was wearing. The low-cut, clingy material wasn't something I would be caught dead in, especially not in public, too afraid my private bits would show, so I wanted to change. I ran into the room to put something more comfortable on, telling her to get the door when he knocked, and by the time I came out, I didn't have a chance in hell.

He looked right through me, and all he saw was her.

The initial rejection only worsened the more we got to know him. Watching those two fall for one another was like a kick to the gut—a double kick when I factored in the shame for crushing on my best friend's guy. It didn't matter that I saw him first. Or that he initially saw me.

I peer at Zaiah, trying not to think about what could have been, and instead, stick out my hand. "Do we have a deal?"

He sighs, staring into my eyes for the longest moment before he says, "Deal."

He gives my hand a hearty shake, and I grin at him. "First, we wallow in ice cream. Then, you can tell me what I need to do to grab Clark's attention."

"Ice cream it is," he says, lying back into my pillows and getting comfortable. "Then we make you a bird."

I smirk at his attempt, but he still doesn't quite understand the concept.

# CHAPTER SIX

## Zaiah

Len studies me over a cup of coffee when I walk into the suite, hockey gear in tow. "How was practice?"

"Fine," I grumble as I head to my room. Truthfully, it wasn't my best. Dropped passes, terrible skating. My neck aches from falling asleep on Len's bed while *The Notebook* played. Plus, I missed a class to help her, and I had to ask a teammate for notes and got relentless shit for it all practice.

I peel off my clothes and step into the shower, staying under the hot spray for a while to relax my sore muscles. If this doesn't go away, I'll have to ask a trainer to take a look at it, which means it will get back to Coach.

I finish up, throw on some joggers and a Warner hockey tee, and walk back out into the kitchen to find

Len still sitting there, nursing her cup. I've never seen her linger this long somewhere, but she has a few pages of printed material in front of her, and I catch the words clock tower. "Any luck on the article?"

"Getting there," she answers. "I have the librarian's help now, so it shouldn't be long. I swear, librarians could save the world."

I'm reaching into the cabinets, but at her words, I peer over my shoulder at her. "I'm sorry, what?"

She nods eagerly. "Solve life's mysteries and problems with research." She waves her hands dismissively. "Everything we're going through now has happened in history. Maybe not the exact same thing, but the root problem. I'm telling you... Save. The. World."

I grab two packets of oatmeal and turn, catching her as she props her glasses up her nose with one finger to the bridge. *Well, that's adorable.* A claw thing pins her blonde hair back, framing a makeupless, fresh face that showcases her clear complexion. However, from the neck down, she's swimming in clothes. Baggy Warner joggers hide everything along with her long-sleeved Warner Gazette shirt that's two sizes too big.

"So." She draws out the *o* and rearranges the papers in front of her, setting them aside. My stomach immediately clenches because I already know what this is about. She went through two pints of ice cream yesterday. I recognize that's a pretty bad problem. Sometimes, half a pint will do. If she chipped a nail, maybe a few bites, but two *pints*? I'm not sure my sister has ever needed two.

Len clears her throat. "Thank you for helping me yesterday. I'm sure I blabbered on and on, and the whole thing was embarrassing."

I shrug her off and pour the oatmeal into a clean bowl, scooping some protein powder into it as well. "What are roommates for?"

"I've had a chance to think about it, and—"

I turn, relief sluicing off me. *Oh, thank God she's come to her senses. All that talk yesterday about changing her was just two-pint worthy feelings. She—*

"I want to start right away."

*Mother...pucker. Shit.*

"Len..." My mouth works but no words come out. She looks at me expectantly, so I drop what I'm doing. "I feel like I need to say this, so hear me out. I have a sister, and I wouldn't want her to do any of this. I had a chance to think on it, too, and this dude isn't good enough for you. Puck what he thinks. It's okay that you're focusing on being a reporter right now."

Her brows shoot up. "Puck?"

I find a coffee mug, fill it with water, and heat it up in the microwave. "Something my mom let me say when I was younger instead of fuck, and it stuck. Listen, you don't want that guy, anyway. Trust me. He's not worth the trouble."

She lowers her gaze, pressing her lips together. "It's not just him." Rubbing the back of her neck, she sighs. "It's all guys. They look right through me, Zaiah. Whether they friend-zone me or worse, pretend like I'm invisible, it stings. This really doesn't have anything to do with Clark, except that he was the causation. Yesterday, that tirade of his woke me up to the idea that it's possible I'm not putting my best foot forward."

I sweep my stare to her face. Her desire is evident, her eyes pleading as she peers back at me.

The microwave beep pulls me out of my inspection. She leans forward on the table, running her hands over her hair until she gets to the hair claw. "I understand where you're coming from, and it's good advice. Puck Clark. I'm not doing this for him. I'm doing this for me. Whether it sounds vain or not, I want guys to pucking see me, you know? If they saw me, then, you know, I'd actually be...puckable to someone."

"Puckable?" *Woah, woah, woah.* My brain goes on high alert. "There's nothing wrong with your puck-ability."

"Oh, so you want to puck me?"

"No." I take a step back, and her face falls. *Shit.* "I didn't— I definitely didn't mean it like that."

She stands from the table, and I stride right up to her. Bracing her hands on my forearms, she forcibly removes me from her space. "It's okay. I understand what you meant, which is why I asked for your insight."

I fold my arms over my chest. Len won't even look at me now. This whole thing has turned into a mess. "Didn't you say research could save the world? What if you—"

"I've Googled it. I've read the magazine articles

about how to get the guy, and though I understand it intellectually, it's hard for me to put it into action. You think this is the first time I've thought about this? It's not. I was a ghost even before ghosting became cool."

"That's—" She shoots me a look, and I clear my throat. "Not the same thing. But you know that," I state quickly as I turn my back to pour the hot water into my oatmeal.

"I was using it as a clever dating analogy." She fixes her glasses to her face again.

A million thoughts run through my head. Mainly, that this is all going to backfire and I'll end up being the bad guy. The one who should've known better. "Listen, in this situation, I would want someone to tell my sister that she's perfect the way she is. And you are, Len. You're perfect the way you are."

She smiles tightly. "Fine. I get it. I'm perfect." She rolls her eyes. "But I want to be puckable."

I should've never let the *puck* thing slip. This is a disaster, but what can I do? I promised her yesterday that I'd help, and if I don't, she'll probably ask someone else. It's embarrassing enough for her that she asked me.

My shoulders slump. "Fine, but I want it in writing that I thought this was a bad idea."

Her hands freak out for a second and then she focuses on me again, her lips turning up into a smile. "But you're still going to give it your all, right? I need you at the top of your game. When I'm researching an article, I write down notes and have questions to follow up on. You can do all that, right?"

"Please. I'll be the best damn dating coach you've ever had. In hockey, we have something called a playbook."

Her eyes widen, breath catching at the same time. "The puckable playbook. That's some nice alliteration right there."

I chuckle. Only she would be excited about a choice phrase. "There's something wrong with you," I mutter before turning to the counter to stir my oatmeal.

"Is that lesson one? Should I dumb myself down?"

"Fuck no." I turn on her. "I swear to God, Len... Len..." I snap my fingers. "Your last name escapes me at the moment *again*, but if you dumb yourself down, the deal is off. Smart is sexy."

Her cheeks flush, and she casts her eyes downward. "Thanks. I really didn't want to act like the girls in *Clueless*."

I spoon some oatmeal into my mouth while I think about our next steps. This is still so tricky. I could step in it at any moment. "I also want it in the contract that you can't get mad at me for things I suggest. We'll probably tread into water that might hurt your feelings."

"Like my appearance."

"You're perfect the way you are."

"I know what I'm getting into," she states. "You don't have to sugarcoat anything. I'm asking you to change me. Yes, I'll put it in the *contract*." She uses air quotes when she says the word.

It would be nice if something I threw out there changed her mind, but she's determined. I check my watch as I shovel another spoonful into my mouth and swallow. "Listen, my parents are coming in today with their RV. It's this thing they do before game days. If you want to meet them, I'm sure they'd love to meet you."

"I met them once."

"Oh." *Why don't I remember that?* It's like she said, she's invisible. Or forgettable. I don't know. Yesterday, I thought she didn't even like guys. The awkward creep of embarrassment heats my cheeks. "That's right. I'm sure they'll want to see you again."

She rolls her eyes at my pathetic attempt to cover up my mistake. "On one condition: don't remind them I'm Trish's ex-roommate."

"Done." Probably a good idea, considering my family hates her.

"Good. Great." She claps her hands in front of her. "I'm going to get ready, and I'll need your help with how to dress. This is perfect. We can use your family as a dry run."

My brain wants to scream at her *"Don't make me do this."*

Instead, I sit at the table and dread the moment she comes back out. It's like waiting on a bed of nails, wondering which one is going to pierce the skin first. I can't actually tell this girl to wear certain things, can I? What she's worn before only shows a lump of a body with no real shape, and if I were going to tell her how to catch a man's attention, I'd address that first. Can I really do it, though?

She texts me that she's coming out over the school app, and I jot down a mental note to give her my real phone number for future conversations.

Her door cracks open. "Okay, go easy on me."

"Just get out here."

She walks out in a crop top and leggings that cling to her body, her bare midriff on full display. My brows rise even though I told myself I shouldn't have a reaction. Honestly, I thought I would have to tell her to show more. Not this.

She pulls on the hem nervously. Her hair, now down, drips past her shoulders in sheets of gold. Makeup highlights her features—most notably, her red cheeks, more prominent from a mix of awkwardness and blush.

"Say something," she snaps.

"Oh, I— I—" She looks...fantastic. Who knew what she was hiding under there? If I saw this girl walking around campus, I'd definitely check her out. I'm nearly speechless, stomach tightening.

"I can't pull this off, can I? *Ugh*."

She turns to run into her room, but I take a few strides to catch up to her and hold back on her arm. "Len, I didn't say that. You look...good."

"Why did you hesitate?"

"I'm trying to take it all in. Calm down." I step backward. When I look at all of her, I get overwhelmed. She's...beautiful, and I feel like an ass for thinking it. The right clothes and a little makeup shouldn't make this much of a difference. I've never been a shallow person. This is— I sigh, turning on my analytical brain, like Len would do, and start from the crown of her head. "Did you straighten your hair?"

She nods.

"I like it. It looks good."

"Thank you."

She pulls on her shirt again. It's obvious she doesn't feel relaxed in it, so I skip that part for now. When I get to her leggings, I have to skip that part, too. I didn't realize how amazing her hips and ass are, and I don't want to be *that* guy. "The shoes look comfortable. And sensible. Fashionable, too."

"Hair and shoes. That's all you got for me? I thought you wanted me to write this hockey article for you, Zaiah?"

She's right. I'm not holding up my end of the bargain. Swallowing, I reach out to her, and she eyes me suspiciously before putting her hands in mine. I need to look her in the eyes when I say this so I don't upset her. "The outfit is adorable," I tell her. "Sexy, even. It shows off your body in a way that you're saying you want to be..."

"Puckable?" she offers.

"Exactly. However...it's obvious you're not feeling it. You look nervous. You keep tugging at the hem, and I'm going to guess that you've never gone out in public showing off your stomach before. If you're nervous around me, imagine when you step outside. You're going to be even more fidgety. All anyone is going to see is you messing with your shirt. If we ever get to the crop top stage, you're going to have to own it. Right now, you don't have the confidence to wear it."

She nods. "So, no on the shirt?"

There's a bit of relief—from me too at how well she's taking this. "It's a no on the shirt *for today*."

She looks away, and it's as if I can see her brain working.

"And it's only a no because you don't feel comfortable," I enforce. "Not because you can't pull it off."

She lifts her head. "You think I can pull this off?"

"I don't think, I know."

"You think guys—um, Clark, or guys like Clark—would look at me?"

I squeeze her hands. "One hundred percent."

"I kind of like the sound of that." She grins to herself.

"Enough not to pull at the hem?"

"Hell no. I have to get this thing off me. My stomach is chilly, and I have a major push-up bra on."

I laugh, watching as she tugs at her bra. "You know what? Let me look at your clothes with you."

"Yeah?"

I shrug, feeling more confident now that she's handling this so well. "Why not? I've seen my sister get ready. How hard could it be?"

The answer: Very hard. Holy shit. For only seeing this girl wear the same type of clothes before today, she has so many.

I check my watch again. My parents are going to be here any minute and we've already gone through five outfits, and all five looked amazing but had her fidgeting. "Okay, listen," I finally say to her. "What would past you pick out if I told you we were going to meet up with my parents?"

She stares at the clothes strewn around the room. "Maybe a pair of joggers and a..." She leaps forward and picks out a white shirt that has some fancy handwriting on it that spells Literature and leads to an old quill.

"Okay, perfect. Keep the shirt, nix the sweats. Either wear jeans or the leggings you tried on earlier. You know that thing girls do when they tie up a shirt if it hangs too low? Do that."

"Like an 80s knot or something? Put a scrunchie around it?"

"No, not that." I hold my hands up. "You know, let's just see what you look like with that on, and we'll go from there."

I scoot out of the room and wipe sweat from my brow. This is taxing. Who would've thought?

My phone pings, and it's a text from my sister saying they're right around the corner. I text back that I can't wait to see them before yelling out, "Len!" Turning, I'm about to tell her they're almost here when she comes out of the room.

She stops just outside, wearing the black leggings from earlier along with her white Literature shirt. It hangs low on her, but already, I'm loving this direction.

"You look great. Tuck the front in a little?"

She pulls her leggings out and shoves the front of her shirt into her pants. I bite my lip and step toward her to help. She freezes when I grab her hip with one hand to steady her, and my mouth goes dry. Quickly, I tug out one whole side, letting it settle at her hip. The other is tucked in, showing off her shape.

"There," I say, backing up, my fingers on fire.

"Does it look okay?"

"Do you feel comfortable?" I counter.

She shrugs. "I'm wearing one of my favorite shirts."

"So, what you're learning is that you can be yourself and still be puckable?"

She drops her head to glare at me. "I bet you annoy your sister, too."

"Well, yeah, I'm the older brother. It's my job." I take her in again. She has far less makeup on than I originally thought. It only looked like a lot since I don't normally see her wearing any. Honestly, I don't know who wouldn't look at her. "You look perfect."

"Just the way I am?"

"Just the way you are."

She turns and peers into a mirror, shaking her head. "New and improved."

# CHAPTER SEVEN

Len

A ɢɪɴᴏʀᴍᴏᴜs ʜᴜɴᴋ ᴏꜰ sᴛᴇᴇʟ ᴡɪᴛʜ ᴀ ꜰʀᴏɴᴛ ʟɪᴋᴇ a Mack truck looms in front of us. Butterflies erupt in my stomach. Trish told me his parents liked to camp. She said she found it primitive. This is anything but. *My God.* "I thought you said RV, not space machine."

Zaiah chuckles, grabbing my hand and pulling me toward it. "Just you wait."

His father steps out and yells, "All aboard!" then peers around like he's planning to welcome a ton of visitors. The way his eyes light up when he sees Zaiah, though. "Hey, kid." He's not bashful about giving him a hug and neither is his son. It's not even a bro hug or that weird thing guys do, it's a straight up hug for several long seconds.

I stand back, a little out of breath from the running,

and watch with a pang of jealousy. But then his dad opens his eyes and sees me standing there.

"Oh, who do we have here?" He practically pushes Zaiah away. "You know you never keep a woman waiting, son."

My cheeks heat at his words. It feels so stupid to admit, really stupid, but the moment Zaiah tucked in my shirt and I walked out of the dorm with these leggings on, I was a new person; a normal human being who could go out into the world and be looked at. I stick out my hand confidently. "I'm Lenore."

Zaiah says it at the same time, but stops at the shortened version of my name, giving me a curious look when I keep going.

New person, new name. Or should it be new person, old name? My father wanted to call me Lenore. Believe it or not, it's after a famous hockey player, but I'll be taking that tidbit of information to the grave.

"What a pretty name," his father says, grabbing my hand and shaking it. He waves me inside like a butler, complete with a short bow. "Welcome to my humble abode. I'm Tom."

"Humble, my ass!" Zaiah quips.

His father shrugs. "There was a bigger one."

I grab hold of the light-up railing and step into the poshest traveling home I've ever seen. It looks like a rock star's bus. Neon rope lights frame the ceiling. White leather adorns everything. I think I've actually found something I wouldn't mind my father spending his money on. "I can't imagine traveling in this."

"If you're going to do something, do it in style," Zaiah's father remarks behind me.

"Oh," a female voice says. I peer toward the sound and see a teenager getting up from one of the plush couches. She eyes me, gaze narrowing. When she reads my shirt, she relaxes a little.

"I'm Lenore," I introduce myself, walking toward her. I almost put my hand out, but then decide that's stupid. "You must be Zaiah's sister."

"Izzy," she confirms.

"Hey."

"Hey."

A little ways back—because let's face it, it's still an RV—another female figure appears, sporting an apron that she's currently wiping her hands on. As if on cue, my other senses open up, and the most delicious smell fills my nostrils.

"Mom, this is Lenore," Zaiah says, wrapping his arm around my shoulders. "My new roommate. *Just* roommate."

"Oh, you dear. Thank you so much for getting Isaiah out of that hell hole of a room. God, he was so miserable."

She pulls me in for a hug, and I stand there in shock for a few seconds before I return it.

"Forgot to warn you," Zaiah whispers. "Mom's a hugger."

"And Dad's weird," Izzy echoes in the same inflection.

"Perfect," I say, smiling, soaking up the attention. I can do affection and weird.

His mother releases me and points at Zaiah. "Keep that smart mouth up and I won't cook for you today."

"Sources say that's a lie," Izzy monotones.

I like her.

First, Zaiah hugs his mom, then he walks over to Izzy and does the same before picking her up and shaking her.

"Did you get another muscle?" she chokes out. "Damn, Zaiah."

"I did, and it's right, oh..." He pretends to point somewhere on his body and then playfully punches his sister in the arm. "How's field hockey?"

The door in the front shuts, and his father calls out for everyone to take a seat. Without having to stand there looking awkward, Zaiah takes my shoulders and steers me toward the white leather couch opposite his sister.

"Buckle up," he whispers. "My father's a terrible driver."

"I heard that, and just for the hecklers in the back, I'll hit two curbs."

Zaiah's mom rolls her eyes and sits next to Izzy. They reach for their seat belts, so I do the same. Zaiah's body is so huge that we're practically touching. When we're all settled, he lifts his brows at his sister again. "Well?"

"I scored the game winning goal yesterday."

He raises his hand, and they give each other a long-distance high-five.

"Mom recorded it so you could see."

"Hopefully, I don't have a seizure from watching it." He mimics someone trying to record something on their phone, only the phone rises up and down haphazardly in front of him.

"I was celebrating!" his mom admonishes with a sly smile. She turns toward me. "I hope you treat your parents with more respect than mine do."

It's obvious she's joking, so I laugh along with everyone else. Hell, I wish my family was this cool. It's just my father and me, and even if I had played a sport, I doubt he would've been there, phone in hand to immortalize it. "Alas, I'm not much of an athlete."

Izzy stares at me, twisting her head. "Not enough people say alas anymore."

"Izzy," Zaiah rebuffs.

"No, I mean it. It's such an old-timey word. Makes you sound smart."

"Lenore is smart." He bumps me with his shoulder.

"More like a nerd," I admit.

He leans down to whisper in my ear conspiratorially, but he says it loud enough for everyone to hear. "It's okay. Izzy's reformed. You could be, too."

The motorhome jolts, and I reach out my hands to brace myself. One of them lands on Zaiah's large thigh. *Jesus*. His sister was right. Is he constructed of muscle?

His dad shouts, "Curb number one!"

Zaiah places his hand on top of mine. "I was

kidding about the driving, by the way. He's actually really good at it, but this thing is so dang big, the campus streets aren't set up to accommodate it."

Relaxing a little, I take a peek outside the windows. "Where are we going, anyway?"

"Zaiah enjoys getting off campus when we come down." His mom peers at him as if he hung the sun and the moon. "We'll be heading to a campsite on the lake. Hope you like to eat."

Zaiah turns to smile at me. "My mom's hobby is cooking and baking. My dad's hobby is buying expensive toys."

His mother shrugs as if he's done an excellent job summing them up.

I glance around, still taking everything in. This isn't anything like I thought it would be. The few times my dad came to visit, we ended up at one of the fancier restaurants in town and sat around and made the obligatory, strained small talk until we could call it a day, saying we tried when we really hadn't.

It doesn't help that he and I disagree about the next step in my life, which is coming sooner rather than later. Despite all my previous objections to his plan, I'm sure it'll come as a shock to him when I don't go running home after graduation.

Zaiah hits me with his elbow. "Lenore is a reporter for the school paper."

His mom and sister look at me expectantly, like I missed a crucial part of the conversation. "Yeah, sorry.

I'm a reporter. That's what I want to do when I graduate in the spring."

"No wonder you used the word *alas*."

I lift my shoulders. "Comes with the territory, I guess."

"Have you ever used it in an article?"

"Pretty sure." I grin. "I try to throw in at least one word that will trip up people." It's become a sort of running joke in the newsroom now.

"She's the one who wrote all the articles about the football scandal."

"Ooh." His mother's eyes flash. "He sent them to us. Very nice."

"Now I see why you like her." Izzy laughs. "Your grudge with the football team."

"It's not a grudge."

His father laughs from the front. "Now who's lying?"

Zaiah's jaw twitches, but he doesn't respond, and soon, Izzy is giving her brother a play-by-play of her field hockey match yesterday with his parents interjecting every now and then.

The motorhome shakes as it picks up speed. None of them seem to notice, but this is the first time I've been in a home on wheels, so every slight shimmy has me peering around to decipher where the noise is coming from and whether we're going to fall apart on the highway.

Luckily, we get to our destination in no time.

Zaiah's father situates the RV so that the windows

in front of me face a good-sized lake. A small firepit, an ancient charcoal grill, and a rocky beach are the only things visible before the water's edge.

"This is so pretty," I muse, stretching in my seat so I can peer out. In the distance, you can see the opposite bank, bare trees painting the landscape.

Zaiah's father releases his seat belt and steps into the main living space. "Perfect spot, huh?" He pushes a button on the wall, and a mechanical whir starts up. "Floor levelers," he says above the noise, nodding and smiling.

I didn't realize we were off kilter, but soon, the noise stops and everyone starts moving about. Mr. James places a hand on my shoulder. "Listen, my house is your house, Lenore. There are beds to take a nap in, my wife will be cooking—you won't want to miss that," he adds. "And I'll probably watch some sports. Go outside. Stay inside. The day is yours."

A warmth envelops me. "Thank you, sir."

He puffs his chest out. "Sir? I like her." Pointing at his own kids, he says, "You two could use some manners."

Zaiah shakes his head. "Thanks for making us look bad."

I pat his shoulder. "Pretty sure you do that well enough on your own."

"Ohhh," Izzy howls. "I double like her."

His mom stands. "So this is what it would've been like with three kids."

"You could've stopped after me and saved yourself

the trouble," Zaiah calls out after she retreats to the kitchen.

"Ha. Ha," Izzy overexaggerates. A pillow flies across the RV, but Zaiah easily snatches it out of the air before it hits him.

The day with the Jameses is so fun. I skim stones along the water with Zaiah. Eat his mother's cooking, which tastes divine. Listen to his father's dad jokes, and witness true sibling interaction. It doesn't take long before I feel a part of the gang, not an outsider asked here by Zaiah. His parents include me in everything. Izzy even asks me what I'm currently writing, and among them, who've never heard the clock tower lore, the opinion is split down the middle on whether it should be fixed or not.

After the second time we eat—yes, the second—I steal away outside to write some notes on my article about the clock tower. Since people will want to make their own opinions, the fact-only piece will help them decide. I could even poll the newsroom or other specific campus groups for sidebar content. Maybe urge the school administration to let the students decide the clock tower's fate with a popular vote.

I write down my last note and come up for air. The wind off the lake whips around for a second, and with it, voices filter toward me. It takes me a minute to realize Zaiah and his sister are doing the dishes in the RV above my head.

"I like her."

"Me too," Zaiah says. "She's fun."

"Would you maybe like her...more?" she pries.

My stomach twists. I definitely shouldn't listen to this, but I can't really get up now. They'll see me.

He groans. "I wish you guys would stop butting into my love life. I'm not interested in being with anyone right now."

"Listen, Trish was a bitch. It's normal—"

"It's not about Trish," he snaps.

"It is."

"Okay, fine, it is. She twisted me up inside. Had me thinking one way, then the other. It was like a roller-coaster."

"And you were in it for the ride."

"Yeah, except the ending sucked." He pauses for a few moments as the faucet turns on, and I'm worried I'm going to miss something. Morbid curiosity and all that. But when it turns off, I can hear them perfectly again. "I don't know if I can trust anyone right now."

"You have to start sometime."

Dozens of images flit through my mind. The kind of person I was around Trish. The kind of person she really was, deep down, when she let the monster come out. The way she used me to cheat on Zaiah. Of course, I didn't know it at the time.

She had all of us played.

When I confronted her about it, she acted like she was some sort of diabolical mastermind instead of someone who truly cared about anyone. I couldn't stand it. For once, I finally stuck up for myself. I told her no more, that she couldn't use my name as an excuse to see her side boyfriend, and if she did it again and I found out about it, I'd tell Zaiah myself.

To my knowledge, she never did, but I told Zaiah anyway. Well, sort of. I didn't go up to him and say, "Hey, I know Trish has been cheating on you." I sent him an anonymous email with pictures I'd taken of a message thread on her cell phone.

I wasn't sure he'd even read the email, let alone put much weight into the content, but before I knew it, he'd confronted her. To her only credit, she didn't lie. She spun tale after tale about how they never said they were exclusive, but she didn't lie.

If you've never heard a manipulator manipulate their way through a situation, it is horrific.

While listening to them argue, I picked out things here and there that sounded so familiar. Things she used to say to me that would make me feel crazy for being upset. She knew how I felt about that. We'd spent countless nights of me talking about my overbearing father, and yet she was manipulating me into submission, too.

The worst part of the whole scenario is that I *let* her take away my voice.

I wish I'd had the balls to tell Zaiah about her cheating myself. Instead, I made it some sort of espionage mission. Call it immaturity or shyness, I'm not sure which, but sending him that anonymous email sounded like the best option at the time.

Hearing the anger still in his voice, I wish I'd given him that answer respectfully and with sympathy.

I'm glad she moved out. I'm glad she yelled all that awful shit at me and left immediately so I didn't have the chance to forgive her.

I blow out a breath, and in my stillness of mind, their conversation comes back. "Nothing is going right, so no sense in starting a relationship with anyone. Plus, I'll be graduating soon. Why begin something when in a few months, everyone will be headed their separate ways?"

"When did you become a nun?"

"I'm being smart. It's called maturity."

"I think you're just scared."

I close my notebook, my stomach turning over. Zaiah doesn't want to date, and I don't even know why I'm reacting like this. I guess there was still a part of me from that night when I was dancing on the table that held out hope...but it's squashed now.

# CHAPTER EIGHT

Zaiah

Lenore climbs into the RV. I peer over my shoulder at her while Izzy's words swirl inside my head. *Scared? Please.* I punch people out on the ice if I have to. I'm not ready to have a girlfriend right now because the idea is stupid.

My sister opens her mouth again, and I hip-check her. Luckily, she looks back to find Lenore there. "Inspiration?" she asks her.

My roomie nods. "I have a mind like a sieve, so if I don't write it down, I'll forget. Then I'll get mad at myself and won't write because I'm convinced whatever thought I had previously was a better thought than any future thoughts."

We both peer at her, my eyes giving her the "you're crazy" look.

"It's a vicious cycle," she explains.

Izzy turns back around, handing me the dish to dry. Under her breath, she says, "For what it's worth, I liiiike her." Rolling my eyes, I turn to put away the bowl, and when I turn back, she's glaring at me. "Maybe a change in the type of girl you go for is exactly what you need."

"I don't have a type," I whisper-yell.

She bursts out laughing.

At that moment, my father comes in from the back. "What's all this laughing?"

"Nothing, Dad. Zaiah thinks he's a regular comedian over here."

He sits on the couch opposite Lenore, and I smile when he peers over at her. My dad is such a people person. Hell, he could talk to a light pole. It was smart to bring her today, forcing her to interact. You'd have to be rude not to be active where my family is concerned.

"Lenore, have you ever seen Zaiah play hockey?"

Her gaze darts up. Every time hockey is mentioned, she startles a little. I'll have to unravel that mystery. Actually, Len has a lot of mysteries. Pulling stuff from her is like trying to make fire out of water.

"Oh, yeah. Yes." She shakes her head. "I have. I'm sure I have."

"I hope you'll come to his game tomorrow."

He barely has the words out before she's answering. "Oh, no, I have to work on my article."

I can't help but grin. *Man, she wants to avoid it at all costs, doesn't she?*

"No, remember?" I ask, turning completely to face

89

them. I dry off a dish until she peers at me. "I already got you a ticket. You said you wanted to come for that *other* article you were going to write."

Her gaze narrows, but she plasters a fake smile on her face. "I don't know what I was thinking."

"I put you in the family section with Mom, Dad, and Izzy."

My dad waggles his brows like a cartoon character. "VIP."

She can barely muster fake enthusiasm. "That sounds...great."

When my dad glances away from her, Len tosses me a look, but I shrug, my lips curving into a grin. She approached me about this, so it's all on her. She needs to experience hockey before she can write about it. Maybe I can even get her to a practice, too.

"You're not a sports person?" my father asks.

"Not really." She clears her throat. "My dad's a big, um, sports person, though. I guess that kind of turned me off."

"Turned you off?"

"Dad," Izzy warns. I swear she has a sense of when to push and when not to push people.

He waves his hand. "I know, I'm prying. Forgive me."

Len shrugs. "It's fine."

I wait for her to continue, but she doesn't. Silence in the RV lengthens.

*Strange...*

Smoothing the towel over the sink, I say, "Well,

Dad, I hate to break up this party, but Lenore and I have to get back."

He stands from the couch, the smile dropping from his face. "Let me tell your mother."

There's a shift in the RV, and I wonder if Lenore can feel it. We've eaten, we've played games, we've talked. But now I have to go prep for the game, and my mom is about to come out crying.

On cue, sniffles sound behind me. "Oh, baby."

"He's twenty-two, Mom."

She swats my sister away and opens her arms. I go into them, rocking her. Her head hits my shoulder, and I rub her back. "I'll see you again tomorrow," I remind her.

"I know." She peers up, tears clinging to the corners of her eyes. "Have a good game. Blow me a kiss after you score."

I chuckle. "Mom, I think that's bad luck now."

She steps back, craning her neck. "It is not. Nothing involving your mother could ever be bad luck. You go out there and put that puck in that net tomorrow. You hear me?"

I lean over to kiss the top of her forehead. "You got it, Coach."

"Alright, let's go, then," my father says abruptly, already reaching into his pocket for the keys.

I squeeze Mom one more time and turn to follow him, waving at Lenore to do the same. "He'll drive us back in the car."

She nods, eyes lighting up. When she saw the Mini Cooper my parents were towing, she freaked out.

Another one of my father's toys.

"It was so nice to see you all," Lenore says, her voice genuine.

My mom pulls her into a hug too. "You too, sweetheart. Come any time."

"Feel free to leave the big dope behind," my sister offers.

I flip her off, and even though my back is to her, I'd be willing to bet she's doing the same.

I wave Len in front of me and then walk down the stairs, leaving Mom and Iz behind. "See you at the game!"

"Go Bulldogs!" Mom yells.

My dad pulls the car up to the door of the RV at the same time. "You're going to have to sit in the back," I tell Len. "I'm too tall."

"Like I'd sit in front," she chastises. "It's your family."

I blink, déjà vu hitting me. The outcome, though, is much different.

Trish told me I was being rude for asking her to sit in the back around my family and making her feel like a second-class citizen. From then on, I was always cramped in the back seat with my knees in my face while my father gave me disapproving looks in the rearview mirror.

Taking a breath, I close my eyes, letting the uneasiness go. I open the door for Len and grab her hand to help her into the car. I don't know why I do it. It's automatic, a gesture of appreciation. "Thank you."

She gives me a strange look. "It's a car ride...you big dope." Her lips turn up, morphing into a wide grin.

The tension sluices off me in an instant seeing her blue eyes shine with mischief. I lean into the back seat. "That's not going to make it into the article, right?"

She taps her chin like she has to think about it.

While she's distracted, I grab the seat belt and pass it around her waist. My fingers graze her hip, and she stills. The seat belt clicks into place, breaking the shocked look on her face, and it's my turn to smile at her. "You good?"

She nods, swallowing. "Mm-hmm. Yeah. Fantastic. All hooked in. As snug as a bug in a rug."

"Did you...eat too much of my mom's dessert?" I tease. "You seem kind of jittery."

My phone pings, distracting me. My father, however, launches into a conversation about Mom's cooking, which Len graciously listens and responds to while I take out my cell and find a text from Iz:

Mr. I'm Not Interested, that looked pretty damn cozy.

Peering up, I spot my mom's and my sister's faces plastered in the RV window. Iz smirks, and Mom is looking on like she's watching a romantic movie.

I slide into the car, typing:

You can mind your business now. Don't get Mom in a tizzy.

93

I sigh, putting my phone away and shutting the door.

My father asks, "Everyone all buckled?"

*No, not from him, too.* I turn his way, and he's giving me the widest grin.

My whole family is crazy.

The rest of the way back to our suite, my dad talks happily beside me as the lake turns to trees, then the trees to houses when we near Warner. Len asks him questions about the Mini, and he answers with glee. If there's anything he loves to talk about, it's the toys he's acquired.

Before long, we're pulling to a stop in front of Knightley. He puts his hand on my shoulder until I turn to look at him. "Good luck. See you at the game."

"Thanks, Dad."

"Thank you for your hospitality," Len says from the back. "I really had fun hanging out with the Jameses today."

My dad peers over his shoulder and smiles. "You're welcome back anytime, dear."

That's more than they said to Trish, and rightfully so, looking back on everything.

I give my dad a mock salute, and Len and I get out. My heart is heavy, weighing my footsteps down. It always is after I leave them. Their presence is a reminder of where I came from and the fact that their lives kept on turning, even when I wasn't there to enjoy it with them.

"Wow, your family is so—"

"Don't," I snap, waving at my dad as he pulls away.

"I was going to say awesome. Or amazing. I was going to say that I wish my family was more like yours."

"Oh." I cast my gaze toward the ground while I walk. "Sorry. Reflex." I open the main door for us, but she's stopped moving, staring at me until I add, "Some people think my family is too much."

She nods, and I might be imagining things, but I'm pretty sure she knows exactly who I mean. She probably heard it all, come to think of it.

"Well, I thought they were great. All of them. If my dad came to visit, you would die of boredom."

"Only your dad?"

"My mom left when I was two." She averts her stare, but I don't think it's out of grief, just another mystery that makes up Lenore.

"I'm sorry."

She shrugs in answer and slips through the open door. We head toward our suite, Len walking in front, and I have to say, those leggings are working for her. Not that I'm trying to look. Her ass is just kind of there, and it's... *Damn.*

I shake the thought off. "Is it cool if I watch some game tape on the main TV in the living room tonight? It's bigger than the one in my room."

She lifts her shoulders, but then whirls, nose scrunching. "Yeah, thanks for telling me about the game so I look like an idiot, and don't make a habit of doing hockey...shit in the living room. That was one of our agreements."

I put my hands up in mock surrender. "I won't." Her attempt at sounding fierce brings a smile to my face. "I don't even have to do it tonight."

"I'll allow it," she says, eyes distrusting, then she breaks into a warm grin. "Only because I want you to blow a kiss to your mom tomorrow. I thought I was going to cry when she started crying."

"Then my diabolical plan is working."

"Huh?"

"Meet my family, fall in love with them, take it easy on me."

"Oh, is that it?"

I nod.

"Well, it is working," she says, shoulders deflating like all fight is leaving her.

"You could watch the game tape with me?"

She unlocks our suite door. "I'd rather throw myself off the roof."

She really hates hockey. How is she supposed to write a positive article about the sport if she despises it? Man, girls are complicated. That was one piece of advice my father gave me that still adds up. The man's a certified genius. Though, I'm not sure you have to be a genius to come to that conclusion.

Len throws up a hand, calling out, "Have a good night," as she walks directly to her room.

I stop in the mouth of the hallway, taking in the

suite. It's nice to have a clean, organized space. To not have some dude passed out, drooling on his bed. And the smells some guys can produce... I shiver.

This is heaven.

A part of me is scared to leave school, but the other part is so ready for it. I can stay with my parents until I'm settled. Not ideal because they are a bit nosey, but it's better than other options.

I grab some snacks and relax into the couch before casting the game tape I asked Coach for onto the TV.

Half an hour later, Len comes out. "How can you still eat?" she asks as I bring a tortilla chip topped with salsa to my mouth. "Your mom can *cook*. I feel like I gained ten pounds."

She's back to wearing her frumpy pajamas, and since I've now seen her in leggings and know the shape of her body, she most certainly did not put on ten pounds. "Carb loading."

She grins, shaking her head all the way to the kitchen. Glasses rattle around and then I feel her behind me. "Number 9, right?"

How does she know my number? The question sits on the tip of my tongue, but I don't ask because it dawns on me that the reason is something I don't want to think about. "That's me."

Surprisingly, she stays there. "You're good, James."

I burst out laughing.

"What?"

"Such a fantastic compliment coming from someone who hates hockey."

She doesn't make a sound, and when I peer up, her cheeks are red. Coming around the couch, she sits on the opposite end. "Well, it wasn't hard to guess. You scored a goal in that footage."

She stays put, and I find myself looking at her more than I do the tape. Her profile is smooth. Pretty, even.

Surprise runs through me. I tilt my head, taking more of her in. She's wearing an oversized shirt and even bigger bottoms, but they tug tight around her ass as she brings her leg up. She's got the sexy girl-next-door look going on right now. Like in that Taylor Swift "You Belong With Me" video, the friend you suddenly find pretty, even though Len and I were never really friends. I looked past her whenever Trish was around, which was a mistake. If today is anything to go by, I would've had a better time with Len.

"Hey."

She spins toward me.

"Why did you introduce yourself to my dad as Lenore?"

She shrugs. "I don't know. I felt like I needed to be someone different to pull off a meeting with your family." She settles back, taking a drink. "Turns out, I'm not sure I had to. They were so accepting."

"They are. So what do you want to be called? Or are we back to square one?"

She shrugs. "I don't know. Shouldn't I be asking you that question, relationship guru? Which one is more attractive, Lenore or Len?"

I wave her away. "I'm not deciding on your name. That's preposterous."

She raises her brows at me.

"I know. Your big words are rubbing off on me."

She grins, peering away. "I guess I don't know. Can't it be like someone who has the name Catherine? Sometimes people call her by her full name. Sometimes people call her Cat or Cathy."

"So, *Lenore* when you're in trouble. *Len* when we're having fun, and—"

"Never Nor," she ekes out, gaze serious.

I make a cross over my heart. My sister went through a phase where she did this all the time, and for some reason, I mimic her here. "Cross my heart."

I wonder why she hates the nickname Trish gave her. Why she doesn't know where Trish is or ever talk about her? Not that I should be thinking about her right now when I should be watching this tape.

I turn my attention back toward the TV, but Len asks, "When did you start playing?"

"Youth hockey," I answer. "My town had a team. I started when I was five."

"Impressive. And you still like it?"

"Still get butterflies when I put on skates."

She smiles. "That's like writing for me. A blank paper is full of opportunities. It's probably similar to when you put on skates. Thinking about all the things you could do..." She swallows. "Don't mind me, I'm kind of a romantic about things like this."

"Like what?"

"Chasing dreams."

I smile at the thought. I almost turn the tape off because talking to Len is far more interesting, but I'm afraid if I do, she'll leave. "Being known for something?"

She nods. "I like getting those bylines, I'm not going to lie."

"Like being immortalized." She nods in agreement, and I continue, "I used to want to play professionally, but..." There's a lot after that but. However, now that I'm thinking about it, it sounds like a lot of sour grapes. "It would've been nice to have my name hanging in a rafter somewhere, so I get what you mean about bylines."

"What are you going to do after graduation, then?"

"Get a job, settle down, maybe even coach for the youth hockey team that started me."

"I love that," she muses. "Full circle."

On the TV, the faint sound of cheering meets my ears.

"Serendipitous," she says.

"If you say so."

She watches the celebration on the TV, then asks, "How long are you going to be up?"

I check my watch. "Not sure. Another hour, maybe. I don't want to be up too late. Have to get my sleep in for the game tomorrow."

"I'll bring my work out here, then, and we can do it side by side."

"Yeah?"

"If I won't bother you. I just don't feel like being alone."

"Yeah, me neither," I say quickly, throat closing up.

She stands, returning a few moments later with her small laptop and a notebook.

"That's it?"

"This is it," she says, settling on the opposite end of the couch. She points to her head. "The magic happens in here."

Her words trigger goose bumps up and down my arms. She gets right to work—head down, fingers flying across the keyboard. I can only stare.

*The magic happens in here.*

I like it. I love it, actually. I go back to watching tape with that in mind, tomorrow's game starting to look like an amazing opportunity.

# CHAPTER NINE

Len

All hockey arenas smell the same. It's the ice. The chill in the air. The required snacks on offer. It's familiar and brings up memories I'd rather forget. I doubt anyone else could've gotten me here but him.

Zaiah James.

His name alone brings up a torrent of conflicting thoughts. Ex-best friend's ex-boyfriend. New roomie. Sweet. Caring. Off-limits.

Heartbreaker.

One thing is for sure, though, I always step outside my comfort zone when it comes to him.

He was at practice when I woke this morning, so I didn't receive his expertise in dressing or makeup. I ended up copying what we did yesterday. One of the shirts I enjoy wearing paired with leggings. My trusty notebook is completing the ensemble, of course. I'm here to write a story, after all.

I spot Izzy in line for some popcorn, and I wave to get her attention. She calls me over. "We got your seat ready."

My stomach dips. "Ready?"

"Oh, oh, oh, just you wait. You're going to wish Z never saved you a ticket. It's slightly mortifying. I'm glad he goes to school hours away now so my friends don't have to witness my humiliation."

I blink, the smile dropping off my face.

She must recognize the look of absolute horror because she laughs. "Yes, it's that bad."

*What has he gotten me into? Should I run away now?*

No wonder he smirked when he told me he had a ticket for me. And the near glint in his eyes last night when he said he'd see me at his game... It all makes sense now. He was pucking with me.

Well, joke's on him because hockey practically raised me. When Zaiah was watching game tape, it was all I could do to keep my mouth shut and pretend I didn't know anything. The truth is, my parents brought me home from the hospital in a hockey onesie—a gift from my father's team. His actual team that he *owns*.

Yes, my father owns a professional hockey team. A pretty damn good one, too.

I attended practices when I was little. The players treated me like their good luck charm. When I was older, I sat in the fancy owner's box, staring down at the excitement of competition below. I loved it...until it became apparent that I came second to a stick and a puck.

Absent due to business meetings and long trips to away games, my father missed dance recitals and school plays. My mother must've felt the same way because she split when I was two. I don't even remember her.

So, I started caring less and less about hockey and found writing.

Sirens would be blaring in the background, the crowd cheering, and my attention would firmly stay on the paper in my lap. People would hug and slap hands over top of me, and I still wouldn't move.

My stomach squeezes as mixed emotions roil through me. It's been ages since I've actually watched a game on purpose, since I cheered for the players on the ice, since I cared about who won or lost.

I offer Izzy a worried smile. "Your brother seems to really love the game."

"Obsessed is more like it. It's all he's ever wanted to do."

I take a breath, reminding myself that cheering on Zaiah and being with my father in the box are two different things. I'm not giving in. I'm not forgiving my father's neglect. I'm supporting a friend.

Zaiah talks about hockey like I talk about writing. He's making his dreams come true out on the ice. Why wouldn't I support him? Plus, I made a deal with him. He helps me, I help him.

To my right, the concessions worker dumps the popping popcorn, sending a whiff of memories my way. The arena smells like my father's only love, but maybe it will eventually smell like Zaiah's hope.

What am I talking about? *My* hope is that this is the last time I have to set foot in a place like this.

Izzy gets her popcorn, then leads the way to our seats. "So, my brother says there's nothing going on between you two. Yet you're here at his game?"

"Oh, yeah, no," I blurt out. "There's nothing going on between us. He's helping me with something."

"With what?"

I scratch the side of my face, feeling like I stepped in it. I should've kept my mouth shut, but I didn't know what to say. Was wading through his family's questions part of this deal? *Ugh.* "Well, I actually like this other guy."

"Another player?" she guesses.

"God no."

We turn the corner near the ice, and she laughs. "You really don't like hockey players, do you?"

I grab the railing, and it wobbles in my hand. This arena is less grand than the one I'm used to, and it's also a little worse for wear. I'll note that down for my story...whatever it's going to be about.

"More like I don't actually like athletes in general," I say with an awkward smile. "Competitive sports turn me off."

She laughs again. "I'm used to seeing girls trip over

themselves to talk to Z. I think you're good for him. Chop down that ego a bit."

I roll my eyes. "You should see the girls with the football players on campus. They're treated like royalty. And for what? Because they can throw a ball?"

"Exactly!" she exclaims. "And it's not reciprocated. I play field hockey and no one cares. No one attends my games except for family members of the other players. No scantily clad hot dudes line up before I get to the locker room, begging me to take them to bed."

"Take you to bed?" a female voice echoes.

Izzy peers up at her mom. "Talking with Lenore about the injustice of female versus male sports and how they're looked at like gods and I might as well be a lesbian."

"I would love you no matter what," Mrs. James remarks in all seriousness.

Izzy scoots down the line past Zaiah's parents, and his mom reaches out to hug me again. She smells of flowers and vanilla...and bacon. She must have made breakfast this morning. Probably better than the oatmeal I scarfed down while staring at my clock tower notes.

"Fancy meeting you here," his dad says, putting his hand gently on my arm when I walk past. "You may continue your boy-bashing. Don't mind me. I'm a girl dad, too."

I snicker, but then I stare down at what's waiting on my seat for me.

My seat is covered in Bulldog blue, complete with

a seat topper with a cushion and a huge symbol of our school mascot, the Bulldog. In the seat is a cowbell; a wiry, blue wig; and a Warner hockey shirt.

I've seen these types of fans before from the box. They're uber fans, and they're crazy.

Izzy nudges me with her elbow. "Aren't you so glad my brother made you come?"

I peer up. The three figures next to me are now wearing the wiry, bright-blue wigs, transforming from three normal people to fanatics in an instant.

"We wanted to ease you into it, dear."

Mrs. James adding a nice sentiment onto the end of that remark doesn't make up for what's about to happen. *I could refuse...*

At that moment, someone bangs on the boards protecting the crowd from rogue pucks. I startle, then glance over to find Zaiah waving at me, his mouthpiece in hand. With his helmet tipped up, the mischievous spark in his eyes is evident.

"You fucker."

Izzy throws her arms around me, her laughter like tinkling bells. "Oh, I knew I was going to like you."

Zaiah skates backward, giving me the biggest grin. "I think you mean *pucker*." I never knew what kind of smile would be considered shit-eating, but I've seen it now. I could describe it with ease if I ever needed to.

I pick up my notebook and point to it. "Watch what I write," I yell, trying to threaten him, but I'm about as ferocious as a caterpillar. My words don't dissolve the pure enjoyment on his face. If anything, they make it worse.

"Maybe there's still time to kick him out," Izzy quips.

Her mother gasps. "Don't say that. Can't you see how much happier he is now?"

Izzy leans in conspiratorially. "Don't let him win. We'll exchange numbers, and I can tell you all the little things that get on his nerves."

"You'd do that?"

"Happily."

"I'm going to take you up on that," I murmur as I pull the wig over my head. I know I don't have to wear it. I could simply sit and bury my head in my notebook, and if it was only Zaiah asking, I might tell him to kick rocks, but his family... I sigh, thinking at least it will be hard to recognize me with this wig on. Not that it matters. The seats in the stands are barely occupied. Only a few students, some family members—as Izzy said—and a cluster of people from the community made the trek to see the game. It's easy to pick the different segments out.

A line of younger girls on the opposite side of the ice, most definitely high school aged, hold up signs. Exactly the type of girls Izzy and I were talking about. Probably falling all over themselves to get the attention of an older hockey player.

"Zaiah calls them puck bunnies."

*Oh, I know.* They ran rampant around my father's arena. His team has a strict "no fraternizing with puck bunnies" rule. In fact, one of the crudest fan signs I've ever seen was held up by a cluster of twenty-something women: "I'll kiss my friends if you score, 17."

The more innuendo the better. Thinking about it now, after talking with Zaiah yesterday, those comments are disrespectful to how much work players put into their sport. I'm sure on some level they love it. They can get an easy lay and a confidence boost, but don't tell me pro players are actually settling down with puck bunnies. The girls let themselves be used, and the players do it because they can.

I jot down a note about that. Seems like I could write a detailed story about putting athletes on a pedestal. Definitely won't be the topic of Zaiah's story, but in the future, maybe. I'd already touched on it in my Warner University football scandal articles, so I know there's a lot more to be explored there.

Then again, I'm not writing about sports long-term. It is the last thing I want to write about.

I mentally cross off the idea when the announcer comes on. The players don't even get a grand entrance with their names called. They just line up to start the game. Pretty sure introducing players isn't only a pro-level thing. They should announce the starting lineup at the very least.

Zaiah takes his spot right in front of us as a winger. The guy lining up across from him is already jawing, but he gets his because as soon as the whistle blows, Zaiah checks him hard.

Izzy and I must have similar bloodlust because we

laugh maniacally, even capturing the attention of the guy who was the brunt of Zaiah's check—now sprawled out on the ice—and I follow suit when she jumps to her feet.

"Go Bulldogs!" she yells.

I don't scream, but I grab the cowbell.

*Oh dear Lord, what am I doing?*

The guy from the opposing team glares, but that has me shaking the thing faster.

"Girl," Izzy starts while we sit back down, "are you sure you don't care?"

"That guy was a dick," I say under my breath.

Izzy's father leans in on the other side. "Can confirm that guy was a dick."

I smile sheepishly, which makes him beam. Izzy, however, laughs so hard she grabs her side. "My parents don't care if you swear," she finally gets out. "Not really. Not since we've gotten older, anyway."

"As long as you don't sound like a trashy teenage dirtbag," her father remarks, waving a white-and-blue pom-pom.

I peer down the line and notice they all have pom-poms, but... "Am I the only one with a cowbell?"

"Think of it as an initiation," his mom calls out from farthest away, her full focus still on the ice. "One of us has to do it, and you drew the short straw."

"I didn't even draw a straw."

"Neither did we," Mr. James says as he jumps to his feet. I glance over at the ice to find one of our players making a run for it toward the other team's goal. He's out ahead of the pack.

"We need the cowbell!" Zaiah's mom yells.

*Welp, if they say they need the cowbell, they need the cowbell*. I grab it and jump to my feet, shaking that thing like I've been doing it all my life.

The player dekes once. Twice...

He shoots, and before I can even tell if the puck went into the net, the siren goes off, and we may be the only ones having a party, but we do the damn thing.

Blue-and-white pom-poms shaking, cowbell ringing, all four of us scream our heads off.

I don't even realize it's Zaiah who scored until he turns toward us while celebrating with his team. I'm mid jump, mid hugging his sister, the cowbell going off like I'm calling everyone to dinner in a three-mile radius, when his gaze flashes our way. Instead of skating to wherever he needs to be, he makes his way to us. I can barely see his face, but he blows that kiss to his mom that he promised, and then he moves his stare to me. "You watching, Len?"

I shake my head. *Cocky little...*

Izzy eyes me suspiciously, her eyes narrowed as I pick up my notebook. "He wants me to write something favorable for the paper."

"Yeah. That must be it," she says, sounding less than convinced.

She turns back around, and my stomach somersaults. This is...fun. Really fun, actually. Butterflies fill my insides, and it's cold in here, but that's not the

111

reason for the goose bumps spreading over my skin. Being here is like seeing an old friend, but even better because that friend is on its best behavior, is dressed immaculately...and looks like Zaiah James.

Is it possible I miss hockey?

*Nah.* It has to be something else.

*Oh shit.* My stomach tightens. After all this time, I couldn't still think about *him* like this, right?

"This is insane," I mutter to myself. Watching an innocent hockey game shouldn't bring up this many mixed emotions. From my father to Zaiah, it's like a tornado runs rampant inside my brain.

For the next period, Izzy distracts me from my thoughts, chatting to me about field hockey, interspersed with comments about the game. I put my analytical mind behind and go with the flow. His parents want a cheering partner, so that's what I do. Besides, I kind of love swinging that cowbell during fast breaks, steals, and fights—especially if Zaiah is involved.

At one point, I peer over to the player's box to find him watching, helmet off, his sweat-soaked hair plastered to the crown of his head, the ends curling by his ears. For a moment, I'm blindsided by the same feelings that surged inside me when I was dancing on that table and he was staring up at me. The initial rush, the flip-flop of my belly. All I could do was look on in disbelief that *I* grabbed his attention.

Like present day, the moment only lasts a few seconds, but it's enough to admire the stubble on his jaw, his easy smile, and dimples. I've never met someone with dimples before. They were a romance novel myth, but not anymore. He's a cover model come to life.

He winks at me, and then his coach calls his line to get back out on the ice. He secures his helmet, grabs his stick, and steps over the barrier, skating away like nothing happened.

Just like when Trish stole his attention, disappointment surrounds me. I had his interest for point three seconds and then *bam*, something better came along.

*It doesn't matter now*, I remind myself. We're only roommates. Clearly. Or maybe leaning toward the friend side. I could deal with that because no matter what Zaiah does, one thing is clear: He's a good person.

He gets the break away again, and we all stand. This time, #9 takes a direct approach and puts it in the net once more.

Before he even celebrates with his teammates, he peers over, and makes a writing gesture in the air, then points at me. I can't see his face from behind the helmet, but he must be loving this.

He's a golden boy...only no one on campus knows it yet.

# CHAPTER TEN

Zaiah

A DULL ACHE SURROUNDS MY RIBS. IT'S NOT THE only pain that makes its way to the surface, but it's the worst. Nothing I haven't felt before, thank God, and at least we can count today's game as a win.

I put my key in the door and find it already unlocked. Pushing it open, I hear shuffling from the living room, and when I close the door behind me, Len stands in the hallway, her hands cupped around her mouth. "And with three goals and one assist, the speed demon himself, Zaiahhhhhhh James!"

I tilt my head at the announcer's voice she's trying to emulate. *Man, she is too cute.*

She shrugs. "Everyone should have a hype man. Also, I figured out your publicity problem."

"Publicity problem?"

She places her hands on her hips. "Yes. You should

be out with your teammates, cruising the town, sowing your wild oats or something." She waves a hand dismissively.

"Sowing my wild oats? Are you in your twenties... or forties?"

"Ha. Ha. Listen, if no one else is going to act like you're a big deal, *you* have to. You should be out at a bar, talking really loudly about how you beat that team's ass today. Showing off your muscular...assets. Preening for your soon-to-be fans."

My mouth quirks. "You think I have assets?"

She gestures toward my body. "I think, you know, *all that* is what most people would consider...very well...put together."

"So, *you* like my assets?"

"I'm speaking generally."

She presses her glasses up her nose, and I can't help thinking her adorable factor is at a ten right now. She literally said *sewing your wild oats* and *assets*. "You can admit it. You were watching my *assets* during the game." I feign shock with a sharp inhale of breath. "Do you think my parents noticed? How inappropriate."

Her mouth drops, a fiery blush blazing across her cheeks. "I—"

"I'm joking."

"I know," she insists, raising her chin.

"I appreciate the welcome. Always love a reminder of how well I played." I stare at her for a few more seconds. Seeing someone else in the stands to watch me always feels nice, but Len wasn't just there casually observing, she cheered like a crazy person right along with my weird family.

"You guys really need the hype guy in the beginning." She grabs her laptop and sits back down on the couch. "Does that cost extra or something? You'd think he would come with the arena."

I walk cautiously to my bedroom and drop my bag before turning and facing Len, who hasn't moved from her spot. "It's been like that all four years."

"Petition for some changes."

"Too late now. Besides, I went to the media. I can feel everything changing right now." She peers up at me, and I make the same handwriting gesture that I made after scoring the last two times. "Taking those notes? Got some good ideas?"

"Yes. Right now, they include the outright fanatical fans some players produce. Cowbells and wigs." She sends me a glare.

"You like that, huh?" I eye up the couch, but I don't think I can sit without hurting myself.

"You could've warned me about the cowbell."

I snicker. "That was your least favorite? I thought it would be the wig."

"The bell was noisy and drew attention to the wig."

I lean against the couch. She can complain all she wants, but I saw something completely different. "You were having fun out there."

"I was," she admits, smiling to herself. "Your family's great. Truly. Your sister and I exchanged numbers, so I have a link to the inside now." She waggles her eyebrows like a cartoon evil mastermind. It's possible she might've spent too much time with my dad today.

I chuckle, cringing when pain shoots through me. Bruised ribs, for sure. The pain is always worse after the adrenaline wears off. Hobbling into the kitchen, I grab some water and take a few gulps before refilling the glass.

As much as I'd like to stay up and talk about the article, rest is in my future. "I'm going to bed," I announce. "Thanks for coming to support me and being good natured about it all. I'm sure my family was ridiculous." I grit my teeth against an upsurge of pain, giving her a wave as I start for my room again.

"Oh," she says. "Yeah, sure. Good night."

"Night."

I hobble to my bedroom as fast as I can and shut the door behind me. Breathing out a long exhale, I head to my attached bathroom and grab the pain reliever in the medicine cabinet. I take a few pills and then undress on my way to the bed, making sure the TV remote, my phone, and the water are next to me before attempting to lie down because I have a feeling it's going to suck for a few seconds, and I won't want to move for at least a few hours.

Quickly, I crawl onto the bed, wincing, but my theory is that situations like this are a Band-Aid scenario. The slower you move, the more torture you endure. Once I'm settled with pillows propped behind me, the rib pain goes back to a dull ache that the pills will take care of soon. Then I put *The Curse of Oak*

*Island* on at low volume and wait to fall asleep. They haven't found the treasure in a hundred years, so I doubt I'll miss it tonight.

Before long, my eyelids flutter closed, and the absolute exhaustion from the game pulls me under.

---

I BLINK AWAKE. My room is still dark. Outside, it's pitch black out, and I shake my head a little, remembering the weird dream I was having. It was treasure related, but not *The Curse of Oak Island*. A girl with curly hair pops into my head, the mountains in Arizona surrounding her.

*Oh, right.* A couple weeks ago, my sister told me about this book she was reading. This chick gets with her stepbrother and his two best friends, but the plot was about the Superstition Mountains and the treasure that's hidden there. A real treasure, apparently—The Lost Dutchman's Gold Mine. I've seen a documentary on The History Channel about it.

I shake my head. *Weird fucking dream.*

I shift to lie on my side, but then my body abruptly reminds me that I played a game recently. Before I can return to a comfortable position, however, a sneeze settles in my sinuses. Bracing would make it worse, so I just let it come. Pain shoots through me, and I grab my midsection. "Ah, fuck."

I groan until I move back, the pillows resting

behind me again. The stupid pain reliever wore off. If only I could get up and grab some more...

A knock sounds on the door. "Zaiah? You okay?"

For a moment, I think the voice is my sister, then my mom, then it comes back around to the fact that I'm in my dorm room and it must be Len on the other side. "I'm okay." My voice cracks. At this point, I'm not hiding anything. "Actually," I bite out, "could you come here?"

The door creaks open after a few seconds. Blonde strands stick out of a topknot haloed by the light in the living room. Her eyes round when she sees me. "Jeez, are you okay?"

"Sore from the game," I force out. "I was hoping you would get me some pain reliever. It's in my bathroom. I think I left the bottle on the sink."

"Of course." She heads that way. "How many?"

She shakes the pill bottle and relief floods me. "Three."

"You sure?"

"I'm a big dude, Len." *And the fucker defenseman that hit me was even bigger.*

"Fine, fine."

She comes out with the three pills cupped in her hand and lays them out on the nightstand next to the water.

"Do you need help sitting up? What hurts?"

"Everything, but mostly my ribs."

"Ohh, yeah. That hit in the third? Your mom flinched."

"I swear she has a direct connection to my brain."

"Would a heating pad help? Or some ice?"

"You have a heating pad?"

"If my cramps get too much."

"Cramps?" I sit up far enough so I can swallow the pills and groan. "Muscle cramps?"

"Period cramps," she deadpans.

I peer at her sheepishly. "If I could laugh without it hurting, I'd chuckle right now." I scoot back, wincing again.

Her lips thin. "Should I call someone?"

"No, this is normal. After a big hit, at least. It's my ribs."

"Do you need to go to the ER?"

I shake my head. "It's a bruise. It'll be gone in a couple days. Promise."

Her brow furrows, her gaze tracing over me. "Okay, well, I'm going to get you both the ice pack and the heating pad."

"Like being at home," I muse.

"Because you're in Knightley now, James. You're moving up in the world."

I snicker as she leaves the room. When she returns, I've taken the pills she left me and I'm nearly knocked back out again, fighting to stay awake.

"You're okay," she whispers. "Sleep. I'll take care of it." She places the ice pack on my ribs as gingerly as possible and the heating pad right next to me. "Text me if you need something, okay? I don't mind."

"Isn't it the middle of the night?"

"Yeah, but what are roommates for?"

Roommates are foul-smelling jerks. At least, in my previous experiences they were. Right now, my pain and exhaustion level want to call her an angel as she slips out of my bedroom, but I'll settle for friend.

---

I WAKE to early morning sun streaming in through my windows, but actually it's the shaking of my bed that did it. Through sleep-impaired eyes, I spy Len jumping up and down on one foot, her hair wild around her. "*Ow*. Son of a—"

"You okay?"

"Sorry," she whispers. "I was checking on you and stubbed my toe on your stupid bed."

"It's okay." I press my hand to my ribs and notice the ice pack is gone and the heating pad is now in its place. Unless I'm losing it, I'm pretty sure the ice was there when I went to sleep.

"I switched it out," she informs me, her foot hovering over the floor. "I figured you wouldn't text."

"Well, I was asleep."

"I know. You mumble in your sleep too. How are those snakes?"

"Snakes?" I sit up slowly to test my limits and surprise hits me when the pain is less.

She disappears into my bathroom, and the shake of the pill bottle sounds. When she returns, she says, "Yeah, you were mumbling about snakes, desert, and I think I heard treasure, but that could've been way off base."

"That's Izzy's fault." I take the pills, drop them onto my tongue and then swallow them with the remaining water on my nightstand. "She was telling me about a book. A romance, but it was about treasure hunting."

"That sounds interesting."

"Izzy thinks so. She says I might even like the smut in it."

"I'll have to ask her for the title. Over text. With my new bestie."

I shake my head at her full grin. "You didn't tell her I was in pain, did you?"

"Nah, I haven't even texted her yet. I wouldn't do that unless you wanted me to, anyway."

Well, that's good to know. I search for my cell. "I should probably get up. What time is it?"

"Nine," she tells me before I can check myself.

I yawn, and when I move my feet over the side of the bed, Len peeks at my abs, her stare lingering. She hasn't torn her gaze away to know that I'm watching her watch me.

Since she's taking her fill, I return the favor. A pair of athletic, dark-blue leggings hug her ass. I don't know if it's the design or the material, but her shape is on point. My gaze travels up to her top. A T-shirt that reads *Peace, Love, and the Oxford Comma* is styled to show off her body rather than hide it...just like I suggested. She's such a good little student.

I move the blankets off me to stand, and a rush of air hits me in places it shouldn't.

Len whirls away at the same time I abruptly pull the covers back up. *Shit, I'm naked.* "Sorry. I forgot."

Peeking over her shoulder, she avoids my gaze. A cute pink hue blossoms on her cheeks. "You should have a holster for that weapon."

"Um, what?" My fists grip the sheets as I try to hold back a laugh.

She squeezes her eyes closed. "Did I say that out loud?"

"I'm afraid so."

"I meant a holster...kind of like boxers. Or briefs. You know, whatever you prefer. They hide things, like a holster. Or whatever. Don't mind me."

She turns on her heels and tries to escape. I lunge after her, keeping the pink sheets around my waist to hide my weapon, a.k.a. junk, but my body protests at the sudden movement. My "hey" comes out more like a groan.

I grab her hand, and she shakes her head, refusing to look back at me.

"Len, it was funny. I enjoyed the joke."

Maybe a little too much. Underneath the polka dots, my cock stirs to life. I ignore it, waiting for her to finally face me again. Eventually, she does, and I drop her arm so I can pull the sheets up.

This time, her eyes don't stray from my face, and an astonishing amount of disappointment threads through me. "Thank you for taking care of me last night."

If I'd been with my previous roommate, I would've been woken up at one a.m. to him finally coming home from being out, and I'd be lucky if he didn't have someone with him.

"I guess you should've added to the contract that we wouldn't flash each other."

This brings a smile to her face, her blue eyes lighting up. "Yeah, I didn't foresee that happening. I was preoccupied with your smelly hockey gear." She swipes a strand of hair away from her lips, and I notice she's done her hair.

I reach out, touching one of the curls. "Did you do something different?"

"I finally used my curling iron, if that's what you mean."

"It looks nice." I can't believe I thought she was asexual. She's funny. Quirky. And...cute. Girl-next-door beautiful, actually. Hidden underneath those oversized clothes was a gorgeous body, and yeah, I'm probably a vain asshole for admitting it, but it took her showing me to see it.

My stomach tightens, desire threading through me. The feeling nearly takes my breath away. Since she-who-will-not-be-named, I haven't been attracted to another girl, as if her infidelity had stolen my ability to look at someone in that way. It was easy to keep the no-girls promise because none of them even tempted me.

"Len..."

She shakes her head again, like my talking broke a spell between us. After a deep breath, she says, "Clark texted and asked to meet."

"Oh." My shoulders sag. That name was nowhere on my radar. *Stupid*, I chastise myself. *She has a crush on someone else.* "Well, you should probably meet him, then."

"Any advice?" Her bright eyes peer into mine.

I gesture toward her. "You look great." It dawns on me that the shirt she's wearing is perfect for him. Mr. Perfect Clark Kent Editor. Why are there two different commas anyway? "And, you know, act like you're someone who deserves to be looked at."

"Yeah?"

She looks so hopeful that I push down any other thoughts. I can keep this strictly a roommate thing. Plus, maybe I only felt things because of the pain reliever and the fact that she saw my penis. She also took care of me all night. I'm just grateful for her and getting the pleasure signals mixed up.

I take a deep breath. "My other advice is to be honest and tell him how you feel. Ask him out on a date."

She grimaces.

The look of worry on her face makes me grin. "I guess you aren't ready for that yet."

She shrugs. "I have to get him to see me first."

"Flirt a little, then. If you can."

She pulls her shoulders back. "I can flirt."

"Of course you can," I agree. "Get out there and flirt. Show him how puckable you are."

"I'm going to flirt," she says, determined. Spinning on her heel, she marches toward the front door like she's on a mission.

Before she leaves, I call out, "Have fun. I'll need a full report later so we can plan your next steps."

She waves without looking, the door closing behind her.

A moment later, she returns. Giving me a sheepish smile, she runs in, then grabs her laptop bag before exiting again.

See? Adorable.

When the front door closes for good, I shut my own bedroom door and lean my forehead against it. *How did I get myself into this?*

I doubt even the author of that treasure-hunting story could come up with this storyline. Dating coach? Rooming with an ex-girlfriend's best friend?

Who does that?

# CHAPTER ELEVEN

Len

ICE CRYSTALS SPARKLE ON THE TIPS OF THE FROZEN blades of grass. An overcast sky lingers, allowing them to shine without being melted away, and every few steps on my way to the newsroom, the air clouds in front of me with a release of breath...and my so-called confidence.

The way Zaiah said *"If you can..."*

If I can? Of course, I— *I can't flirt. What am I doing?*

I physically, possibly even mentally, don't know how to do such a thing.

My stomach churns. It'll just be me and Clark, like it always is. Me, getting all the tingles while we work on the formatting. Him, being his cute little pre-Superman self.

I should be ecstatic. So why does my mind wander back to Zaiah?

Holy penis, that's why.

I flush all over, remembering the accidental flash. For a split second, I'd imagined he meant to. That his smirk was pride in showing me his...let's face it, *thick* cock.

*"See what you do to me?" he says in my erotica daydream.*

*He runs his fist up and down his length. My body floods with desire.*

*"I can't wait to take you, Sexy Girl. On your knees."*

I squeeze my eyes shut, willing my heart to calm. In what world would he ever call me *Sexy Girl*? Plus, thinking about Zaiah that way permeates into dangerous territory. Not only are we roommates now, but given my history with him, I could get carried away. Fast.

I'll admit, I was jealous of Trish. When I spilled the beans about her cheating, I worried I was being selfish. If my envy over their relationship clouded my judgment. Don't get me wrong, I knew what she was doing was terrible and selfish, but who was I more loyal to?

Trish didn't have a problem bringing that up in that last fight.

Zaiah deserves so much more than her, though. He shouldn't be second to anyone, and neither should I.

The fact is that he doesn't see me like that. He

never has. I need to put all thoughts of him away and focus on someone I could possibly have: Clark.

I get to the newspaper building and stall because that realization still doesn't help me with flirting. Calling Zaiah now and asking him how to do it would make me want to crawl under a rock, so I gather other resources. One, I send a quick text to Izzy. I've just met her, but I miss having a girlfriend I can talk about this stuff with. Two, I pull up trusty Google since I don't have the time to look for better resources. In some instances, however, Google can be good, and I hope this is one of those times.

*Top results: Playfulness, Authenticity, Respect, Kindness.*

*Teasing and joking.* Okay, I can do that. I do that with Zaiah.

*I do that with Zaiah?!*

Before I can look too far into it, my phone buzzes with a text from Izzy.

Cleavage. Zaiah likes cleavage.

My fingers fly across the keyboard.

This isn't about your brother!

Oh, right. Sure. Well, I think every guy likes cleavage.

I peer down at my shirt. There's no way a pop of

boob is going to come out of there, so that nixes that idea.

> Then again, this guy sounds like the opposite of most guys. He probably wants you fully covered. Standoffish. Be cold. Ignore him.

I eye my phone screen. I don't even think I said much about Clark. Clearly, she doesn't know how to flirt either.

Playfulness it is.

With a deep breath, I pull open the door and walk toward the newsroom. I glance past the glass windows and find Clark there, his laptop open in front of him. He bites down on a pencil, and besides how unsanitary that is, he looks cute.

My heart springs into action, beating harder. Before he can see me watching him, I move to the door and open it. He glances up when I enter, smiling. "Hey there."

"Hey," I say. My brain fires, telling me to add a flirty nickname, so I quickly conjure up, "My super—" *NO, NO, NO. ABORT!* "My super...editor, you."

His smile grows wider. "Not feeling it today, though. This layout has got me stumped."

His gaze immediately tracks back down to the screen. Maybe I should've come in butt first? Zaiah did say my butt looks good in leggings.

My stomach flutters all over again, but I push that thought out of my mind. "I'm sure we can figure it out."

I would normally set up across from him, but not

this time. I stride to his side of the table, drop my stuff in an empty chair, and move in close. First, I just stare at him. Clark is the right amount of good looking. Perfectly cute. Though, his jaw isn't as nice as Zaiah's. His frame is smaller, too. Most guys our age are, so it's not his fault. I'm one hundred percent sure Clark isn't packing the six-pack Zaiah has. Or the—

My face flushes.

I need to get his dick out of my brain.

"Any thoughts?"

Clark still hasn't *really* looked at me yet. Had I worn a shirt for cleavage purposes, he wouldn't have even noticed.

I sigh, finally looking down to see what he has. Clark has many talents as an editor, but layout isn't one of them. One glaring error is that he has my clock tower article on the front page. "Oh, Clark, I'm not done with the clock tower piece. Maybe next issue."

He peers over. "Really? You're usually so much more prompt."

A pang of pain hits me square in the chest. I search for the right words because I did tell him I'd have it done this upcoming week, but I didn't mean Tuesday's paper. "I don't have enough right now, and I got another idea over the weekend that will take some time to put in place."

He sighs. "Well, that ruins that idea."

"Run the piece Murphy is working on," I offer.

"He said he needs another week as well."

"Hasn't he been working on it for over a month?"

Clark shrugs, and I have to take a deep breath to calm myself. *He's saying I'm not prompt?* "I'm sure someone has something worthy of front and center."

"I'll figure it out." A quick, hard tap on the delete key cuts the placeholder title for my article from the doc. Guilt laces through me. I've really been working on that article when I can, pretty much all available hours, but it's a bigger piece than I imagined when I pitched the idea.

I shake those thoughts away. *He's not mad at me,* I tell myself. *He's overwhelmed by the layout.*

"Of course you will." Placing my hand tentatively on his shoulder, I rub my thumb over it. However, as soon as I do it, I stare at my hand in horror. It feels weird. Wrong, even. Heck, I touched Zaiah's naked chest all night changing out his heating pad to ice every hour or so, yet this is so much more awkward.

"Thanks," he mutters.

He still doesn't look up, so I drop my hand, shaking the odd feeling off. Maybe if we get the layout over with, he'll finally notice me.

I stare at the project, and my brain starts clicking. "Why don't you ask Aimee for that piece she's been working on? Pretty sure she had something for you. Run with Flora's piece on the side column, then our sports box... Oh, the hockey score is wrong. It was five to two, not four to two."

"How do you know?"

"I was at the game."

He peers up. We're hunched over the laptop

together, but I can feel his gaze on me. Slowly, I turn to face him. He cocks his head. "You don't like sports."

"Oh, I, um... Well, I was kind of coerced." I push my glasses up my nose.

He studies me a moment, then takes out his phone. "I'll text Dev to confirm."

I could text a better source than that but whatever. While he's busy, I switch the football score and the hockey score around, putting the hockey score on top. *Ha.*

"While he gets back to me," he trails off as we start to work on the rest of the paper.

We go over each page, and I have the whole thing done in about half an hour. When we're through, I shrug. "I think you get caught in the weeds," I tell him. "You can't do it wrong."

"You're a whiz," he says in awe. "It's like you have a sixth sense."

He's not even looking at me, but I feel his compliment down to my toes. I bump him with my shoulder. "Look who's talking."

It was supposed to be a playful gesture, but Clark stumbles into the chair next to him, and I watch in horror when he catches himself on it, flailing.

"Oh my God. I'm so sorry!"

He blushes as he rights himself. "Maybe you should try out for the football team. You'd make a good linebacker."

My shoulders slump, and I groan internally. Just

what every girl wants to be compared to, a hulk of a man. I barely touched him!

His phone pings, and he peers down at it. "Dev says the score is right."

"It's not," I tell him, rolling my eyes. "Here, I'll text Zaiah."

"Zaiah?"

"Zaiah James. He's a winger."

"You know a hockey player?"

"Mm-hmm. You know, the guy who was in here the other day?" While I'm talking, I text with Zaiah:

> Hey, what was the score of the game yesterday? Need it for the paper.

Is this a cry for help? You were there.

> I know but pretend I don't because the sports reporter is saying something different, and I need proof to show Clark.

Just tell him you're right.

> I did.

Then?

> Please text the score.

> Wait...

I send a few periods in a row to bury the rest of the conversation so Clark won't read what we're saying.

What the fuck was that?

The score, Zaiah.

Aren't you going to ask me if I'm feeling better?

I smile, shaking my head. *So stubborn.*

"What are you smiling about?" Clark asks.

I nearly jump out of my skin. I'd almost forgotten he was waiting. "Oh, Zaiah's being...Zaiah." I point to the phone like the evidence is all there, but when Clark looks over, I angle it out of the way.

Since I nursed you back to health all night, I know you're fine. The score.

For the record, I think this is ridiculous.

> 5–2, sexy butt.

> You ass.

I cover up the sexy butt and show my phone to Clark. "From a player himself."

"Okay." He sighs as he changes the score, not even realizing that I switched the order around. "Wonder if the rest of these are even right."

"Dev should probably pay more attention. All of them could be wrong."

He shudders, and I agree. We're here to report the news, not give out misinformation.

My phone buzzes again.

> How's the flirting?

> I flirt adequately, thank you.

> Adequately? I can already tell this is going terribly.

> That's where you're wrong. I don't only nurse jocks back to health, I can flirt with the best of them.

"You sure do smile at your phone a lot."

"I smile at you, too, if you would pay attention."

The words fly out before I even realize. It's all Zaiah's fault. I was in a combative and playful mood texting the stubborn jerk.

My hand flies over my mouth, my phone forgotten.

Mortification flits through me, and my face heats like a raging furnace. "Sorry, Clark. I don't— I just—"

He grins, and it warms his face. Pushing his glasses up his nose, he stands up straight. "I'm always in business mode when we're in here, aren't I?"

I nod, holding my phone to my chest. "Which is honorable," I state. "Very honorable. Please, I'm so embarrassed. I didn't, um...."

"It's okay. I kind of like the idea of you smiling at me."

"You do?" My heart thumps, a rush sounding in my ears. It's like I'm living in a vacuum as I hear my voice ask, "Maybe we could go do something sometime? Coffee? Or..." That's all I've got. Coffee. "Or something other people do?"

He places his hand on my shoulder. "That would be nice. We should do...something."

I can't tell if he's as nervous as I am or if he's trying to joke with me about my complete and utter lack of eloquence in this moment, but I did it. I did what Zaiah told me to do, and now Clark keeps staring at me. It's kind of unnerving, actually. I feel like I have to say something. Anything. I laugh nervously and peer at my feet. "Sorry, I'm bad at this."

"Me too." He chuckles, and I feel a little better, but only a fraction.

*At least we can be bad together.* I think about saying exactly that, but the innuendo stops me. "We could go for coffee now. If we're done here?"

He checks his watch. Disappointment hits me, but then he answers, "Yeah, I can do that."

I gather my things and wait as Clark saves the file and shuts his computer down. He doesn't look at me again until he says, "Ready." I make sure to walk away first, hoping Zaiah isn't lying about the way my butt looks in leggings. The more I wear them, the more comfortable I'm getting, too.

He locks up, and then we start off toward the small café on campus. It's not the first time we've gotten coffee together, but other people are usually involved and there isn't a layer of discomfort hanging around us.

"So, how's your article coming?"

"Good," I explain. "I had this idea about polling some of the student body. Different segments, for instance, athletes versus science majors versus a random slice. Then comparing the data."

"That would be cool."

He doesn't sling his arm casually over my shoulder or bump me with his elbow like Zaiah would. He isn't the type, but if he was, it would make things so much easier.

"How are classes?" I ask because I've only crushed on this guy for two years and that's all I can think to bring up. Before I can eye-roll myself to death, I remind myself that the alternative is letting him know how much of a creeper I've been and sling all of his interests out at once.

"They're okay. I'm ready to graduate and start my life, you know?"

"Any job prospects?"

"Just worrying about graduating for now. I'll have to stay with my parents, then do the whole send out resumes and stuff. What about you?".

"I don't know. I'm thinking of freelancing for a bit."

We finally arrive at the coffee shop, and it's overrun with people. Luckily, a spot opens up in the far side when two girls wearing workout gear stand to leave, so we take it, and Clark offers to get my coffee.

My leg jumps up and down as I watch him walk up to the counter. Everything I wanted is happening right now, and I'm overwrought with awkwardness. It's like I've never talked to a guy in my life, let alone the one I'm on a date with.

"Hey," a voice says.

I peer up to find one of Zaiah's teammates, but I'm not sure of his name. "Oh, hey."

He sits down. "It was so cool seeing you at the game. We were all talking about it."

I laugh, nearly choking. My gaze flits to Clark at the counter and back to the seat he's supposed to occupy that's now been confiscated by a much larger frame. "Lovely, I can imagine."

"The Jameses are hilarious. You took it in good stride."

"Thanks. I think the blue hair really fit me."

He pulls out his phone, taps it a few times, and then brings up a picture of the four of us yelling. I have the most ferocious look on my face.

I cringe. "Tell me not everyone has seen that picture."

"My parents took it. They were sitting a few rows ahead of you guys, and no, I won't tell you that I sent this to the team group chat."

My stomach squeezes. "You didn't..."

"I did." He grins, and he has a charm about him because I really want to throw up right now, but he's making me feel better about it. "It was too good to pass up. Plus, it was nice seeing someone in the stands other than family."

I rub my temples, still staring at me in my open-mouthed, God-knows-what-I-was-screaming glory. "Glad to be of service."

"Is that you, Len?"

I sit straighter, my elbow slamming down on the table. Clark's holding two cups of coffee and peering at the picture.

Zaiah's teammate stands. "I take it this is your seat?"

Clark laughs, still peering at the picture. "You look ridiculous."

Zaiah's teammate gives him a funny look. "It was all in good fun."

"Who are the others? Is that your family?"

I stare at him, sure I've mentioned before that it's only me and my dad, which would mean this obviously couldn't be my family. But it's okay. He can't be expected to remember every little thing about me. "No, that's Zaiah's sister and parents."

"Oh, jeez."

My stomach twists. Zaiah's teammate is still giving Clark some major side-eye and shuts the screen off, finally taking the picture away. He steps out of Clark's path, his look frosty. "See you later, Len."

"Yeah, later."

Clark offers me a cup, and I wrap my hands around it, watching Zaiah's teammate leave the café. I've only been Zaiah's roommate for a few days and the hockey team already knows me. Wonderful.

Clark shakes his head, then takes a sip.

"What?" I ask.

"You don't seem the type."

I'm sure I should come back with something flirtatious, but my mind is stuck on *type* and won't move on.

I can't do anything right. Not studious enough for Clark. Not pretty enough for Zaiah. Not that *that* matters now.

When am I ever going to be enough just the way I am?

# CHAPTER TWELVE

Zaiah

THE CLANG OF STICKS REVERBERATES AROUND THE
rink. I stand from the bench and knock my own against
the sidewall while my team scrimmages. Luckily, the
rib pain is nearly healed thanks to Len. The trainer
should okay me to come back to practice in a couple of
days. If they don't, I'll revolt.

Adam skates up to the bench and stops quick, sending
ice shards flying my way. "Dick." I give him the universal
sign for what I think of that move, and he laughs it off
before throwing his legs over the wall during a line change.

He takes off his helmet and shakes his head, his
sweaty hair moving with his momentum. "You seem
pissed."

"Just want to get back out there," I answer, staring
longingly at my teammate handling the puck.

He shrugs. "That's not all."

*Not this again.* I shouldn't have told Adam what I think of Mr. Super Editor Douchebag because the asshole keeps bringing it up. "Listen, I'm fine."

His gaze bores into the side of my face, but I don't give him the satisfaction of looking up at him because *'I'm fine'* is an utter lie. It's Adam's fault. He texted the team group chat almost a week ago with a pic of Clark and Len at the coffee shop. Before she even got home, I knew she'd gone on her first date with Clark. I also knew that he'd made fun of her for what she looked like at the game.

Adam putting Clark on blast in the group chat was like hanging up a wanted poster with his face on it. The team and I are watching him very closely.

Len endeared herself to my teammates when she was such a good sport at the last game alongside my parents. They took to her immediately. Like big brothers, response after response to Adam's callout were all colorful ways to say they'd kick his ass.

We don't play around when it comes to one of our own.

"You should talk to her."

"I can't butt into her life like that." No one on the team knows that I'm her dating coach. I practically pushed her to get the guy. Hell, I'm the one who told her to ask him out, to flirt. Truthfully, I wasn't sure she had it in her. I thought she'd figure this guy out before it got this far.

Now, how am I supposed to tell her she's making a huge mistake?

Coach blows the final whistle, and I follow the guys into the locker room after slapping their hands one by one. When Coach goes into the office, I pull a freshie aside and tell him he needs to be more aggressive. He skates like a dream in practice, but he's tentative during games, and he's not getting many minutes because of it. If he wants to play more, he needs to impress Coach when it counts.

He nods, slapping my shoulder. When I turn, Adam's in a hushed conversation with Jonesy, a sophomore. He sees me heading back over, and he turns Jonesy's shoulders to face me.

"Oh, hey," Jonesy says, shifting on his feet.

Adam smirks, shucking off his gear before leaving for the showers.

"'Sup?" I ask, getting my bag out of the locker.

"A few of the guys and I were wondering about Len..."

"What about her?" I shut the door a bit too hard.

He stares at it, and Adam's voice comes wafting toward us from God knows where, like he's narrating this from some unseen place. "Say it."

Jonesy sighs. "A few of us were wondering if she's available?"

"Excuse me?"

He wipes his hands down the pads at his thighs. "We weren't sure if you were interested. She was sitting with your family in the stands and she's your roommate, yet she's dating this other guy. We don't want to step on toes, but we could give her some other options to get this douche away from her."

I blink, suddenly wishing I was suited up because I'd check this guy into the lockers for even thinking about Len that way. "You want to date her?"

"She's got this sexy librarian thing going on."

I look around, noticing some of the other guys are peering our way. I swear to God, they're like vultures. "She's off-limits," I snap before I even realize what I'm saying.

He brings his hands up in front of his chest. "Okay. We're cool. We just wanted to know."

He walks away, and I stare at the ground. Len would kill me if she knew I did that. Jonesy will put the word out that she's mine, and it'll only take a few minutes for this to travel through the whole team. If they were protective over her before, they'll be doubly so now.

*She's off-limits.*

I don't know what came over me. I grab my bag and turn toward the exit, my mind a whir of so many things. I had no grounds to claim her at all, but for some reason, it feels more than right.

*Fuck. How did this happen?* I meander in the direction of Knightley, not sure what to do about Len. As observant as she is, she'll know the guys are acting differently toward her. A couple of days ago, she mentioned they were extremely nice to her, initiating conversation and greeting her in the hallway.

145

One of them might even say something about this to her now.

*Shit.*

I march up Knightley's steps, stomach flipping. Fishing out my key, I place it in the lock and twist once I get to our suite but realize it's already open. I enter and hear a giggle. For a moment, I smile, thinking Len is up to something, but when I close the door behind me and walk down the hall, she jumps up from the couch and smooths her shirt.

The tool is with her, and the smile drops off my face.

I glare at him as he fixes his glasses. "Hey," I say.

"Hey. We were..." She trails off, red rushing to her cheeks.

Clark elbows her, and I want to knee him in the crotch. How dare he? I don't care if she were to say they were getting busy on the couch, you don't shut her up like she's a child.

I take a deep breath and give her a smile. "It's okay."

"I should go," Clark states.

*Yes, you fucking should.* It would be polite to leave the room, but I stand my ground.

He grabs her hand. "Gotta get ready for tonight."

My gaze zeros in on their interlaced fingers. "What's tonight?"

"Clark and I are going out to celebrate my article."

I peer up at her, taking her in. She's beaming, and jealousy ricochets through me. "Where to?"

"Bubbles."

I lift my brows. A nightclub doesn't sound like a place either of them would go, but okay. Every so often, they have a special night when they pump in bubbles from the ceiling. Trish and I went before. It was a blast —or so I thought at the time. "Cool."

"You should come," she says, gaze lighting up.

Clark gives her a look. I wasn't going to turn her down at all, but now I'm going to make him pay. "That's awesome. I would love to. I did read your final draft, after all."

She grins, pushing my shoulder. "Catches one missed period and this guy thinks he should get a byline."

"It was a crucial period."

She shakes her head, and the way she laughs does something to me that I can't explain.

Clark clears his throat.

*What kind of motherfucker clears his throat like that?*

"I'm going to take off." He glances my way. "Other people are going tonight, so, unfortunately, there's no room for you in the car. You'll have to find your own ride."

"No problem. I got a car." My smile stretches so tight it could crack at any moment.

Without warning, Clark swoops down and kisses Len on the cheek. I watch it all, wanting to rip him away from her. I'm beyond telling myself it's because he's a jerk to her. These feelings came on gradually, then all at once, nearly plowing me over. She's smart and funny, and no matter how many times I try to talk myself out of it, I'm still going to feel this way.

I move next to her while he strides down the hallway. He turns at the last second, and I'm right there, taking his spot. For good measure, I put my arm around her. His smile falters, and he quickly closes the door behind himself.

"Sorry. He was kind of rude."

"He probably feels threatened."

"Yeah, okay," she says doubtfully, taking her glasses off to stare at the lenses and then putting them back on.

"I mean, you live with me."

She turns to face me, and my arm drops off her shoulders. "You, sir, live with me," she says, pointing first to my chest, then to hers. "And don't you forget it."

"Oh, is that how it is?"

"That's how it is."

She walks over and sits on the couch, and I follow. She bites her lip, and the empty stare she gives the wall prompting me to move closer. She jostles toward me, our shoulders touching. "What's wrong?"

Leaning into me, she sighs. "I don't know."

My immediate instinct is to ask her what that asshole did, but I fight it back. "You can talk to me. We're friends, you know."

"I know." She drums her fingertips over her skin. "It's kind of embarrassing."

The heat of her body beckons me, so I lean into her. "Tell me. I am your dating guru. Life coach."

"Life coach? Now you're just tossing out job titles."

"Possibly, but if this is about Clark, I can help." *Help throw him under the bus.*

This close, it's hard to battle back the thoughts I've been having about her. I rub my thumb against her thigh.

"Well, we..." She squirms before finally blowing out a breath. "We kissed today."

Silence fills the space between us. My stomach squeezes, even though I kind of figured that's what was going on when I walked in, but to have her verify it impacts me more than I thought. Before I can say anything, she blurts out, "I'm not sure I liked it. I'm not sure I did it right. I'm not sure I actually felt something."

Relief fills me. Call me a terrible person, but I feel it all the way to my toes. I can work with this. "Maybe he's a bad kisser?"

"Maybe?"

I turn toward her, propping my knee on the couch. "A first kiss can be awkward. Maybe it was the newness."

"Maybe. Have you ever had disappointing first kisses?"

My gaze inadvertently drops to her lips. "Not since I knew what I was doing."

She frowns. "Of course you haven't. I shouldn't have asked you."

"What's that supposed to mean?"

"Well, look at you." She waves in my direction.

149

"You ooze testosterone. You sweep a girl off her feet, lay one on her, and steal her soul."

"Wait, how did I become a soul stealer? That sounds bad."

She shakes her head. "It's the opposite." Peering away, her eyes dance. "It's when it's so good it hurts."

I reach for her.

She jumps up from her seat, backing away. Her cheeks blaze red.

"You think I kiss like that?"

"I'm a writer. I don't know what I'm saying."

I rise to my feet and grab her hand before she can turn away. "Len, you deserve to be kissed like that." I can picture doing it now, swooping in and claiming a little piece of her for my own, but I want her to want it, too. I want this guy to be only a memory before I make my move. "So, if you're not feeling it with Clark, maybe that means something?"

"Maybe..."

She tightens her grip on my hand, and the connection between us sparks like live wires. Possessiveness takes over—the same kind that overtook me when Jonesy asked if Len was available. I want her to forget all about Clark, especially with the way she's staring up at me.

A second later, she swallows, extracting her fingers from my own. "Um, will I see you tonight?"

She avoids my gaze, and I don't like it. "Bubbles. What time?"

"Eight."

"Maybe."

"It would be cool if you came."

Yeah, cool to have me sitting there, watching them make eyes at each other, knowing there's no chemistry. God forbid they kiss in front of me.

I tell her I'm going to lie down for a little while before I do something stupid like ask her to drop Clark so she and I can go to Bubbles tonight alone. I'd give her the best damn first date she's ever had *and* the kiss she deserves.

———

BLINKING, I yawn and stare at the ceiling for a second before I reach for my phone, turning the screen toward me. *Shit.* It's already eight p.m. All I wanted was to lie down to think about things, and I ended up conking out for a few hours.

I grab my phone and text Adam.

> Want to go to Bubbles?

> Sure, man.

> Be ready in thirty.

I don't wait for him to respond. I jump in the shower to rinse and am brushing my teeth when he texts back that he'll be ready. I put on some cologne, find my outfit, and style my hair with the clay stuff my sister bought me.

When I open my door, a white flutter moves in front of me, and then a piece of paper slides onto the floor. I pick it up reading:

*Don't forget about Bubbles. Hope to see you there.*

She has such pretty handwriting. I find myself tracing the swoopy lines with my fingers. There's no way I wouldn't go now.

Within the next fifteen minutes, Adam's in my car playing DJ as we drive out to Longville, the same town the hockey arena is in, and he's peppering me with questions about Len. "So let me get this straight," he says, "this asshole clearly doesn't want you to go, but you're going anyway?"

"That's about it."

"Well played."

"You should've seen the look he gave her."

"Ha. Bro is worried." He taps the dash. "He should be. You got the whole hockey team thinking she's yours already. They won't even breathe in her direction now."

"Don't think I don't know you set that whole thing up. Jackass."

He gives me a grin. "You needed a push."

"You told me she was going to be a stalker." I park the car on a side street and feed the meter.

Adam meets me at the front of the car. "That was

before I saw how awesome she was." He looks like he's going to say more but gets caught up in staring at a cluster of girls ahead of us as we walk toward Bubbles. The hem of their dresses barely covers their asses. I doubt Len owns an outfit like that, but I'd love to see her in one...privately. Maybe I can convince her to start wearing sweats again so her body can be a treasure just for me.

I elbow Adam, who hasn't taken his gaze off the girls in front of us. "Make sure you keep your phone on."

"Oh, I'm sticking by you," he says. "I need to see how this plays out."

We pay at the door, and the bass of the blaring house music reverberates through my chest as I step inside. Adam follows. "We'll have a hell of a time finding her."

The place is set up with a bar on one side and the dance floor in the middle with seating on the opposite side. Big columns slice up the floor, holding up the second level where more people dance, some leaning over the railing with drinks in their hands, staring at the crowd below.

I peer to the right and spot Len against a wall, a drink in her hand, head bobbing to the music while Clark leans against the wall, hands shoved in his pockets. They'd barely made it inside.

"Found her."

"Huh?"

I point toward Len, and Adam pushes me that way.

My gaze travels down the length of her, and I nearly stumble over my feet. A form-fitting sequin dress hugs her in all the right ways, the strobe lights reflecting off its iridescent shine. That definitely wasn't in her closet before.

She looks fucking fantastic.

I move in front of them, and Clark sees me first. If it's possible, his face gets even more sour.

"Hey!" Len says, throwing her arms around me.

I squeeze her, closing my eyes as I do. She backs away. "Mmm, you smell good."

I cock my head, taking her in. Her unfocused eyes and the way she laughs staring into her drink give her away.

*Oh, here we go.* "Been drinking a little, have you?"

She lifts her shoulders, but it's an exaggerated motion, and I can't help but chuckle. "Hey, this is Adam."

"Hey, Adam. I know you." She opens her arms, and the fucker smirks at me as he hugs her. He'll pay for that in practice once I get my ass back out on the ice.

"This is Clark," Len announces. "He's the editor for the newspaper."

I grin, noticing she didn't introduce him as her boyfriend or her date.

"Hey, Clark." Adam shakes his hand, and I have to hide a snicker when Clark's eyes widen. The big lug is squeezing the hell out of him.

"We should get a seat," I say. "No sense in being wallflowers."

"Clark said they were all gross."

"Well, that's half the fun." Turning, I roll my eyes. Too gross to sit? Why'd they even come? On the way to the seating area, I grab a waitress and motion toward a free booth that will fit all of us. "Can we spray this down?"

"Sure thing, handsome."

She wipes both the table and the booth, then stands there as we sit. "Can I get a drink order?"

"Beer for me. Whatever you got on tap."

"Same," Adam says.

"I'll have another one of these," Len says, pointing to her cup.

"Is that the Bubble special?"

"I think so."

Clark asks for a rum and coke.

When she walks away, I wrap my arm around the back of the half-circle booth that happens to also go around Len. "Have you guys danced?"

Len slurps up the rest of her drink. "Nope."

*Let me guess, the floor is unsanitary, too?*

"Where are your friends?"

"No one else could make it," Clark answers.

*Yeah, I bet. If there ever was anyone else going.*

"Have they dropped the first Bubbles yet?"

"Nope," Len says, and I swear to God, she's so cute like this. Unreserved. "I can't wait, though."

"They'll set off a siren when they do," I tell her.

"Huh?" She points to her ear when the music picks up.

I lean into her. "They'll set off a siren when they do."

Her eyes light up, but then the waitress comes over to drop off our drinks. Adam immediately starts flirting and has the girl blushing as I give her my card.

"I got it," Clark says.

I hold up a hand. "No biggie. You can get the next round."

He sits back in his seat looking even more pissy than when we showed up. Len turns toward me and drunk-whispers, "I don't think he's having a good time."

I lean over and say into her ear, "Maybe because he has a giant stick up his ass."

"Huh?"

I smile. "Maybe it's not his scene."

"He won't dance."

Well, fuck that. I'll dance with her. As if on cue, the siren sounds. I sit back and wait for Clark to ask her, but when he doesn't move, I speak up. "Come on, fancy reporter. You have to get the full experience."

"Yeah?" She turns toward Clark. "Do you mind?"

"What?"

"I'm going to dance with Zaiah, unless you want to?"

I swallow. "Come on, we're going to miss it."

Without giving him a chance to answer, I step around Adam and hold out my hand. She fits hers in mine, and I pull her to a spot on the floor as the bubbles start to drop.

She looks up, the bubbles falling all around us, the strobe lighting them up like a kaleidoscope. Holding her hands out, she turns them toward the ceiling.

For fuck's sake... She's beautiful. How could I have looked past her before?

I'm the biggest walking cliché in the world.

"You ready?" I ask her.

"Hmm?"

I step in close, wrapping my arms around her. "Let's dance, Lenore."

My hips take over, moving to the hard beats of Taylor Swift's "Are You Ready For It?"

# CHAPTER THIRTEEN

Len

I MIGHT BE TIPSY—AND I AM—BUT ZAIAH DANCES like a dancing queen. No, that's not right. Like Channing Tatum in *Magic Mike*. Or maybe a mix between the two. Whatever, I mean, Zaiah's hips should definitely not be pressed this close to mine, but I can't push him away.

It feels too good.

Like we're in sync.

Like it's only the two of us as a rainbow of bubbles cascade from the ceiling. The bubbles hit my arms and pop, making me giggle.

"This is fun," I sigh.

He moves his lips to my ear. "How much did you drink, sweetie?"

I shrug, not wanting to tell him. I know exactly how many I've had. I needed a couple as soon as we arrived to muster up the courage to not keep pulling on Trish's dress. The same dress that caught Zaiah's attention in the first place. Then, I drank a couple more because Clark kept saying he'd never seen me wear anything like this, and even though it sounded like a compliment, he never actually complimented me.

"Do you—" I stop myself. Pretty sure fishing for compliments is not a good look.

"What?" he asks, pulling away, his hips still moving against mine, making mine sway.

I bite my tongue, and he touches the corner of my mouth. An electric shock moves through me. I blink up at him, lips buzzing. "Sorry."

"Don't say sorry. Tell me what's up."

I move closer, hugging him as I whisper-yell, "Does this dress look okay?"

He reaches up, holding the back of my head to say into my ear, "I think I heard wrong. *I thought* I heard you ask if you looked okay in that dress, but that can't be doubt in your voice. Not when you are owning that dress like you are."

"Really?"

"Really. It hugs every part of you in the best ways, Lenore."

The husky tone in his voice sends a shiver through me, but that could also be the alcohol making me hear what I want to.

*Do* I want him to want me? No, I'm here with Clark. Right? Right.

"Clark didn't compliment me."

Zaiah steps back, and suddenly, my whole front is like a frigid iceberg. My body moves toward him, trying to recapture everything, but he holds me back with two arms. "Then he's a clown, and you don't need his approval."

I give him a small smile, but he looks away.

My stomach drops. "Are you done dancing?"

Just as I pose the question the song stops, and my shoulders deflate. The moment is gone, stolen away like the few bass notes that end the song.

Without answering, Zaiah leads me through a throng of people that have moved in around us. When I fall against a few of them, he puts me in front of him and holds my hips.

"I'm fine."

"Said every drunk person ever."

"I'm feeling good," I tell him. "I'm okay."

Peering up, I spot our table and move that way. The closer we get, even darker clouds descend across Clark's face. He's been miserable since he picked me up. First, it was that Zaiah was coming. Second, it was that he hated the place I picked out. Who knows what it is this time.

"You got some moves, Len," Adam says.

"Nah, it was all Zaiah." I put an exclamation point on that comment when I trip over my own two feet. "*Oops*." I giggle, embarrassment ringing through me. "Not used to heels."

"She's fun," Adam says as I sit back in the booth, making Clark scoot in.

Clark puts his arm around me, and I sink into it. It's the first time he's done that. We've kissed a little, still trying to perfect it like Zaiah said, but it's not improving much. Or at all.

Zaiah takes one look at us and stands. "I'm going to get another drink."

I pop up. "I'll go with you."

Both he and Clark help me sit back down. "Not this time," Zaiah says, then spins and walks away.

"I'm perfectly capable," I murmur.

Clark puts a hand on my bicep. "You're drunk, Len."

"So?"

He leans over. "It's kind of embarrassing."

I sit back, deflated, the area behind my eyes heating. "Sorry."

"Hey," Adam's snap of a voice sounds from across the table. "She's not embarrassing."

Next to me, Clark stills. He waves his hand dismissively in the hockey player's direction, and I watch as Adam's eyes turn cold.

Clark leans in closer so he can speak into my ear. "You were all over him."

"I..." Swallowing, I stop there. Maybe I was all over him. It certainly felt like it. I should probably apologize. "We're just friends."

"Are you sure about that?"

My answer, "Positively," is shadowed by Adam jumping to his feet.

He eyes us, jaw working. "She's fine."

Clark sighs. "You don't know her."

Adam's hands clench at his sides, and for a moment, I think we might have an issue, but then he pulls out his phone and turns his back, walking a few feet away.

How fucking embarrassing. Maybe I was acting stupid? Then Clark calling me out was even worse.

I turn toward him. "Are you going to dance with me?"

"With your instability?" he scoffs. "I don't think it's a good idea."

"But you wouldn't dance with me when I was sober either."

"Why are you being combative? It's hard for me to dance when I don't drink, and I have to drive us home."

He's right. I'm drunk and he can't let loose with me because he's being responsible. "I was celebrating," I explain, less bitchy now.

"I know," he says, patting my back. "The article was great. The poll, your resolution, it was fantastic, Len. You should be proud of yourself. Maybe, you know, you went a little too hard. You're not used to drinking, right?"

"Yeah."

"It's okay." He moves my head to his shoulder, and I take a deep breath. My body is jumpy, like it doesn't want to sit still. It wants to do the first thing that pops into my head. It wants to say the first thing that dangles on the tip of my tongue.

I probably have been acting strangely. Freer than I normally do, so I should rein it in.

Adam comes back to the table holding his hand out. "Want to dance, Len?"

"I'm acting strange, I can't."

He gives me a weird look. "You're one hundred percent fine. I want to see those moves."

Clark pats my shoulder. "Actually, we're going to head out."

I sit up. "We are? I was having fun."

He gives me a hard stare, and I shut my mouth.

"If she wants to stay, Z and I can take her back."

Most of me wants to do that, but that seems inappropriate, doesn't it? I second guess myself. I came here with Clark. Staying with two hockey players is a bad idea.

Two *hockey* players. *Ugh, what am I doing?*

Clark's my date and he said I'm drunk, so we should get going if he wants to. It's only right. Natural. Normal, even.

*How many more adjectives can I come up with for natural?*

I giggle, and now two guys are looking at me like I've lost it.

Scooting down the booth, I stand, grabbing the table so I don't look like I'm drunk and do something extra embarrassing like fall over in front of everyone. I don't need to be showing everyone my hoo-ha in this tight dress.

"Drunk Lenore Bares All" would make a funny headline, though.

I smile but hold back a little so I don't have to spout the inner workings of my mind.

"We can take care of her," Adam offers, moving in front of us and effectively blocking the exit.

"It's cool," Clark states, this time a little more forcefully.

I pat Adam's arm. "Rain check on that dance. Then maybe I can convince you to burn that photo you have of me."

"It's digital. You can't burn it," Clark states.

Irritation slithers up my spine. "Metaphorically."

Ignoring Adam altogether, Clark grabs my elbow and helps maneuver me through the crowd, but it's not as stable as when Zaiah had my hips. Now that felt good. I can still feel his steady hands on me.

"Should we say bye to Zaiah?" I shout.

"I'm sure his pal will tell him."

I laugh. "You said *his pal*."

Despite Clark's words, I search for him, and I'm pretty sure I spot him dancing with a girl.

Immediately, I turn away, swallowing. For some reason, my steps are more confident as I walk toward the exit.

The ride from Longville back to my dorm goes by in a blur. Clark isn't talkative at all, so I keep replaying everything that happened over and over. First, through my eyes. Then, through Clark's. Then finally, through Zaiah's.

He had no problem dropping me for someone else. Which he should, really. But that probably means Clark was right. I was too drunk. I was embarrassing.

Clark pulls up to the curb by the front door and doesn't even put the car in Park. I freeze for a moment. He's not going to walk me up to the suite?

"My parents are coming to visit in the morning, so..."

"Yeah, I'm fine," I say, fiddling with the doorknob. "What time should I be ready?"

"For?"

"To meet your parents."

"Oh. Um..."

*Oh shit. He wasn't going to invite me. Jesus. I should throw myself off a bridge right now. Of course he doesn't want me there.*

"You know what? I'm going to bed," I tell him, pushing the car door open. "See you."

I nearly trip over the curb, but luckily save face before closing the door and walking up to the building. Clark pulls away and is out of sight when I get to the door and search for my key. I dig all through my little purse and don't see anything but my ID, credit card, a few dollars, and my phone.

Maybe it dropped in Clark's car? No way am I calling him now. Not when I just put my foot in my mouth.

I hug my arms around myself and brace against the cold wind before looking through my contacts for Zaiah and pressing his name, my stomach churning.

He's half an hour away, and I don't want to pull him from having a good time, but another burst of cold air rushes past me, and I run my hands up and down my arms.

"Len, are you okay?"

"Hey." I nibble on my lip.

"Hey, are you okay? Where are you?"

The concern in his voice makes my voice crack. "I'm locked out."

"Sweetie, where are you?"

"Outside Knightley." An entire body shiver sends my teeth chattering.

"Where's Clark?"

"He dropped me off. Are you in the vicinity to come let me in?"

A tinny voice in the background that must be Adam asks, "He dropped her off? Dick."

"Oh wait, here comes someone," I tell them. *Ugh, could this day get any worse?* I wave at the person coming up to the door. "Lost my key."

"Yeah, I've seen you around. I'll let you in."

"Lenore?" A pause. "Lenore?"

"Yeah, I'm here," I respond as another shiver runs through me. "I'm in the vestibule now."

"Okay, I'm coming. I should be there in ten."

"No, stay. I can ask someone here to let me in."

"Sweetie, I'm already in the car heading your way. Be there in ten."

That same tinny voice says, "You're a—" before the line goes dead.

I peer at the screen to confirm he's not there anymore, then call out thank you to the person who let me in.

Warmth wraps around me, but I still keep my arms folded in front of me. This is exactly what I didn't want when I decided to wear this dress. The harsh florescent lights spotlight me. At least at the club, I could hide in the dark, in the brief respites between the strobe and laser beams.

I'm halfway up the stairs when I realize I should've taken the elevator. The banister is my lifeline, and I cling to it before getting to the second floor. Then I realize I went the wrong way down the hallway. Not because I'm drunk, but because my legs are pale. Too pale, and it's all I can look at as I make my way around.

I look ridiculous.

Our room number is like a beacon, and I finally get to it and lean against the door. My knees want to give way, but I can't sit on the floor in my dress or I'll definitely be showing off my hoo-ha to anyone who walks by.

I stare at my phone, checking for the time I called Zaiah. I simultaneously regret and can't wait for him to get here. Crawling into my bed right now sounds like a good plan. How am I going to face Clark the next time I see him? And I'm definitely going to have to see him because I'm pretty sure he has my key. Plus, there's work and all that.

I'll blame it on the alcohol.

Hey, isn't that a song?

*Blame it on the a-a-a-a-alcohol.*

I've only sung the chorus more than a dozen times, since I don't know any of the other words, before loud thumps echo on the steps.

Zaiah moves into view, and I have to press my lips together. Half relief, half this icky feeling I can't shake fills me.

"Hi," I start.

His face is grim, his lips a straight line.

"I'm sorry."

"Don't say sorry."

"Well, I am."

He slides his key into the lock and peers at me. "You're going to have to step away so I can open the door."

"Not until you say it's okay."

He tilts his head, confusion etching into his perfect features.

"Say it's okay, and you're not mad at me."

He cups my face. "Lenore, I'm not mad at you. I'm worried about you. There's a difference."

Maybe that's worse. My skin tingles where he touches me, and I wrap my arms tighter around my front, feeling more than exposed in this outfit.

I step aside, breaking the connection, and he opens the door. After it swings out, he grabs my hips like he did at Bubbles and guides me backward. "I'll get you some water."

The way he's staring is unnerving, and I can't help but gaze right back, noticing for the first time that gold flecks dot his brown eyes. Immediately, I look away. He's so handsome it hurts. Before today, it was easier to think of him as only my roommate. My stomach squeezes with the thought that I'm screwing all of this up. "I'm not sure I'm feeling good anymore. The cold breeze stole it away."

"The cold breeze, huh? You're definitely a writer." He leads me to the couch and helps me sit, lingering to make sure I'm okay before going into the kitchen.

A cupboard slams, and I jump. Whirling to peer over my shoulder, I spot Zaiah there, hands gripping the countertops with a furious look on his face. I *am* screwing this up, and the thought is sobering. "See. I knew you were mad."

"I'm not mad at you."

"Well, that's obviously a lie because I'm the only one here."

I sit back on the couch with my arms folded over my chest. I must look like a petulant child, so I let my arms slide down, but my pout remains. This night was supposed to be a celebration, but it has turned into a nightmare. Clark ditched me, he doesn't want me to meet his parents, and now, Zaiah is mad at me.

I swallow. "Is it because I stole you away from dancing with that girl? Or made you come home early?"

"Girl? What girl? I only danced with you."

"I saw—"

Suddenly, he's in front of me, gaze in shadows with his lips a straight line, effectively cutting me off from my thought. I haven't seen him this angry before, not even when facing down a defenseman.

He hands me the water. "I'm not mad at you, Lenore. I'm going to kill that editor, though."

"Clark? Why?"

"You don't leave a girl outside her dorm."

"He didn't know I lost my key."

"He left without taking you safely upstairs to your room when the whole reason he wanted you to leave Bubbles is because he thought you were too drunk. Do you get that, Len? He leaves a drunk girl at the curb to fend for herself and then drives off? What kind of asshole does that?"

"He's busy tomorrow," I repeat Clark's excuse on autopilot, like it's the only justification necessary.

"I don't care if he was prepping for the end of the fucking world, you get a girl home safely. Especially when she's your date."

His chest heaves, and his sharp words cut like a knife. He's right. Embarrassment sinks its ugly claws into me. I can't even get a guy I'm dating to treat me well, and to make matters worse, Zaiah witnessed the whole thing.

I look away. "I'm sorry."

"Stop saying that!"

I gulp down some water, willing myself not to cry.

"None of this is your fault," he says, voice softening.

"You're being so nice." I try to smile for him. "Are you sure you're a hockey player?"

His face morphs to confusion then a slight smile. "Your brain is being funny, sweetie. I'm not sure where you're connecting some thoughts to others, but if I was your date, no way in hell would I be leaving you outside your place. Alone. In the cold. Freezing, in that dress."

He sweeps his gaze across me, and goose bumps sprout in its wake. "Well, you wouldn't have to because we live together."

"Even if we didn't."

Unfortunately, this scenario he's conjuring in his head would never come to fruition. He doesn't see me like that. I place the water on the end table. "I need your expert dating advice."

His shoulders fall forward. "Lenore, I don't want to be your dating coach anymore."

My mouth opens in shock. "We had an agreement." He studies my face, but I don't give him a chance to back out. "He doesn't want me to meet his parents... But you let me meet your parents."

"Good, he's a dick."

I scoff, meeting his hard stare. "He is not. I wouldn't be attracted to dicks."

He presses his lips together, eyes glittering. I watch him until the realization of what I just said hits.

I groan in frustration. "Obviously, not what I meant. Dicks are perfectly fine. I wouldn't call them cute or beautiful. I saw yours once. It was..."

*Magnificent.*

*Drool-worthy.*

*Puckable, for sure.*

He drops to his knees. Grasping my head between his large palms, he says, "Don't finish that sentence. I'm wearing thin tonight, sweetie, and the last thing I need is for you to test my scruples."

The warm and fuzzies swarm my stomach, and my face burns at his touch. "I like when you call me sweetie."

"You're killing me," he groans, his brown eyes staring straight into mine.

A heaviness blankets us, anchoring this moment. My heart slams in my chest, the beat urging me forward. My gaze flicks to his lips. "We should kiss."

He blinks. "What?"

*Yeah, what?* My brain fires a red flag, and I pivot from my original thought. If he rejects me, the aftermath would be devastating. I must have misread everything. "You should kiss me to see if I'm a good kisser. Maybe it's me who's the problem, you know, with me and Clark. Maybe I kiss like a dead fish. You'll be honest with me."

His thumb strokes my cheek. He studies me for so long it feels like he's read me from cover to cover. Like the book of my life is in my eyes and he's just indulged. "I'll kiss you because I want to, Len, and for no other reason. Do you understand?"

# CHAPTER FOURTEEN

Zaiah

"I don't think I heard you correctly," she slurs.

I stare into her innocent blue eyes, then track down to her lips. Every fiber in my being wants to kiss her, but not while she's in this state, and I certainly don't want to so she can pretend it's because of that dick. "It's okay. I'll explain it some other time. Put your feet up here." I pat the couch.

She takes a deep breath, watching me as I move away. As soon as I create space between us, the mounting tension releases, like a balloon has just been popped. I sit, and she pulls her feet up rather expertly, given her state. I grab them, placing them on my lap.

She giggles when I slide my fingers across her ankle, slumping on the couch. "My feet are sensitive."

I have to close my eyes for a moment to help minimize the fact that I want to find out which dorm Clark is in and pummel the motherfucker. Seeing how fragile Lenore is right now coupled with the way she's dressed makes me think he doesn't have a protective bone in his scrawny little body. Crime on campus is minimal, but her heels might as well be weapons to herself right now.

I work on the small clasps, keeping my mind on the task at hand. If I let it wander, I might do something we'll regret, so I change the subject. "I'm glad you were able to let loose tonight. Did you have fun?"

"I had fun when you got there, but Clark was a dud the entire night." She frowns. "First, he was mad I invited you, then he made it perfectly clear he didn't want to be there. I think I embarrassed him and then I made the biggest mistake ever, Zaiah. It was embarrassing. I am embarrassing."

I smirk at the part where he didn't want me to come, but the rest of it pisses me off. "You aren't embarrassing. You were letting loose. There's a difference."

She runs her fingers over the sequins at her front, pouting. "He didn't even compliment my dress. He made comments about it, but none were exactly flattering. He probably thought it was too slutty."

I nearly grind my teeth together. If I look at that dress for too long, I'm going to want to kiss her. I swallow, peering back at the clasp. "He's a dumbass."

"Zaiah..."

174

I finally slip the clip out and get the first shoe off, dumping it to the floor. "I'm serious." I couldn't give a shit about Clark.

She's quiet for a moment while I work on the other shoe. I don't know why they make these clasps so damn small. My fingers are too big. They should have drunk-girl shoes where the buckles are ten times the size.

"Zaiah..." She uses her other foot to push the strap down her heel and slips easily out of it.

I gape at her. "You could do that the entire time?"

She ignores me and asks, "Do you recognize this dress?"

I swallow, peering at it briefly before moving my gaze to her face. "You look great in it, Len. Don't let that asshole—"

"Never mind," she sighs before I can even finish my thought.

"What?"

"Nothing." She reaches out her hands, and I pull her to a seated position.

Instead of staying upright, though, she cozies up to me, dropping her head on my shoulder and twisting her legs underneath her. The vulnerability wafting off her pricks at my protective side. I lift my arm, and she moves in closer, laying her head on my chest.

My heart kicks into gear, and I drop my arm to her shoulder, rubbing my thumb up and down her skin.

"There are things I wish I could tell you," she mumbles.

She's killing me. If she was sober, I'd let her say anything she wanted. I'd kiss her without hesitation. I'd tell her she should drop Clark and go with me. There's something here, and she feels it, too. The way she's cuddling me. The way she looks at me. I swallow. "You can tell me when you're feeling more yourself."

"That's the thing. I am more myself." She picks her head up to stare into my eyes. "Usually, there are all these thoughts swirling in my head, but I push them down. Way down. They're coming out easier now."

I run my hand along her temple and down over her ear. "I don't want you to regret anything you might say. I want you to mean it."

She reaches up, cupping my cheek. "You're so handsome, hockey player."

"Lenore, *you*—" I start, thinking of all the things I want to say to her. How pretty she is. How smart she is. How she's far and away the brightest part of my life right now.

"Don't." She pulls back. "I know it's not true. Unless you were going to call me boring, then continue. But no lies right now, okay? No lies. Promise?"

She doesn't even see herself. "You are the furthest thing from boring, Lenore. Don't you see that? Look at you. Whether you're wearing this dress, leggings, or your baggy T-shirts, it doesn't matter. You're beautiful, and no one should make you feel otherwise. Not me. Not Clark. Not anyone. You're the same as you've always been, except you're more confident. You're practically glowing. Len, you're gorgeous."

Her eyes widen. She stares at me for the longest time, pressing her lips together. "I wanted someone to see me, you know?"

"*I* see you."

Her gaze drops to my lips, and my heart hammers. I'm trying so hard to be a good guy. "Before you look at me like that, I have something to say. Clark doesn't see you." I reach out to brush my fingers along her cheeks. "He made you feel less today, and someone who likes you would never want you to feel less. You should be able to invite whoever you want to go out. You should dance under the bubbles, and a real man would never leave a girl outside her dorm like that."

She pushes air through her lips until they vibrate briefly.

"Clark doesn't deserve you. Tonight, he showed you the kind of boyfriend he would be. Is this how you want to feel after a night with him?"

"He was mean," she agrees, then lifts her pretty blue eyes to me. "I only had fun with you."

I take a deep breath, letting it out slowly. "Does that tell you something, sweetie?"

"It tells me I would have fun with you, but you don't like me like that. You never have."

My fingers sink into her upper arm, bringing her close. "What do you mean I never have?"

"Nothing. Forget I said anything."

Not likely.

My stomach dips, and she looks away, red staining her cheeks. "What would you do if you knew I liked you?"

Turning back, she eyes my lips. "Kiss you. Like I've been wanting to."

I thread my fingers into the hair at the nape of her neck. Her lids flutter closed at the contact, like she's anticipating the most precious moment.

*Fuck my scruples.*

I hover over her mouth. "I'd do the same." Then I slide my lips over hers.

A softness greets me, reminding me of sweet innocence. Of purity. I want what lies underneath. True emotion and feeling. I nudge at her lips, begging her to open for me, and when she does, I tip her head back, sweeping my tongue inside her. She moans into my mouth, and my dick responds. *Fuck.*

She grabs my shirt and angles forward, meeting my lips with hungry kisses of her own. Our tongues clash, and my heart beats like crazy. I work my fingers into her hair, tugging her closer, keeping her there until I'm ravishing her mouth. I kiss her like she deserves to be kissed, filled with passion, and I've awakened a vixen.

"Zaiah," she whispers against my lips, her breaths coming in harsh pants before she seals her mouth to mine again. Tiny moans rip from her throat, breathy and intoxicating. Her body starts to move with mine, and I yank her dress up to her hips, moving her so she can straddle my lap.

She breaks the kiss, wide-eyed. I can see the point when the vixen retreats and rational Len takes over. Her lips plump and open, she takes a deep breath before saying, "You're a great kisser. I knew you would be."

I run my fingers underneath her chin, making her look at me again. "It wasn't just me."

"You think I'm good too?"

"I'm hard as a fucking rock, sweetie."

Her gaze drops to my lap. "Well, that's a normal physical reaction. It's our brain chemistry that sends pleasure signals through our body and—"

"It was you, Lenore," I tell her, pulling her forward so she can feel what she did to me. My dick meets yielding flesh, and I use everything in my power not to take this further. Not tonight.

She gasps. "Oh my—" Rocking forward, she moves my cock. "I didn't think that was ever going to happen."

"You thought about this?" I rasp, watching her slide over me, slow and steady.

She nods. "Even when you were with her."

I grip her hips. I don't want this moment to end.

Her breaths deepen. "I would want to touch myself thinking about you."

*Jesus Christ.* I roll my body upward to feel her, and another soft gasp escapes her mouth.

"Did you..."

She shakes her head. "It felt wrong. You were—"

"With the wrong person," I finish, angling my hips into her again. Something inside me mends when I think about Len waiting in the wings while I was ruining my life with Trish. Like a higher power was looking out for me the entire time, lingering to see if I'd get my head on straight, and Len is the prize for all the anguish and mindfuck I went through. "Show me now," I urge.

"I shouldn't. I can't."

"Look at me, sweetie." Her eyes open, and somehow, the connection between us sparks even brighter. "I want you to."

"Zaiah..." She swallows, gripping my shoulders. "I'd be embarrassed."

"Do you feel good right now? Working over my cock?"

She peers down, and she gasps a little when she realizes she's still moving her hips against mine. "I'm sorry." She stops immediately, but then she groans a few moments later. "I want it. I can't stop."

"Don't stop, pretty girl." I guide her over me again, but she takes control.

"You don't know how many times I thought about this."

"Show me. Show me there was something better out there for me."

Wonder lights her gaze. "Better?"

"So much better."

I wait with bated breath until her hand snakes down between us. She circles her fingers over her clit, slowly at first, then picking up speed. Her mouth opens in a silent moan, head falling back.

180

"Let me hear you. I want it all."

Her fingers don't falter. They swirl faster, matching her release of breaths. "Zaiah, oh. Yes." A long moan escapes. "Please."

I grit my teeth to keep from moving with her as she continues to rock against me.

Within no time, her movements become jerky.

"Yes. Yes," she pants.

Fuck. I love to see her like this. No inhibitions, just beautiful, sensual pleasure. The noises clawing from her throat are addictive, and I can't tear my gaze away.

"I'm going to—" She lets out a short scream before collapsing on top of me, hips moving ever so slowly against mine.

Surprise ricochets through me. Her chest rises and falls rapidly, and I hold her, tightening my arms around her protectively. That was so quick. So responsive. "Sweetie, that was all for me. That was so perfect."

She moans into my chest, her fingers clawing into my pec like she wants to be even closer.

My thoughts exactly. I stand, and she wraps her legs around my waist, but she immediately pulls away, eyes wide. "You can pick me up."

"Sweetie, you weigh nothing. I probably deadlift triple your weight."

She barely contains a smirk as I carry her to her room. For a moment, I keep her in my arms. Her fingers lightly stroke the back of my neck. When I stare into her eyes, I see a whole new Len.

I was with the wrong girl the entire time. I know that with absolute certainty now.

Placing her down on the bed, I caress my fingers up her throat to her chin so she'll look at me. "Thank you for sharing that with me. To watch you do that?" I swallow. "You don't even know, Len."

I'd been kicked around too long. Confidence in the dirt because of what Trish did to me, but to think there was someone there all along?

Her gaze drags down my body. "Do you want me to..."

Reaching for my dick, I squeeze it through my jeans. God, I want to let her. I want to see those innocent eyes stare up at me as she takes my cock into her mouth, but on the chance that she's not one hundred percent sober, I can't do it. Not for any gentlemanly reasons, but because I have a feeling her lips around me will be life changing, and if she retreats afterward, I won't be able to stand it.

She reaches out, and I quickly grab her hands, lowering to kneel in front of her. "Not tonight, sweetie."

Her lips press together. Rejection flashes in her eyes.

"No, listen." I slide forward to cup her face. "I vow no one—not even myself—will touch me until you're ready. Because this, right here, it's all yours, Lenore."

"What if I am ready?"

I brush my fingers over her cheekbone. "This is no judgment whatsoever. It's my own possessiveness.

Next time, it'll be our date. You'll squeeze your body into a dress like that for me. From start to finish, you'll think about me and only me."

"You're mad about Clark?"

"I'm not mad about Clark. You've been in your bed, lying awake, thinking about us."

"He was the safe choice," she admits. "While you were...never going to happen."

Her words punch a hole in my gut. She's right. It took me being in her face twenty-four seven to see her. It makes me question my own judgment.

I start to stand, and she reaches out to grab my shoulder. "Stay with me tonight? Just to sleep?"

Nodding, I undress down to my boxers as she watches. When I start to slip into bed, she turns her back to me. "Can you get my zipper?"

I find the white tab at the top and pull it down slowly, revealing every inch of her bare back. My mouth goes dry.

"Thank you."

I trace my finger down her back, and she shivers.

"No fair," she breathes out. After a brief moment, she stands to grab a shirt. It's dark in the corner without the light from the living room spilling in through the open door, but I see the outline of her body as she drops her dress then tugs on an oversized T-shirt.

Turning, she walks back over slowly, setting her glasses on the nightstand. She kneels on the bed before getting in and settling onto her pillow. I scoot closer, sliding in next to her and wrapping my arm around her midsection.

We both lie awake for some time, breaths steadily evening out. My lids start to flutter, but not until she's already asleep next to me.

# CHAPTER FIFTEEN

Len

THE STEAM OF THE COFFEE FILLS MY NOSTRILS AS I stride into the newspaper room. The place is nearly full, which tells me I'm late. Well, not really late, just not early like normal. We don't have hours I could actually be late for, but I like to spend as much time as possible here to accustom myself to being in a newsroom for the rest of my career.

Flora lifts her gaze when I drop my stuff across from her. "Someone looks like she got laid. Did you and Clark..." She waggles her brows.

I'm about to launch into the story about Clark and the disaster that was our date at Bubbles, but a hand touches my shoulder. "Hey."

I nearly jump out of my seat and peer up to find Clark staring down at me. We haven't talked since he dropped me off outside Knightley a couple of nights ago and so much has happened since then.

"Hey," I eke out.

"I got your text. I didn't find your key in my car."

Turns out, my key had been in my purse the whole time and my drunk ass hadn't seen it. What are the odds? "I actually found it. Thanks for checking, though."

He rubs my shoulder. "I feel bad that you were locked out."

I maneuver away from his touch. "Zaiah was there."

"Oh." He pauses for a moment. "Good."

Zaiah and I got together because I thought I'd lost that key. It was fate. He swooped in like a knight on a white horse. The whole thing was meant to be. Plus, now that I'm sober, I agree with him. Clark had no business making me leave Bubbles only to drop me off at the curb of my place.

My phone starts ringing, and I scramble to get it, heart pinging in my chest. I hope it's Zaiah checking in about how I'm dealing with the Clark situation. He knew how nervous I was.

"What are you working on now?" Clark asks.

*Ugh, can't he see that my phone is ringing?*

I stare down at the screen, and my stomach free falls. It's not Zaiah. It's Dad. I point at my phone. "I have to get this."

Quick footsteps take me to the side of the room. "Hello?"

"Hey, Pumpkin."

"Hey, Dad."

"I haven't heard from you in a while."

Clark eyes me warily before turning and heading back to his office. I sigh. "That's because the last time we talked, we got into a fight."

"Fight?" he complains. "What fight? It was nothing but a disagreement. I just want to know how my daughter is doing."

"Doing good, Dad." I swallow, my throat suddenly dry because I have never been this interesting in my entire life. Went on a date with one guy and ended up on top of another by the end of the night. Since I doubt my dad wants to hear updates about my love life, I go with a safe topic. "My new article went to print the other day."

"Well, send it my way. I'd like to read it."

"It probably wouldn't interest you."

"Lenore, everything you do interests me. It doesn't have to be about sports."

That sounds like a gigantic lie, but if I call him out on it, we'll end up arguing again. God, isn't it ironic that my next article will be about sports? I have to make it different from an individual game, though. Or the sport. I have to make it something *more*. "I can send it to you."

"Perfect. I'll read it between meetings. Listen, Pumpkin, we're playing the Ice Eagles this weekend, and since it's so close to you, I'd like you to come. I miss you."

My absentminded finger-drumming against my side stops. Dad isn't often vulnerable. He doesn't say things like that. Not really. "You'd be interested to know I went to a game myself. Here. The Warner college team."

"You did? Is the team any good?"

"Actually, they're having a great year. One of the best in history." My mind wanders. I could write about that... I dismiss the idea. I'll mention it, but I'm not going to make my whole article about winning. This is for Zaiah, so it has to be bigger than that.

"I bet the coach is pleased."

I snicker. I bet the coach is terrible at marketing. And the school. And the players. "Yeah, they're thrilled, I guess."

"Well? The Ice Eagles game?"

"I don't know, Dad. It depends on how much work I have to do."

His pause has my stomach squeezing. I can almost hear him contemplating on the other end of the line. "Well, just in case, I'll grab two seats for you and your roommate. Let me know if you need more."

"My roommate?" Fear punches into me. *He knows about Zaiah?*

"Yeah, the girl. What's her name?"

I breathe out a sigh of relief, but part of me is annoyed. I shouldn't be surprised he still thinks Trish is my roommate, but it's aggravating. "We don't live together anymore, Dad."

"You don't?"

"No."

Guilt rears up. I don't want to take back what happened between Zaiah and me, but was it wrong? Trish was my best friend. She'd be so pissed if she knew what happened. Friends don't get involved with each other's boyfriends. Or even ex-boyfriends. Right?

Not that I can call her my friend anymore. Or that I should've called her a friend before.

My father's voice butts into my pity party. "Well, I'm sure you have someone else to take. I'll leave the tickets, Lenore, and like I said, if you need more, let me know."

"Sure, Dad. I'll let you know."

*Like I have friends who are dying to go to a hockey game.*

"Bye, Dad."

"Miss you, honey."

I pause as surprise hits me. "Miss you, too."

It's evident that he's trying. I'm probably the only one not.

The call ends, and I clutch my phone in my hands. Zaiah would love to go to a pro hockey game. But then I'd have to tell him how I got the tickets and who my dad is. Would he be mad I didn't tell him sooner?

Peeking up, I spot Flora. She's pretending not to look at me, but for once, her fingers aren't flying over the keyboard. God, she'd be a horrible undercover reporter.

"Hey..." I walk toward her. "Do you want to take this workday to the café?"

She peers at the coffee cup I sat on the table, but my gaze immediately moves to Clark to make sure he's still in his office.

She grins like she knows I'm about to spill the tea. "Hell yeah. I've been waiting for you to ask."

I grab my stuff I hadn't even unpacked yet, and Flora and I take off. Clark looks up at the last minute before I can escape, but he's on the phone, so he can't say anything. He watches me go, his face full of unsaid questions.

"Girl, what's going on?" Flora asks as soon as we make it outside. "There was some major weirdness going on between you and Clark and not the usual you pining after him when he doesn't notice."

I give her a look.

She holds her hands up. "It's the truth. Look at you. Clandestine phone calls. Clark staring over like a star-crossed, jaded lover. How did your life get interesting all of a sudden?"

Maybe I asked the wrong person to talk to about this. I don't need another friend to make fun of me when I really need them to listen.

"Hey." She pulls me to a stop. "I'm sorry. I didn't mean it like that. Genuinely. I was only teasing."

I peer into her eyes. There's a subtle difference from the way Trish used to apologize to the way Flora just did. Trish used to do it like she couldn't believe I was upset. She did it begrudgingly and with a hint of annoyance. I don't see the same in Flora.

"Apology accepted. I'm sorry."

"No," Flora says. "I apologize, you say okay, and that's it. You don't apologize back."

"Okay, I take my apology back."

"Well, now you're just being a bitch."

She smirks, and I understand the teasing that time. "Get used to it."

She nearly jumps up and down. "I cannot wait to hear what happened. This is going to be so good."

I laugh as we turn toward the café again. She places her arm through mine, and we walk linked. Campus is sparse, only the occasional person meandering between classes, but the closer we get to the café, the busier it is.

"I hope we can find a seat," I muse.

"Oh, we're getting a seat. Even if we have to sneak these into the library. By the way, you already have a coffee."

I grin, sipping. "Then I'll grab the seat while you catch up."

She pulls open the glass door, and we step through. There are about five people in line, and I look around, scoping out the edges of the café so we can have a little privacy. I spot an empty booth in the back. It's too big for the two of us, but I don't care. Huge groups aren't waiting around for it, so I point it out to Flora and head over.

I sit facing the entrance. While I wait, I scroll through my emails without really seeing them as I think about what I want to say to Flora. I'll tell her about Clark first, of course. Maybe I could even ask her about what I should say to Zaiah. Do I tell him I'm the one who threw Trish under the bus? What about the dress and the fact that he saw me first? What about *my dad*?

"You look like you're thinking too hard," Flora says.

"A lot of information to process," I tell her.

"Well, I'm here for it." She sits, wrapping her hands around her coffee.

I lean back. "I need advice, and as you might have noticed, you're the only girl I talk to, so..."

She gives me a small smile, and for a passing moment, I feel like an idiot. I had other friends. Well, Trish had other friends, but when I cut ties with her, I was shy about making new ones. And keeping the old ones. People like Trish breed other people like Trish, and they're not people I wanted in my life anymore.

Flora reaches across the table to set her hand on mine. "Len, we're friends. It's okay if you call us that, you know?"

Panic shoots through me at the word *friend*. It's as if I have PTSD from my relationship with Trish, obviously at a much smaller scale than someone who went to war. However, sometimes our exchanges felt like mini battles. Subterfuge and counterattacks. I shiver just remembering.

"So?" Flora asks, lifting her brows. "I'm on the edge of my seat. Clark seemed off. You seemed great at first, and then..."

Taking a deep breath, I let it out. "I'll start with Bubbles. Clark was miserable." The whole story spews from my mouth like an exorcism, and as I'm telling her, I'm getting more upset about the things Clark did.

She slaps the table at one point. "Zaiah was there?"

I shrug. "I invited him."

"Woah, woah, woah. Back this horse up. You invited Zaiah to your date with Clark?"

"Well, first off, Clark told me other people were going. He said we couldn't take Zaiah because the car was full."

"Then it ended up being only you and Clark?"

I nod.

"Hmm," she says, taking a sip of her drink. "I think someone was jealous."

"He was upset, for sure. We were supposed to be out celebrating my article, but he wouldn't even relax. He was mad that it was loud. He was mad that I drank."

"Wait." She holds up a hand. "He gave you shit about drinking?"

"He took me home early because he said I was making a fool of myself."

"Okay, Len, I'm going to say this in the nicest way possible so I don't hurt your feelings... This is not the guy for you. Fuck him. He's not the guy for anyone. Run away."

"I did. I mean, that's why I'm so weirded out this morning. He took me home early, then he dropped me off and left before I realized I didn't have my key. Plus, his parents came to visit on Sunday, and I mistakenly thought he was going to invite me, and he was like, straight up, no."

She sits back and shakes her head. "Dick. I always suspected. The way he takes advantage of you in the newsroom—"

"He doesn't—"

"Len, if you didn't help that loser, nothing would ever get done."

"I don't know..."

"I *do* know, and I'm telling you as your new best friend. From now on, don't help him. Watch how everything falls apart. I'm actually getting giddy thinking about it. Promise me you'll pull back. You need to draw a hard line because this guy is toxic."

I swallow, trying to recuperate from Flora's battering ram of truth. Trish was toxic, too. I realized that on my own, so why did Clark escape my notice? Why didn't I see it?

I open my mouth and close it.

"Hey, if I said something..."

"No." I stand. "It's not you. Sorry, I need to be alone right now."

I start to grab my stuff.

"Len."

"It's not you. Promise."

I rub my chest as I make my way through the crowd of people at the café exit, nearly knocking shoulders with a towering figure. "Sorry."

"Len? You okay?"

I turn to see Adam standing there. "Fine. I'm good. Sorry."

Turning, I head out the door and start for the dorm, praying Zaiah's in class or at practice or just not there. My phone rings, and I pull my bag around to see who it is. *Clark.* I come to a stop. His name scrolling across my phone used to send goose bumps through me. What kind of person lets two toxic people into their lives? *Welcomes* them? Begs for their attention?

I clench my phone and do the first thing I can think: I pull back and heave it into the air.

"Hey!" A body jogs over and snatches it before it hits the ground. I recognize the shoulders, the frame, and I want to die of embarrassment before he spins around and it's confirmed.

The universe fucks me again.

I'm still alive when Zaiah turns, my phone dangling from his fingers. I stand still, my feet frozen in place as he jogs up to me. "You should try out for baseball."

I peer at the ground, and within a few seconds, my phone enters my view.

"You missed a call."

"Good," I snap, grabbing it and shoving it back in my bag.

"Hey, are you okay?"

"I'm fine," I say, hiding a sniffle. "I'm overstimulated, I think."

Flora calls out from behind me. "Len, are you okay?"

Zaiah reaches out, but I slide away from him. "Sorry, I'm good. Everyone can stop worrying." I back away like I'm a mouse trapped in a corner by a big, hungry lion. "I'm A-Okay. I'm suddenly tired. I'm going to take a nap."

"I can make sure you get back alright," Zaiah offers, stepping forward.

The concern on his face is so pure. But do I trust myself anymore? Apparently, I'm a horrible judge of character.

"I'm perfectly capable of doing it myself. Thanks."

I turn before they can say another word. My feet pick up the pace, and when I'm about thirty yards away, I glance back to see if anyone is following me. Luckily, no one is.

My phone buzzes with a text from Zaiah when I hit the steps to Knightley.

DON'T THROW ME.

Text me when you're home. I mean it. If you don't, I'm going to come looking.

A smile starts to curve my lips, but I stuff it down. When I arrive at my suite, I lie in bed and text him that I'm okay, then pull the covers up over me to hide away.

# CHAPTER SIXTEEN

---

Zaiah

THE LOUD THRUM OF THE AWAY BUS CHUGS TO life, spitting out exhaust from the back end in white smoke that clings to the air while it ascends to the sky. I climb the steps to find a seat, the game we just played running through my head.

A loss.

We didn't play hard enough. Good enough. Like we wanted it enough. Maybe I'm the worst offender. Things have gone to shit lately.

A text comes through, and for a split second, I hope it's Len, even though we're barely talking. She might text me if the dorm was on fire. Or if she forgot her key. Or...

I shake my head. It's from my mom. My family always makes her text first.

Well...

I put my phone away, but it goes off again. Adam sits next to me, and I lean my head against the window, hoping to get some shut-eye.

"That blew."

*My sentiments exactly.*

"You played well, though."

"You too."

"Bro, do not placate me with that shit. I gave up a bunch of pucks."

I shrug, but the truth of it is, I can't get my head straight about the game because it's on a different topic.

Len.

First, she wants me to help her date Clark, the douchebag. I help her. Clark, unsurprisingly, turns out to be as douchey as I thought. Then, we have the most amazing evening. She was so free, so uninhibited. She danced like a seductress. She touched herself like a queen. The day after that, a flip switched.

My first thought was that she'd gotten back together with Clark. She hasn't spoken about him and I haven't seen them together, so I don't think they are, but my brain can't turn away from it. Regardless of what happened, she pushed me away.

Maybe we took it too far too soon?

Adam leans back, and I shut my eyes, hopeful that a nice, quiet ride back to campus awaits me, but that's immediately thwarted.

"Have you seen Lenore again?"

I swallow. "What do you mean? I see her all the time."

"I'm just, you know, curious."

My stomach twists. I side-eye him, and he holds his hands up. "Dude, I'm only checking in. I thought for sure you were going to lock that shit down, but you haven't said anything about her in over a week."

"I don't want to talk about it."

He's quiet for a moment...until I glance over. "Sorry. I didn't realize she turned you down."

"She didn't turn me down." I sit, straightening my legs as far as they can go under the seat in front of me. These buses weren't meant for guys like us. Too fucking tiny. Add Adam with his blabbermouth, and my space is getting smaller and smaller.

"Okay, man. I thought that might be the reason you've been so quiet lately."

Luckily, that's the last thing Adam says all trip until we grab our things and file off the bus.

The chill air coats me, my breaths coming out in a fan of white clouds while I walk toward Knightley. The creak of the door sounds when I open it and trudge up the steps, dreaming about my bed. Tomorrow will come too fast at this point.

I turn down the hallway and peer up when a door closes. The figure walking toward me stops me in my tracks. Clark. Coming out of *our* suite.

So they are together. She's been hiding him from me because of what we did.

I see how it is.

I drag my bag back up my shoulder and avert my gaze, my hand twitching to take my anger out on him. Skinny little shit. He wouldn't survive one check into the boards.

He sneers when he passes me. "Have fun with that one tonight."

That one. *That one?* "Have a little fucking respect."

"Oh, you're pissed at me? That's rich. You know how long she's been drooling over me?"

I shake my head, stepping toward him, crowding him against the wall. "Let me make one thing very fucking clear: You're a piece of shit. You treated her like garbage because you're a narcissistic pig, and I swear to God, if I see you doing it again, I'll use your head as a puck. Do you understand?"

"Zaiah..."

I peer to my right, and in the time it takes me to see Lenore standing in the doorway in her turtle pajamas, Clark makes his escape.

Should've punched him. Dick.

She pushes her glasses up her nose as I stride toward her, dragging my bag. "What did he say?"

"I don't know what you see in him," I grind out, rejection nearly knocking me off my feet. I thought we'd turned a corner, but I was wrong.

She moves out of my way so I can walk in with my gear. "I don't see anything in him, actually." Her voice is so low, so tiny. "What I saw before was a figment of my imagination. I had a crush on someone who didn't deserve it. That happens to me a lot."

I spin on her. "What was he doing here, then?"

She studies the floor. "Trying to get me to sleep with him."

I drop my bag, heart pumping.

"He didn't take it well when I finally told him off."

I swallow hard. "You did?"

She gives me a soft smile and walks toward the couch, taking a seat and wrapping her arms around her knees. "I also used the term narcissistic pig. To think I was even trying to get his attention." She blows out a breath. "He said my attempts were so desperate that he assumed I'd be an easy lay."

I turn and march toward the door until Len's voice breaks through the anger spinning in my head.

"He's not worth it. He's not worth anything. Especially not hockey."

I stop with my hand on the doorknob. She's right. If I get into a fight on campus, I'll be punished. I'll probably get benched for a couple games, and in my senior year, that's the last thing I want.

"I still might," I say, turning back to her.

We both stare at each other for the longest time. With a sigh, she lets her knees go. "Can you not go right to your room?"

My shoulders relax. Finally. "I don't have to be anywhere but where you want me to be."

She struggles to smile, but her cheeks flush, giving her a pretty, pink hue. "We should've had this conversation before, and I'm sorry I was such a coward. I was embarrassed. I was confused. I—"

I walk toward her. "You don't have to apologize."

"Let me get this out. The day you saw me at the café?" She sniffles. "My friend Flora was pointing out how Clark is toxic, and it dawned on me that I let so many people like that into my life, and I don't know what that says about me."

Her eyes tear up, and I sit next to her, bringing her to my side. "You're a nice person."

She doesn't allow me to comfort her. Instead, she blurts, "I need to bring up Trish."

My body stiffens.

"She was a shit friend as much as she was a shit girlfriend. You've probably already guessed, but I don't talk to her anymore. We got into a huge fight the day you guys broke up."

I swallow the sudden dryness in my throat and scoot away so I can look at her, tilting her chin up to peer into her eyes. "I'm sorry she was that way to you too."

"Zaiah, I'm the one who told you about her other boyfriend." A tear runs down her cheek. "I, um, I was a coward and sent you that note. I should've done it differently. In person probably, but I wanted you to know above anything else, and I wasn't strong enough to tell you in person."

My lids flutter closed as I remember what it felt like to open that note. Trish's infidelity had devastated me. She'd had me in a chokehold. She was exciting.

Alluring. But looking back, I can see the manipulation. That took me weeks, though.

I let out a breath.

"Don't hate me."

I run a hand down my face, surprise upending me for a moment. Across from me, however, Len's nearly shaking, a worried shell of a person. I reach out to grasp her hand. "I wouldn't have believed it unless you sent the evidence the way you did. Trish was a manipulator, Len, and she would've been the same for you, too. You're too...pure for her. You did me the biggest favor."

"Yeah?"

"I always wondered who sent it. I have to say, I never thought about you. I figured you hadn't spoken to her, but I thought you grew apart when she transferred schools."

"No, it ended pretty badly. She found out I sent the note. You know how you look back on fights and wish you said something differently? I replay our argument in my head all the time, and I come up with the best things to say, but I just let her hurl insults at me until she was done. Then she left. I actually felt bad about it."

"Well, don't."

"She was the only friend I had."

Every word she says breaks my heart.

"Also, um...I don't even know if I should bring this up, but...you saw me first." Her voice cracks, and she looks away. I reach out to turn her face back toward me.

She wipes her eyes. "If you think about the night you first saw Trish, you might remember you saw her through a window—"

"Dancing on a table."

"You asked to come up."

I nod.

She smiles a little. "It was me on the table, Zaiah. Trish let me borrow one of her dresses, and when you saw me, I was on cloud nine. Then you asked to come up, and I was buzzing all over. I thought... *Ugh*, this is so damn embarrassing... I thought maybe I would actually get a college boyfriend."

"But you didn't answer the door," I tell her.

"I was pulling on the dress and fidgeting, so Trish told me I should change because I looked like a middle schooler playing dress-up. By the time I got back to the room, she had you tied around her pinky."

I clench my jaw so hard it gives me a headache. Manipulated since moment one. Trish knew what she was doing. She never mentioned it was Len on the table, and when people asked how we met, she told them how I was smitten from the beginning, watching her dance. She made it sound so romantic. "I guess I'm a big dick, too."

"It wasn't your fault."

"Oh, I know about Trish's manipulations, but I wish it'd been you."

"You...do? But I'm nothing like Trish."

"That's a good thing."

"But, I mean, she was so bubbly and cool."

"Cool is overrated."

"Coming from someone who is cool."

"That's how I know."

Len's quiet for a moment, and I don't push her. Eventually, she says, "When it was all over, I saw what she was from the very beginning, but I didn't see it at the time. She was always getting mad when I would get mad. She had this way of wording things so that I would apologize when I was the one who really deserved an 'I'm sorry.'

"I think she even told me to change out of the dress so you'd see her and not me, and honestly, it was probably for the best. If the two of us were standing right next to each other, who would look at me? Even if I'd kept the dress on, it was only a façade. The next day, you would've run screaming."

"Give me a little credit."

She shrugs. "I know where I stand."

My hands turn to fists. No one will talk down to Lenore on my watch. Not even herself. "The only thing you lack is confidence. You're beautiful, Len. You not only hold up to Trish, you blow her out of the water—inside and out."

Blinking at me, she parts her lips. I can tell she's thinking about what I said, but not believing it. Guess I know what my next task is.

"By the way, she didn't have everyone fooled. My family disliked her from the beginning."

"They did? They like me."

"Like is an understatement. They love you, sweetie."

She sits back, leaning against the armrest and slipping her toes under my thighs. "After what happened between us, I should've told you right away. But I had the revelation about Clark and Trish, and I've been—" She shrugs.

"None of this is your fault."

"It must be," she whispers. "There's something about me that doesn't see through bullshit. I can't trust myself."

"Well, you made progress today. You told Clark off. That's a great start. You could contact Trish and tell her off, too." The way she looks at me tells me that's the last thing she wants to do, so I pivot. "Or... Okay, don't laugh. When I was a kid, I had anger issues. My mom would sit me down and tell me to write a letter to get it out. On a side note, I have really good penmanship now."

Len presses her lips together, amusement dancing in her eyes. "Did you ever give the letters to the person?"

"No, they were for me. It was a way of feeling it and letting it go. You love to write, so write Trish a note. Get everything out. *Everything*. Even all those one-liners you came up with after the fact. You'll feel so much better."

She taps her chin. "I like that idea. I think I will do that."

"Then, maybe we can play hockey?"

Her cheeks flame. "Um, what now?"

I beam at her. "My parents also put me in hockey because I was aggressive. The doctor thought I had too much energy."

Instead of making fun of me like I expect, Lenore grows quiet. "Speaking of that..." She runs her hands through her hair. "There's something else I have to tell you."

# CHAPTER SEVENTEEN

## Len

Most people wouldn't care who my dad was, but to not tell Zaiah would've been a chink in our armor. If there is an us.

God, I want there to be an us.

I step out of the car, and he rushes over with an umbrella so I'm not pelted by the cold rain. The arena lights reflect in the puddles as we rush past the parking attendant, laughing when the water splashes up our legs.

"Where are we going again?"

"Will call," I shriek, and a car passes in front of us. We narrowly avoid being doused head to toe in water. "Holy shit."

"Close one." He places his hand on the small of my back and leads me across the now-clear road as we head toward the main entrance. A bunch of others have shown up last minute and are doing the same. We trudge along behind them and end up under a cement roof so Zaiah can finally lower the umbrella.

"Thank you," I tell him.

His eyes spark when he looks at me, and I pray I'm not being a hopeless romantic, finally looking into the gaze of the guy who should've been hers all along. I'm obsessed enough to imagine things when they aren't there.

This past week has been nothing short of amazing. Zaiah sees me. He wasn't mad that I didn't tell him face-to-face about her cheating. In fact, he understood. Turns out, we have similar stories about Trish. And it was like looking in a mirror when I told him about my dad and why hockey is such a sore subject.

He got that, too.

The feelings for him that had been growing inside me solidified, anchoring to my bones. I'm so far gone for Zaiah James.

If I'm all wrong about this, it's going to be devastating. I'm willing to take the leap off the cliff, though. Dive so hard and so fast that I subject my own body to possible injury I may never recover from.

I hand over my ID to the person at will call, and they hand back tickets. A quick peek inside the envelope says Dad was very good to me.

Zaiah's eyes round as I angle them toward him.

"Am I wrong or is that on the boards?"

"On the boards," I confirm. His eyes light up, and I

laugh. "You know you usually watch games from much closer, right? Like, actually on the ice."

He bumps his shoulder into mine. "But I don't get to enjoy them. This is going to be awesome."

I hand him one of the tickets, and we get them scanned and head inside. The announcer is still introducing the players, the sound reverberating around the stadium like the big man himself is a hockey fan, his booming voice ricocheting off my ribs.

"We didn't miss puck drop. Come on."

He takes my hand, sliding his fingers through mine. I already knew watching a hockey game with Zaiah was going to be one of the better experiences I've had in a place like this. As of right now, it might be tied with watching him play.

When we get to the lower level, Zaiah leads me down the steps, and I peer up into the suites, wondering which one my father is in. Afterward, we'll go to dinner. I told him I brought a plus one. Didn't tell him it was a male, though, so that will be interesting. The first ever time this has happened.

Zaiah holds my seat down, offering up the aisle. This front row allows him to spread out his legs, which is the first thing he does. Immediately, he brings out his phone as I place my bag on the floor and then I'm being dragged up and turned around. "Selfie," he says, and I have just enough time to take in the fact that he has his arm around my shoulders and our faces are close together before the camera flashes.

"You two look adorable," a woman with an

opposing team's jersey on coos from the row behind us. "I'll take a picture if you want?"

"Please," Zaiah says, handing her his phone.

Butterflies erupt in my stomach. I couldn't be any more awkward. I'm more nervous about this than when I straddled his hips on the couch and touched myself in front of him.

Zaiah leans down to whisper in my ear, "Put your arm around me, sweetie."

I do as he says, smiling. The lady takes a few pictures, oohing and aahing. I'm sure it's all Zaiah. Everyone probably thinks I'm his sister. Or his cousin. Or some sort of platonic friend he's taken pity on.

She offers up the phone, but before Zaiah grabs it, he kisses my temple. I swallow at the contact, my throat dry like brittle leaves on the ground in winter.

We sit, and Zaiah fiddles on his phone while the players skate onto the ice.

I nudge him. "Tell your sister I say hi."

He grins back at me. "Tell her yourself."

At the same time the crowd starts to cheer, I feel a vibration in my bag that rests against my ankle. I lean over, taking my phone out, and my jaw slacks when I read the screen. Zaiah added me to a group chat...with his family.

"You—"

He jumps to his feet, and I quickly peek up as the puck lands on the ice. The game has started, which is entertaining in itself, but my phone keeps vibrating in my hand, and what's more fascinating to me is each time Zaiah's family responds.

Mom James: You two!

Dad James: Pair of fine-looking young people.

Iz: I'm dying!!!!

Zaiah's hot breath hits my ear. "The game's up here, sweetheart."

My whole body tingles. "You put me in a group text with your parents."

"They love you."

I search his gaze. It's as grounding as ever, but at the same time, it makes me soar right out of the building. I'm on a cloud, watching this from afar, or on a couch salivating over this scene in a movie.

This is not my life.

His lips peel into another grin. "Are you okay?"

I nod. "Having a little trouble breathing."

"Here. I'll resuscitate you."

Zaiah leans over, his lips moving closer and closer. I watch them until my lids flutter closed. His lips take possession of mine, working over me. Sure, I'm kissing back, but I'm enthralled and dazed, caught in a spell of Zaiah's own doing.

He could rule kingdoms with these lips.

He pulls away, and I'm sure I look like a goober, but my eyes stay closed, savoring the moment. His fingers drag over mine, sinking between them until we're holding hands, his large palm sitting on top of mine against my thigh.

Without looking at him, I scoot closer and only open my eyes when I'm facing the ice again, in time for someone to get checked into the boards right in front of us. To our left, the people stand, slamming their palms on the glass, but Zaiah and I stay right where we are. Together.

The first period passes like a fairy tale. The longer the game stretches, the more comfortable I am. I'm able to enjoy the game with Zaiah, not just be a girl riding high on dopamine hits.

I should do an article about love being a drug. I can't be the only person who thinks of it this way. Not that I'm in love with him. I don't think. There must be some scientific explanation for feeling high around someone you care about.

"I'm going to head to concessions. Want anything?"

"Popcorn?"

He nods, kissing my forehead. After he's disappeared, I take out my phone. It would be rude of me to not respond to his family, so I send the score of the game. No less than five texts appear one after the other.

Iz: See any hot players?

Zaiah: Shut your mouth.

Mom James: He didn't like that. LOL.

Iz: He's worried Len will run off with a bigger, better player.

My stomach squeezes, but I respond, sending a laughing emoji. It's a safe response. I could be laughing that they're even thinking that, or I could be laughing along with them. I could also be laughing that I would even do that, which is my true response. There isn't a bigger, better player than Zaiah.

Zaiah returns soon after I put my phone away. He dangles the popcorn in front of me, but when I go to take it, he sits, moving it out of my grasp. "Explain something to me, pretty girl."

"What?"

"What does your emoji mean?"

"It's clearly a laughing emoji. I'm laughing."

"At what?" His eyes dance.

"Your family."

He sits back, digging around in my popcorn and throwing a couple pieces into his mouth. "Be more specific."

I can't help but smile. "They're asking weird questions."

He eats a couple more pieces before looking back at me. "I'll let you in on a little secret. My family and I have another text thread going, and they're all dying to know whether we're a couple. They're trying to goad you into saying it."

"Well, what did you tell them?"

"I told them I was taking things slow because you seem to want to go slow."

He inches nearer, and my gaze drops to his lips. My own buzz with excitement.

"So I hope that emoji meant you find it hilarious that you would ever look at another guy when you're around me."

"You think so?" I tease.

"I do because you look like you want to kiss me right now."

"Ahh!" The lady behind us screams. "You two are on the kiss cam! Kiss! Kiss! Kiss!"

I peer up, seeing Zaiah and I on the larger-than-life screen. I analyze it for a few seconds, but then a strong hand grips my chin, moving me to face him again. Then, he lays one on me. His tongue sweeps over mine. It's not a sweet kiss like other people give when they're on a Jumbotron bigger than some houses. This is a *kiss*.

A kiss people write about in literature. The kind of kiss little girls dream of when they fantasize about their Prince Charming.

The crowd erupts. Zaiah lingers, pressing his lips against mine before breaking apart. Everyone around us is in a frenzy. The guy behind Zaiah slaps his shoulder. I don't dare look back at the screen for fear they're broadcasting my red face to the entire arena. I'm sure they are.

"I got it on video!" the woman informs us excitedly. "Let me AirDrop it to you."

Zaiah spins, gladly arranging the video, and I slink down in my chair. "Thank you," he tells her. "This is great."

Turning, he thrusts his screen into my face, and I watch the shaky video the lady behind us got of the

Jumbotron. Red lips kiss the screen over top of us with the heading Kiss Cam, but you clearly see Zaiah taking control. To my surprise, I'm no slouch. If I were an outsider looking in, we look like a couple in love.

My phone buzzes, and my gaze flicks to Zaiah. "You didn't."

"Didn't what?" His lip twitches.

I scramble to get my phone out and peer at the screen. He did. He sent it to the group text.

"Oh my God."

"What? They wanted proof that a beautiful, smart girl would ever fall for me. I had to show them."

"You're—"

"Handsome. Adorable. Perf—"

"—lying." I swallow, trying to push down the panic rearing up and failing miserably.

He cups his hand around the back of my head. "It's time to get out of Len Land and move into reality. Check your phone."

I tilt my phone as it vibrates with incoming texts.

> Iz: I KNEW IT!!!

> Mom James: I'm so excited! Lenore, what's your favorite meal? I'm cooking for you.

> Dad James: Really happy for you two.

My stomach squeezes. A smile has somehow forced its way onto my face, and I can't make it stop. I don't want to run away with assumptions, though. "Zaiah, your family thinks we're..."

He waits for me, his gaze locking onto mine, as if pleading for me to say it.

"...together?"

"I hope that's not a question because you'll hurt my feelings."

"It's just, I'm so different from you."

His gaze turns hard. "Lenore, you are fucking perfect, so start realizing it. You're sexy, beautiful, smart as hell. I'm in awe of you. Is all that clear? Did I break into that stubborn brain of yours? Talk bad about yourself again and see what happens."

"I—"

Leaning over, he whispers, "I plan on showing how I feel a lot more, so get on board. I know you'll win against that willful brain of yours eventually."

He hands me my popcorn and places his arm around me. His grip on my arm tightens, and it's comforting and possessive and sexy as hell. I bite my lip, sinking into his touch.

This might be the most perfect day.

# CHAPTER EIGHTEEN

### Zaiah

Leaning forward, I squint through the rain-splattered windshield to see the top of the building in front of me. Lights pour from windows here and there, but the highest level is all lit up. "It's in this one?"

"That's what the website says." She pauses while I search for a parking space. "We can cancel."

"You'd love that, but no." My own stomach squeezes. The way she's laid out her dad's personality, he sounds like a bit of a bully. Family is important, though. Personalities can change. We grow up, and our parents are forced to recognize that eventually.

However, hearing her stories makes me immensely grateful for my family. They played the perfect wingmen tonight. They might be a little off-center, but they're the greatest.

"There's one," Len says, pointing at an open spot on the street. "No parallel parking either."

I smile as I put my blinker on and scoot into the space. The rain has stopped. Streetlights reflect off the remnants dotting the windshield but at least we won't get more wet. Putting the car in park, I peer over at Len, who has her hand raised in the air, brows lifted.

She frowns. "You left me hanging."

I slap her hand, making sure to grab it and pull her over the console to place my lips on hers. Kissing her is like an adventure. She takes us through a story. Soft and gentle, then the climax, ending with a caress that has me wanting to do it all over again. I could write my own stories in her lips. In her body. In her.

And I'm not the writer.

"You ready?" I ask.

She bites her lip. "It'll be good." Despite her words, she peeks up at the hotel, forehead crinkling.

I get the feeling someone is trying to convince themselves to take the next step, so I do it for her. Opening my door, I start to get out. She follows.

Once we're on the street, she takes my elbow while we head inside. "Looks swanky," I mutter as we enter a foyer with the biggest chandelier I've ever seen. Everything is highlighted in gold, right down to the flourishes on the columns. "You're rich, aren't you, Len?"

She squeezes my arm. "I mean, *I'm* not rich, but my dad's owned the team for a while."

I'm not a stranger to his name. In fact, when she

first told me, I'm pretty sure my mouth unhinged from the rest of my face. What are the odds that his daughter would go to the same college I go to, let alone be dancing on a table when I happened to walk by?

Those are divine odds, if you ask me, and I don't believe a wink in that stuff.

"We probably should've dressed differently," I say, realizing how we completely clash with the old-money charm of the hotel.

"Look who's nervous now," she tells me, hitting the button for the elevator. "Act normal. One thing my dad doesn't do is throw his money around, so there won't be a dress code. He'll probably show up in khakis. He hates pretentious people, so there'll be none of that."

"What does your house look like?" I ask as the elevator lifts, beeping through the floors.

"It's a...house."

"Is it a mansion?"

She laughs. "No. I mean, it's not small, but my dad came from nothing. You'll see when you meet him. He prides himself on work ethic. He's more blue collar than white collar, I promise."

The elevator doors open, and I fit my hand through hers. "Is this okay?"

She nods, squeezing me. I stare down at where we connect, her long, slender fingers clutching mine. Honestly, it feels better than I could've imagined.

"You with me?" Len asks.

"I wouldn't want to be anywhere else."

The way she lights up is a beacon beckoning me out of the darkness Trish left me in. She's like a lamp that's been finally turned on.

She's gorgeous.

Len gives her last name to the host, and we're seated in a small, offset room with only a few tables, making me feel better about the jeans I'm wearing. If I'd known where we were eating, I would've gone to the game dressed nicer. I was so looking forward to spending time with Len that the dinner afterward was the last thing on my mind.

"Oh, here he is," Len states, standing with a smile on her face.

I rise with her, looking over my shoulder to find a man my father's age, though his hair is slicked back and gray. Not the kind of gray that denotes their age, but the kind that says *distinguished*. She was right. He's wearing khakis with a button-up, the two buttons at the top left open.

"There's my Pumpkin." He hugs her, and they embrace for a while, making me wonder when they saw each other last. I know she hasn't seen him since I moved into the suite, yet I've seen my parents.

When they back away, she gestures toward me. "Dad, I'd like to introduce you to Isaiah James."

Her dad spins, holding his hand out. "Nice to meet you, Isaiah. I'm Chad Robertson."

"Mr. Robertson, nice to meet you."

His grip is firm, and for a moment, I forget he's

Len's dad as I peer into the eyes of a well-respected man in my sport. He's like Jerry Jones, the owner of the Cowboys or Vince McMahon of WWE. Everyone knows who they are. They're at every game and event. They're a symbol of the team as much as the star is.

He pats my bicep and walks around me. "Isaiah James, I feel like I've heard that name before."

Len clears her throat. "Dad's a walking stat machine, so don't get too big of a head." She smiles at me and then at her dad. "He plays for Warner, Dad. You probably saw his name mentioned."

"Well, you're right. Isn't that something? My only daughter dating a hockey player. I never thought I'd see this happen."

Len chokes on her water, and the both of us laugh.

"You didn't think I saw you two on the Jumbotron?" He winks at me before turning his attention toward Len, who's sporting a cherry-red face.

"Sorry about that, sir," I intervene. "I often find myself taken by her."

"I just like to make my daughter embarrassed, that's all."

I sit back in my chair, relaxing more and more. I half expected a tyrant to walk into the room. When I saw the foyer, I was pretty sure we were meeting a Rockefeller and I'd have to know what spoon to eat my appetizer with. But as Len promised, he's down to earth.

A menu moves into my vision, and I thank the waiter while he hands the rest of them out to the table.

"So, Isaiah, are you any good at hockey?"

"Dad!"

I laugh along with him, and Len sends me a look.

"He's the highest scorer for the Bulldogs. He's a winger. He's had three hat tricks in his career, including one this season, and his stats are solid."

"Wow. Stalker."

Her mouth drops a little. "I requested your stats for...the thing I have to do."

"Then memorized them?"

She shrugs. "I have a very proficient memory. And if you're wondering, yes, I'll remember this moment for a very long time." She draws the last words out, trying to give me a hard stare.

Her dad laughs. "I like you two." He takes a sip of his water and is still smiling when he places it back on the table.

"Well, I hope you like me."

He waves her away. "You know what I mean. I like you two together."

"He could be a serial killer."

"Is he?"

"No."

I shake my head. Her mind is still an enigma to me, like an exquisite puzzle I love trying to work out.

"I'm only saying, you've known him for five seconds."

"I trust my daughter's judgment implicitly."

She keeps her eyes on him, and I avert my gaze to scour the menu. I can't even pronounce half the

223

items offered. I look for a safe word like chicken or steak—

*Holy shit.* The steak is a hundred dollars.

I'm scanning the menu for chicken when her dad says, "Feel free to get what you want, I'm paying."

I smile at him, but there's no way I'm getting a hundred-dollar steak from this guy. I just met him. I find a menu item with chicken and as much as I can decipher from the words around it, it's edible.

Soon, we're giving our orders to the waiter as another server comes over with a bottle of wine and fills our glasses. I don't even know if I like wine.

"Only the one glass if you're driving my daughter around," her father says, playfully glaring at me. I recognize the tease in his voice, too. My father has dad humor for days.

"So, what are your plans when school ends?"

For a few seconds, I mistakenly think he's talking to Len, but then he looks at me expectantly. "I plan on coaching peewee back home, sir. I'll be graduating with a degree in business economics, so a job offer close to home would be nice."

"Sounds like you want to be a team owner with that kind of degree."

"I...never really thought about it before. Seems out of reach."

"Well..."

"Oh, here we go," Len interrupts.

"You could learn a little something from this, too, sweetheart."

"Dad, I've heard your rah-rah speech a bunch of times."

I glance between the two of them. "I would like a rah-rah speech."

Her father hits the table with a hammer fist, making me jump. "You can do anything you put your mind to. You just have to work at it. One foot in front of the other. You keep solving problems, eliminating obstacles one at a time. I wasn't born into a hockey family. I didn't have any hockey friends. All I had was a love for the sport, and look where I am now. I'm sitting in a rooftop restaurant with a panoramic view of the city that my team —*my* team—played in. I have a controlling factor in what they do. I'm set for life. I could retire right now. If you want something, you go out and fucking get it."

I sit up straighter. "Len says you weren't rich growing up?"

His gaze morphs into a sort of sad recollection. "My dad was a factory worker, and my mom worked part-time at the local library shelving books. They're wonderful people. But I had seven brothers and sisters, so we didn't have much. I knew from the time I was a little boy that I wanted more. I hated seeing my father come home tired and angry only to get up the next day and do it all over again. He worked his body to an early grave. That's not the life I wanted."

I take a deep breath, letting his words consume me. My father's an accountant who owns his own business.

He's always pushed me to create something of my own, like Len's father. "It's inspiring, sir."

He leans forward. "You have your whole life ahead of you. It's scary, for sure, but start now. It's never too early. It's never too late. It's all about what's in here." He hits his chest.

"Dad, can we get off the Ted Talk, please?"

He peers at Len, then back at me. "She's heard it all before."

She glances away, staring out at the panoramic view. Tension rises after that, and confusion flickers through me. I don't understand where her head is at, and by the time we're pushing away our desserts, I'm hoping Mr. Robertson will leave for the restroom so I can ask her what's wrong.

Her dad seems fine—nice, even—but I'm cautiously optimistic. Len isn't the type to overexaggerate when it comes to people.

"Thanks for dinner, sir."

"Yeah, this place was good. One thing I love is a good, hearty meal."

"You've had your fair share of McDonald's, Dad," Len says.

He lifts his shoulders. "An indulgence from a past life. I can't give up those cheeseburgers that barely pass for meat. Addicting."

"I can't even tell you the last time I had McDonald's."

He hits me on the shoulder. "Young guy like you has to stay in shape for the season. I know how it is.

Oh." He stands, waving. I glance behind me and see another gentleman enter the room and make his way toward us. "Jenkins, this is my daughter who I was telling you about. The writer."

"Ahh, nice to meet you. Lenore, right?"

"Yes," she says, bluntly. They shake hands, but Len acts anything but cordial.

"I look forward to meeting with you after you graduate."

I peer between the two, not sure who the guy is.

When Jenkins leaves, Mr. Robertson settles back down again, but Lenore remains standing. Her hard stare focuses on her father.

He looks up. "What?"

"Who's Jenkins, Dad?"

"He's the marketing arm for the team."

"Dad."

"Oh, it couldn't hurt to meet him, sunshine. You act like you hate the sport, but we both know you're only being...difficult. You grew up a fan, and here you bring me a boyfriend who plays hockey. You can't detest it that much."

"I don't want to work for your team."

"I don't see any other job offers coming through."

Her jaw clenches. This is the first time I've seen Len mad. Furious, actually. "I haven't even graduated yet."

"You have to do something."

"Obviously," she grits out, throwing her napkin on the table.

"Lenore..." He peers at me and back at her. "We can discuss this later."

"There's nothing to discuss. I'm sick of you not hearing me."

"Just...calm down."

Len starts to shake. I've been around my sister enough to know that those words are like putting a lit match on dry timber. Tears spring to her eyes, and I can't anymore. I see what she was saying. He turned from a fun-loving father to someone who doesn't even see what he's doing.

"Excuse me, sir. I know it's not my place—"

"It certainly isn't."

Nerves skate over my skin, but I'm not going to let anyone talk badly about her and that includes her father. "Lenore's going to make you proud no matter what. Even if it isn't what you want her to do. This scenario reminds me of your story about growing up. About how you did the seemingly impossible. She may not know what she's going to do yet, but she's more like you than you might think. She's going to be someone, and she's going to do it without your help."

Mr. Robertson presses his lips together. I stay staring at him because I don't know what else to do. Soon, though, a soft touch caresses my arm, and I peek over at a gorgeous face, eyes rimmed with tears.

"Come on," she states, pulling on my arm.

I let her take me away, but over my shoulder, I call out, "Thanks for dinner. It was nice to meet you."

She tugs even harder, and when we're out of the

room, I wrap my arm around her shoulders, kissing her temple.

"I think that went well."

She chuckles, wiping the tears from her eyes. "Only you, Zaiah James. Only you."

# CHAPTER NINETEEN

Len

THE DRIVE HOME PASSES, AND I CAN'T STOP
staring at Zaiah. No one has ever spoken up for me to
my dad. No one.

I place my hand on his leg, and he slides his fingers
through mine, squeezing while he steers with his other
hand. I didn't think anyone held hands like this
anymore. So connected that they have to take up every
available space, even the in-between.

Zaiah is like that, though. He likes the parts of me
that others don't. The parts that don't glow all the time.
The parts that aren't perfect. The parts that I hid away
because I wasn't sure I was good enough.

"So, Zaiah?"

"Hmm?"

His brow furrows like he's engrossed in some

twisted riddle, but as the silence stretches, he peers over at me.

"Since you're my puckable dating coach..."

A smile peels his lips apart. "Yeah?"

"What should I do if I really like a guy?"

His Adam's apple bobs. "You should tell him. Sometimes guys can be thick in the skull."

"And how do I do that? Seduce him when I'm drunk?"

The laugh that escapes him makes my body vibrate with a giggle. He peeks over. "You could do that."

*More like did do that.* "Do I tell him my deepest, darkest secrets?"

He squeezes my hand. "Yes."

"Do I invite him to a hockey game I don't even want to go to?"

A small grin ghosts his lips. "You could, especially if he's loved hockey since he was a little kid."

I tap my chin like I'm really thinking about something. "What if he adds me to his family group chat and kisses me in front of a whole arena of people?"

"Then he's a goner for you, sweetie."

My heart does funny things, stopping and starting in a strange cadence. My brain, however, keeps telling me that this is too good to be true. That Zaiah would never talk to me this way, and that I must be in some sort of daydream. "That's good to know," I say softly.

"Oh, that's good to know?" he teases. "Okay."

I rub my thumb over the side of his finger. "Well, I

can't take your advice right away. That'll make me look silly."

"Maybe I should take my own, then." He glances in the rearview mirror and pulls over to the side of the road. The car vibrates over the ridges in the pavement lining the white lines until we come to a stop.

A car speeds past us, but it's the time of night where the stars and the moon and the outline of the trees are all I can see as Zaiah twists in his seat. He squeezes the hand interlaced with his own on his thigh. "Lenore Robertson, I like you. Your awkwardness, your unbelievable brain, the way you can be a dictionary one second and then yell, 'Looks like you need to borrow my glasses!' at a ref the next."

My face flames. Pretty sure I yelled that at his game. "You heard that?"

He runs his thumb across my skin. "I always hear you."

His words settle around me like an embrace, wrapping me up tight. "Well, to be fair, he missed a lot of calls."

Zaiah shrugs. "He's a college ref."

He stares into my eyes, and nerves skate over my skin. "Well, back to what you were saying," I say, dragging in a long breath. "I think you were telling me something important."

He reaches out to swipe a loose hair around my ear, then threads his fingers through my hair to cup my neck. "You're special, Lenore, and I'm going to make sure you know it for as long as you allow me to. What else is a boyfriend for?"

I inhale a deep breath. "Boyfriend?"

He nods, leaning in for a kiss. My lack of hesitation surprises me when I move in, bridging the gap between us. He digs his nails into my scalp, and I let out a moan as he traces my bottom lip before kissing me with an intensity that has my mind spinning.

*I'm kissing Zaiah James. It's really happening.*

I smile against his lips, and he returns the favor before we start again, my mouth seeking his first, relishing the way we meld together.

When we break apart, my breath comes out in short pants, and I'm clutching the collar of his shirt in my fist. I smooth it down. "I like you, too."

The corner of his lips teases upward. "I know."

I can't keep a smile off my face. "So it's official?"

"It's been official. You're a little slow on the uptake."

"Oh, really?"

He squeezes my hand on his thigh again before sitting back, checking his side mirror, and pulling back out onto the road.

"So, how long have I had a boyfriend without knowing?"

"I'm torn between two instances. The moment you touched yourself in front of me..."

My face burns hot.

"Or when I walked in on you and Clark kissing

that day after practice and realized I wanted to tear him away from you."

"That...then?" I mutter incoherently.

I retrace his every word and sigh. My brain doesn't kick in nearly as much, and when it tries, I bat the ugly thoughts away with a spikey mace.

Not in this world. In this world, the geek gets the guy.

I'm on a high until he parks outside Knightley, then up the stairs as he holds my hand, and finally when the suite door closes behind us.

"I don't think you've stopped smiling," Zaiah remarks.

"Sorry, that's probably dorky."

He pulls me toward him, his hand trailing down my spine until it cruises past my hips and over my ass where he takes a handful. "The opposite."

I move into him, the hard outline of his cock on my hip urging me closer. "How do we do this? We live together. I don't want to go too fast."

"We take it day by day, sweetie. Tonight, though, I'm sleeping in your bed. I'm going to hold you and tell you that you can do whatever you want after you graduate. Then tomorrow, we can make a plan."

"I like plans."

"I know."

"You're okay with that?"

He kisses my forehead. "I want you to be comfortable. I'm just not giving you a choice tonight because I'm selfish." He pats my ass. "Now, go pull your cute pajamas on, and I'll be there in a minute."

He wasn't kidding when he said he liked my ass. He squeezes it again, and a rush of heat flares between my thighs.

There's not a chance we're not having sex tonight, right?

I need to brush my teeth. I need to see what panties I'm wearing. I need to—

When I get out of my head, Zaiah's already in his room, so I sprint toward mine. I brush my teeth first because if all else fails, that's the most important. While I change into my pj's, I check my panties and decide to go with a different pair, but instead of changing right into them, I turn on the shower and wait for it to heat up.

Jumping inside, I execute the quickest wash of my life, then a record-breaking towel-off session before I pull on the new panties. I realize my pajamas are in my room, so I walk straight to the dresser in my underwear to rifle through my drawers.

"Did you take a shower, sweetie?"

I jump, letting out a scream. I turn to find Zaiah spread out on my bed, smirking.

Oh my God, I totally walked in nearly naked. I flashed him.

I do everything in my power not to cover up.

He presses his lips together to keep from laughing.

"My pajamas are in here," I mutter.

This time, he lets the laugh out. "Do you think I

mind the full frontal? I'm tempted to ask you to come to bed like that..." His gaze drops to my breasts, taking his fill until he finally looks up again. He must see something in my face because he says, "Get dressed and come here."

With my back turned, I tug on my pajamas, opting for a tank top and shorts with monkeys all over them. My body flushes with heat, and I take a deep breath before spinning toward him again.

"Those are cute. I especially like the way I can see your nipples poking through."

My hands fly to my chest and I peer down, worried there's a hole in my tank, but that's not it at all. I'm nipping, and the tank is so thin you can see it.

"Get over here," Zaiah demands.

I walk his way, kneeling on the other side of the bed. He pulls me the rest of the way to him, settling me on my side with his arm around my shoulders. When he talks, his breath fans over my lips. "I put in a movie. Hope that's okay. It's one of my favorites."

"You're not the type of guy that hogs the remote, are you?"

"I doubt I'll even pay attention to it."

He hits play, and I peek over to see he's started *The Mighty Ducks*. My mouth drops. "I love this movie. Pretty sure I wore my copy out as a kid."

"I had a feeling."

"Quack, quack, quack, quack, quack, Mr. Ducksworth!" I say, imitating a line in the movie.

He grins, eyes shining.

"I had a crush on Charlie."

"Of course you did."

"Especially in part two."

"It's knucklepuck time."

I drop my head to his chest, body shaking as I hide a laugh. All the fears I had melt away in the blink of an eye. I cuddle next to him, and he places my arm across his stomach.

Maybe I should write an ode to abs. *"Ladies, don't settle for less. They aren't the thing of fiction."*

*Dear God.*

The movie plays in the background, but I'm more invested in real life. Zaiah's thumb on my hip, tracing my curves. My fingers flexing over his abs.

Before I know it, the movie is nearly finished, and I peer up to find Zaiah's eyes closed, his chest rising and lowering rhythmically.

I raise my arm, staring down at him. The hem of his shirt has lifted, and I spot a peek of his toned stomach. Behind me, the ducks are going into a Flying V, and if I could tug his shorts down a little more, I could see Zaiah's V too.

"You checking me out?" He stretches his hands over his head to yawn, his shirt sliding up.

He goes to pull it back down, but I stop him with a hand on his. "I want to see you."

I tug on his shirt, and he sits up, tugging it over his head before reclining against the wall again. I walk my fingers up his chest, tracing the muscles of his pecs.

"This hardly seems fair."

"You already got a peek of me," I tease.

"But you were so far away."

My stomach clenches as I try to pull bravery from somewhere. "A piece of clothing for a piece of clothing?"

"Like strip poker without the game?"

I nod.

"Good. Because I don't want to play games with you."

Does he always know the right things to say? He takes my hand from his stomach, kisses it, and rests it next to the hem of my tank. I finger the stitching. "You want me to do it?"

He gives me a short nod, staring at me. My fingers shake. I've never undressed for a guy.

I find confidence in his gaze, in the way he swallows while he waits with his eyes glued to me. My clumsy fingers grab the hem and lift, dragging it past my stomach and over my breasts until I drop it off the side of the bed.

"God," he breathes.

I shut my eyes for a moment, clinging to my fading bravado. He's not running away screaming, so that's a good sign. I open them again, and his eyes are still on me, tracing me. I can almost feel his concentration like a physical touch.

I let him get his fill until I get antsy. "Pants?"

"Just pants?"

I nod slowly, watching as he hooks his thumbs under the waistband of his joggers and yanks down, bringing his feet up to free his legs. I don't watch them fall to the floor, my gaze honed on his bulge. He cups it, and I decide I'm a big fan of boxer briefs. They leave nothing to the imagination.

"Now you. Though it's hardly fair. You've been teasing me with those skimpy shorts since you put them on."

"A deal is a deal." I lie back, shucking my monkey shorts off and returning to the same position I was in. Zaiah reaches out and tugs me close, my breasts pressing against his bare skin.

"Give it to me straight. How drunk were you the last time we did something?"

I swallow the dryness in my mouth. "I wanted it, Zaiah. I wanted you."

"And now?"

I take a deep breath, letting my thoughts ruminate. It's hard expressing them. They could bring rejection, but this newfound certainty I find in him shoves me forward. He'll be careful with me. He has been since day one. "I want you in a different way."

"Be completely clear, Lenore. What do you want?"

"I want to feel you inside me."

"My fingers?"

I shake my head, tracing my hand down his chest and brushing against his length. "Your dick. What do *you* want, though?"

"To bury myself inside you." He lifts my chin so I can see his eyes. "I want to feel it when you come this time."

I suck in a breath. "You do?"

"More than anything." His hand leaves my chin and lands on my breast, his thumb tracing my nipple.

A surge of pleasure jolts through me. "Zaiah…"

He circles my nipple until it's hard, his strokes making me breathless.

"We need to get rid of these," he instructs, dropping his other hand to my panties.

We lean back, both pushing our last pieces of clothing off while we look at each other. Immediately after his boxer briefs are on the floor, his hand fists his cock.

I watch in awe as he strokes himself. "Condoms?" I squeak out.

He leans over, pulling a box from my bedside table. I lift my brows at him, and he smiles. "You're not the only one who likes to be prepared."

He beckons me over, grabbing my face. The kiss is so fierce, so passionate, that I lose myself in it. In the captivating way his mouth and tongue work in synchronization. I'm so engrossed that I nearly crawl out of my skin when his fingers find my hips.

He smiles into my mouth. "I need to get you ready for me, sweetie."

He parts my legs, sliding his fingers up my inner thigh until he finds my folds. He teases me there, and I buck into his hand. Pleasure warms my core. "Zaiah."

"I know," he says, lifting up to take possession of my mouth. Miraculously, his fingers don't stop. They tease my entrance before he pushes a finger inside, and I shift against his palm.

My stomach twists. "Zaiah, I'm worried I won't last..." I ride his finger, the pressure building until it explodes in a frenzy. A cry flies from my lips, followed by, "Sorry!" as I break into a million pieces.

He moans into my mouth. "You're killing me." He strokes his finger inside me, teasing out my aftershocks. "Tight and wet. Lenore."

I moan, the sound coming from somewhere deep within. "I'm sorry. I wanted to wait."

"Don't you dare say you're sorry. That was fucking beautiful."

He pulls out, then switches to two fingers. I grip his bicep like an anchor when he restarts his rhythm.

"I don't know if I..." I swallow. "If I can."

His jaw sets like I've laid down a challenge. Leaning forward, he captures my lips again. His whole body works in tandem to fire me up once more. I move with him, moans pouring from my mouth.

He brings me to the brink again, my mouth dropping slowly... Then he pulls away.

A sound of protest hums from my lips.

"Fuck," he breathes, ripping his lips from mine. "You're so responsive."

My nails sink into his skin. Heart thundering, I peer over, pressing my thighs together to somehow recapture the feeling. When nothing works, I pout. "What happened? Why did you stop?"

"It's called teasing, sweetheart. Don't you worry. You're going to have more."

He rolls my back to the bed, following after. Spreading my legs, he teases my clit while he kisses a trail down my chest, stopping at my rib cage and making his way over to the curve of my breast.

He flicks his tongue across my nipple, and my hips jerk up when he closes his mouth over me, his tongue circling.

"Zaiah. I want to feel you. Please."

"Feel what?"

"Your dick, baby. Your dick."

"Not this?" He drives two fingers inside me, pumping as I grip his shoulders and hang on. He doesn't stop until I'm breathing heavily, the familiar sensations swirling through me.

"Oh," I cry. "*Please.*"

He strokes inside me a couple more times, then retreats again, leaving me empty.

"Zaiah," I groan.

"I want to feel this perfect pussy come around me." He reaches into the condom box and brings one out. After ripping it open, he slides it down his length. I watch him between my legs, a thrilling sensual picture. He fists his cock, moving his grip up and down. "Did you think about this?"

I nod. My skin buzzes in anticipation, my hips searching for something that isn't there yet.

"You touched yourself, naughty girl?"

I moan, something about his words firing up my nerve endings. "So many times."

He grabs my hips, tugging me closer. The head of his dick rubs against my clit, and I jump. The sensation doesn't stop, and I stare down to find him fisting his tip in circles over my clit.

Warmth spreads through me. My knees fall to the mattress, and I grip the sheets in my hands. "Zaiah, are you trying to drive me crazy?"

"One hundred percent."

"It's working." I moan. "I want to feel you."

"You wouldn't believe the view I have of you right now, Len. You're the most gorgeous thing I've ever seen. Tell me you believe it."

I swallow, trying to imagine what he sees. I'm desperate for him. Flushed. Squirming.

His voice grows darker. "Tell me."

I shift on the bed, and he follows, still keeping the same maddening swirls.

"You're gorgeous. I want to fuck you so badly. Sink my dick into your pretty pussy. You feel the connection, don't you?"

I nod, breathless.

"So beautiful. You were made for me."

I moan as the heat starts to envelop me. It's everywhere and growing stronger. Building. Building.

"Say it."

"I was made for you."

"Good girl."

A jolt surges through me at his words, like a precursor to pleasure.

"Now say you're beautiful."

"Zaiah..." My hips move with him. *I'm almost...there.*

"These breasts. These hips. These curves. Fuck, Len. Say you see it." He angles his cock down, and the head slips inside.

"Ahh!" I try to rock with him, but he expertly moves it back up to my clit, not missing a beat. "Zaiah."

"You're gorgeous."

I press my lips together. Again, I try to imagine what he sees. My hair fanned out over the bed. My body ready, waiting, dying to be fucked by him. "I'm...beautiful."

"Again."

His harsh command whips through me, triggering my orgasm. "I'm—"

"Len!"

"Beautiful!"

He thrusts inside me as my body starts to contract. My walls close around him, and that sensation sparks a surge of pleasure as he rocks into me at a gentle pace. I ride out the long aftershocks like waves crashing onto the shoreline again and again. Unrelenting.

"You're trying to kill me," he pants.

He thrusts, sinking so far into my sensitive flesh that I cry out.

He moans into my neck, kissing me softly. "Better than I imagined, sweetie."

"You felt me?"

His forearms move to the bed, propping himself up so he can continue his strokes. "Every perfect part of you." He ravages me with kisses across my sensitive skin, my mouth, my neck, my collarbone. He doesn't stop. "I see you."

Those are the sexiest words I've ever heard. Who doesn't want to be seen? Who doesn't want all the little parts of them to be bare to the world and accepted? And that's what this is. A complete and utter acceptance in the most perfect way.

"I see you, too," I whisper.

He drives inside me harder, faster. Sensory overload has my body shaking until I'm trembling beneath him.

It's a different sensation—more powerful in some ways—the reaction he has to me. The furrow deepening in his brow. The way his muscles tense. The moan that escapes his body like it was dragged out of him from the depths of his soul.

Knowing I'm doing that... No feeling can compare. "Zaiah."

He drops his forehead to mine. Our breaths mix in heady pleasure.

I run my palms down his muscular arms, then back up, threading my hands around the sweat-dampened nape of his neck.

We move against each other in earnest, my brain switching off and letting my body takeover while we eke out every pleasure we can. We're joined for a long time. A steady state of connectedness, of acceptance, of chasing after the next sigh and the next, our moans a chorus of contentment.

My third orgasm builds and builds until, at the exact perfect moment, it throws me over while he buries himself inside. I gasp, clinging to his back. It takes control of my whole body. I have no say in the noises that fly from my mouth or the movements of my limbs.

He makes one more short pump until he, too, follows, his cock pulsing inside me. His whispered words into my skin fill me, bolstering me like a therapy session I didn't know I needed.

Once we both come back down, I rest my head against the pillow, closing my eyes, savoring the last remnants in utter bliss.

Zaiah stays seated there for the longest time, comfortable in silence. When he finally pulls out, a groan sounds straight from his chest. He cups my face, his thumb tracing my cheekbone. "Perfect."

# CHAPTER TWENTY

Len

When Zaiah told me he wanted to take me somewhere, I wasn't expecting this.

He leads me into the arena with the goofiest grin, his golden-retriever energy turned up to the max.

"Do you have practice or something?"

He shakes his head.

"A game I suddenly don't know about?"

If it's possible, his grin widens even more. "You know when my games are, Little Miss Stalker."

I bump him with my shoulder as he squeezes my hand. We've barely been able to stay separate since last night. We slept in each other's arms. We showered together, a flirty explosion of bubbles and shampoo, both of us now smelling like my body wash. "Please," I retort. "I'm the opposite of a stalker. I'm like the anti-stalker."

He reaches up to move a strand of hair away from my face. "What about now?"

I blink. Sometimes staring into his eyes transfixes me, as if he's standing in a spotlight and I'm the only other person in the room. "What's that song? 'I messed around and got addicted.'"

Ahead, the ice looms beyond the open Zamboni doors, and I instinctually breathe in, taking in the aromas that uniquely belong to a hockey rink. The ice, the tang of forgotten, sticky sodas and old popcorn. It's like a stale candy shop. But today? Today it smells a little better. Like I can inhale every part of Zaiah.

He bends over to retrieve something and comes back up with a pair of skates. "I hope you skate better than you sing."

I mock gasp, taking the skates from him. "You'll have to get used to my concert showers. They happen every morning."

"Your lips will be otherwise engaged, I'm afraid."

A shiver flutters through me like the light touch of a butterfly's wing. Yesterday, I wanted to make ground rules so we wouldn't take this too far too soon, the idea of having a live-in boyfriend freaking me out. What if he gets bored with me? What if he chews with his mouth open? What if he snores and I can't get adequate rest?

But the way he spoke to me last night, the tender way he broke down my fears, I'm floating on a cloud d'amour. A love cloud.

"And you got my skate size how?"

"I looked at your shoe size like a proper stalker. You really could take some cues from me."

I grin. The idea of Zaiah pursuing me is still preposterous in my head, but here we are. We sit on the nearby bench and pull our skates on. I peek over at the expert way he laces up, his nimble fingers wasting no time. "And you miraculously have yours here too? They weren't in the car."

"The general manager here loves me."

"Oh, does he now? Do you want me to take photos with you guys kissing?"

He shakes his head. "He has a beard. It would sting too much. Face rash and all that."

I laugh. It's been forever since I've skated, and I pray my legs will hold me.

Zaiah offers me his hand when I'm finished lacing up, and I take it as we walk toward the open ice. He does it effortlessly, and I think he looks like a graceful swan, but that was before his blades hit ice.

I stand back in awe, watching while he glides. Hockey is all sharp angles, fast breaks, and severe stops. I didn't get to admire his fluidity on skates before, but it's all here in front of me now. The way he shifts from one edge of his blade to another. His hair billowing up on the side. And of course, there's no pesky helmet blocking his handsome face.

That little, negative voice inside me sneers, *You can't pull in a guy with such good looks. What are you thinking?*

But then he skates up to me and reaches out his hands. "Lenore, sweetie, you ready?"

I place my hands in his, like a symbol of faith. Our connection sizzles, the tips of my fingers buzzing with electricity as he urges me out onto the ice.

"I've secretly wanted to bring you here for a while. I thought the girl who cheered for me at my game and spouted stats couldn't hate hockey as much as you said. Then I met your dad..."

His words are softened by my concentration of getting my legs to work in tune with the blades, syncing them up so I don't make a fool of myself. Zaiah watches me and talks at the same time like some sort of savant.

"Then I figured you out. It wasn't hockey at all. It was him. It was your whole life being smothered and you wanting to break free. I saw it all," he finally says, squeezing my hand. "That's why you don't want to work with him, isn't it?"

I skate a few clunky strides, thinking about how I want to say this. My dad is a touchy subject. It's not like he's a bad person. He's not mean, he's actually just trying to do good things. "I want to be my own person," I start. "His whole life is hockey, which meant for a very long time, my whole life was hockey. I never had a mother figure—that I remember, anyway—to steer me another way. To add another layer. It was hockey and dad all the time. And I guess I don't hate it. I just don't want it to be my identity. I don't want to live in the Robertson shadow my entire life. You know?"

"I get it," Zaiah says. "Admittedly, I was confused

when he first showed up at the restaurant. I was expecting a tyrant twirling a thin mustache. Which is ridiculous because I've seen pictures of your father." He laughs to himself. "But there's more than one way to be...overbearing."

"I do love him."

"He knows that."

I shrug. "Sometimes I think we're the exact same. He wanted to make something of himself, and that's how I feel. I just don't understand why he doesn't get that it doesn't have to be hockey for me. It can be something else."

"I think...and I may be completely off base, but I think because he made this bigger-than-life *life,* he wants to pass it on to you—or at the very least, share it. He wants to give you the best things, and this is the only way he knows how."

"I want to show him that whatever my life turns out to be, it's what I want. I might not be rich by his standards, but I want to be fulfilled. No offense, but hockey isn't going to fulfill me."

He nods as we make the turn around the back of the goalie net. "I've been thinking. Our whole deal is off. You don't need to write the article about the team. I never would've asked you to if I understood everything."

I stop sloppily, my skates unsteady. He turns on his edge, facing me, and I place my hands on my hips. "A deal's a deal, Coach. Plus, I've already started writing it in my head, and I think you're really going to like it."

He skates toward me, threading his fingers through mine. "I don't want to be your dad in your eyes."

I swallow, his gesture nearly melting me. "You aren't, Zaiah, because you're not dictating what I write. I won't give anything away, but I'm doing the article my way. It will still be about the team, but I'm putting my spin on it."

He starts skating backward, pulling me along. "If you're sure."

"I'm sure," I tell him, staring into his eyes. I'm sure of a lot of things at this moment. Like how right it feels to be here with him, to hold his hand, to have this primal reaction to him in my stomach. A tug. A yearning.

"What did you think about my dad, anyway?"

He smirks. "For the answer to that, you're going to have to catch me." He untangles his fingers from mine and skates backward, easily skimming over the surface and picking up speed.

I wobble after him, my movements becoming less jerky as I try to pick up speed. I get into a rhythm, and he smiles when I reach out. He dodges out of the way, of course, then turns around to skate faster, and I know I have no hope of catching him. Before we get to the other turn, he slows so I don't hurt myself, capturing my hand again.

"So?" I prompt, though there's no way I actually won.

"Honestly, I was inspired."

"He is inspiring," I agree, smiling to myself. "I

really don't hate my father."

"I know," he says, rubbing my hand with his thumb. "I was inspired by how he took action and made his life what he wanted. He strikes me as the kind of person who wouldn't let setbacks get in his way. As he said, he just kept solving problems that made a big difference. I envied him."

A pride-filled bubble surrounds me. My father, the walking TED Talk.

Zaiah stares down at the ice as we skate. "I was thinking all last night about the future, and it made me come to terms with the fact that I really want a career in hockey. I want to play, I want to coach. I want to be around it, and I'm mad now."

"Mad?"

"I stayed at Warner all this time for nothing. An underrated hockey team. No scout visits. No interest from the next level whatsoever. And now I'm a senior with no prospects."

His shoulders slump forward. Seeing him like this kills me. "There has to be a way," I say softly. "If it's what you really want, you have to try. We can brainstorm. We can figure it out together." Immediately, my mind starts sparking with ideas. "You need a lot more than local interest in your hockey team. My article isn't going to cut it."

He tilts his head back, the strong line of his jaw more cutting in the arena lights. "I'm mad at myself," he admits. "It's a lot easier living in complacency, isn't it?"

"Oh God, yes. If I wanted a job right out of college, I'd go to my dad. He'd pay me handsomely and give me a generous time-off package with great benefits. Writing hockey bullshit is enticing. Complacency is enticing. But that's not what I want. The easy way out isn't necessarily the best way."

"Hockey bullshit, huh?"

I grin. "No offense."

"None taken because you're cute."

My face heats. I search his gaze and say, "I want to help. Call it the Robertson in me, but we can figure this out."

He slows us to a stop, pulling me in, his hot breath fanning over my lips. "You'd really help me?"

"Why wouldn't I?"

His arms band around me tighter. "You keep surprising me."

"It's nothing," I assure him.

His low expectations are due to Trish. Thankfully, she's no longer in either of our lives. Maybe her temporary appearance wasn't as much of a curse as I originally thought. Her manipulations taught me that I needed to be stronger. That there's a difference between having a backbone and being a bitch. Most importantly, her exit from my life taught me that people need to accept me for who I am.

Zaiah helped with that, too, except his influences were positive ones. When I asked him for help, he never changed me. He never told me to act like a different person. He never told me to wear clothes I would've been embarrassed in. He guided me toward better decisions to take ownership of myself.

Maybe I can repay the favor by doing the same thing? If anyone deserves to have his dreams fulfilled, it's Zaiah.

He peers down, staring at my skates. "I think you passed the test, by the way."

"There was a test? I'm always good at those, but I usually know I'm taking them."

"Let's see..." He traces his thumb over my cheekbone, leaning down ever so slowly. My gaze moves to his lips, my mouth opening slightly, and then my lids flutter closed as we connect.

His kiss is a promise, a new beginning, a balm. All gifts I need, and he gives it to me with his whole self.

He pulls away, squeezing my hips. "Definitely passed."

I swallow at his attention, my throat suddenly dry, and a thought rings true. He's said it before, but I didn't actually believe it until this very moment, wrapped in his arms on his turf.

He sees me.

There are so many words on the tip of my tongue but sometimes, it's just as potent to communicate in other ways. I pull him back down, sealing my lips to his this time, letting my mouth tell him what I feel because I'm scared to do it any other way.

I never take chances, always calculated decisions, but I will for him. I'm all in.

# CHAPTER TWENTY-ONE

## Zaiah

My dad's rumbly RV pulls to a stop in front of Knightley Hall. He honks the horn in rapid succession, the sound echoing through the air, and Len laughs, her dancing eyes finding mine as I squeeze her hand.

The RV door flies open, and Izzy jumps down the steps. She runs forward, arms open, and envelops Lenore in a big hug. I stare, wide-eyed at the way Izzy giggles and bounces on her toes.

"Hey, hey," I tease. "You're smothering my girl."

Izzy whispers so loud I'm sure my parents hear her in the RV, "You bitch, I knew you liked him."

Len hides a smile with closed lips.

I elbow her, the corner of my mouth twitching. "What's this about telling her you didn't like me?"

Mom saves her from answering. She's half hanging

out of the RV, waving at us. No, that's not right. She's waving at my girlfriend. "Lenore, I made you chicken and dumplings. Just like you wanted."

The way Len's eyes light up... "I thought that face was for me?"

Izzy's nose scrunches up. "Ew."

Len rubs her hand down my forearm. "If you knew how much chicken and dumplings meant to me, you wouldn't be jealous."

She barely gets the words out before Izzy tugs her toward the RV where my mother gives her a half hug, one hand still holding the railing. Izzy and Len go up around her, but Mom waits for me. She wraps her arm around my shoulders. "She's a good girl, Isaiah."

"Thanks, Mo—"

She lowers her voice. "I seem to have gotten myself stuck. I can't wrangle myself in, and I don't want to fall."

I kiss her cheek, helping to right her on top of the RV steps again. "That excited, huh?" I tease.

"Infinitely better than the last one. Times a hundred."

"Infinite is already the best number you can get."

She smooths down her apron. "I'm just making sure you know we approve."

"Are you calling me thick? Pucking unbelievable."

She gives me the mom look, pointed and glaring. "We wondered there for a while."

I sling my arm around her, chuckling and kissing

257

her temple. When I look up, Dad's embracing Len. "Hi, Sweetheart."

My smile widens.

He pats her on the back before letting her go and saying, "Let's get this train a rollin'."

"Remember, only a short one today, Dad. I have to be back in time for the game tonight."

He salutes me, then pulls his jacket apart to show off his T-shirt, a huge grin transforming his face.

Is that...?

No...

I squint, taking in a cartoon me in my Warner Bulldog jersey riding a unicorn that poops out blue hockey pucks.

"You can't be serious."

My mom swats him. "Those were a surprise."

"I got excited," he explains. He takes one look at her disappointed stare then turns his back and heads to the driver's seat with an overexaggerated cringe face.

"Well, if the cat's out of the bag." She takes off her apron, showing the same shirt.

"Wait for it," Izzy says.

My mom turns slowly. *Mom* is spelled out across the shoulders. Izzy maneuvers her jacket down and turns to show off the word *sister*.

My dad bounces his hand off his forehead. "I forgot. This one's for you."

Lenore nearly gets blindsided by a shirt sailing through the air because she can't stop laughing. I catch it before it hits her and hand it over. She jumps up and down, the RV rocking with her excitement. "I've never been happier to wear something in my life."

She immediately pulls it on, her smile wide.

"Yeah, *girlfriend*," Izzy enunciates, playfully punching her arm.

"Is that what mine says?"

I turn her around and trace my fingers over the letters spelling out *girlfriend* on the back. "What else would it say?"

She lifts her shoulders, but the laughter has died somewhere inside, replaced with something else. She goes quiet. Stoic.

"Alright, get saddled up, unicorns," my dad announces. "This train's about to jet off to a park!"

I lean into Len's ear as I guide her toward the couch. "I hope you're not quiet because you don't want to be my girlfriend."

"That's not it. I'm worried people will make fun of you."

She thought the shirt was hilarious before she found out hers said *girlfriend*, so this isn't about the shirt itself, this is about her.

While my mom and sister buckle in, I sit her in her seat, pull the lap restraint over her, and whisper, "If we weren't with my parents right now, I'd fuck that worried look off your face, sweetie."

Her eyes flash to mine, desire and heat overtaking the mixed emotions.

Standing up, I ask, "You in?"

She nods, and I sit as the RV starts rolling. I lock

my seat belt into place and grab her hand, interlacing our fingers. Her palm is sweaty, and she moves incrementally closer to me.

"Look at them," Mom says to Izzy, poking her with her elbow.

Izzy grins. "He did good for once."

I scratch my face with my middle finger, and my mom pretends not to see Izzy return it subtly.

Keeping to his word, Dad doesn't go far. After a few minutes of Izzy talking about her recent game, he pulls into a park. Mom serves up the chicken and dumplings, and we eat, talk, and laugh through lunch. Lenore fits in seamlessly, like she was always a part of the James puzzle.

"So, what are you writing right now?" my dad asks her.

"Oh, she's not giving it up," I warn. "It's some sort of top-secret document."

"Oh really?" he asks, clearly intrigued.

"Well, only to your son. I'll be happy to tell you later when he's playing."

My dad winks at her, and I scoff, "Are you kidding me? I didn't know that."

She shrugs, and Izzy holds out a fist, "Well played, sis."

"Aww, I always wanted a sister," Len muses as she touches her knuckles to Iz's.

Izzy's eyes widen. "Me too!"

My mom starts laughing. "She once wrote me a document with bullet points of all the reasons why we should have another daughter. When I pointed out we couldn't guarantee the baby would be a girl, she dropped it."

"I didn't want to be outnumbered."

"I always wanted two," my mom says, reaching out her hands to both Izzy and me and squeezing.

"Too bad only one is going to make you proud," I quip. "And you are outnumbered because I'm twice the size of you."

Izzy shoots her napkin at me. "I'll have you know Mom made me fudge because I aced my math test."

I gasp with over-the-top exaggeration, placing a hand on my chest. "*Blasphemy.*"

Iz shrugs with all the poise of a powerful queen.

"You know how she struggles with math," Mom whispers.

"Hey," Izzy contests. "It's hard, okay?"

"Lucky for you two..." Mom gets up, going to the back of the RV. She's gone for a few seconds and comes out with two baggies. I'm about as excited as a meth addict on a downward spiral when she hands me a bag of fudge.

"Thanks, Mom." I know I shouldn't before a game, but one piece can't hurt. I drop a chocolate square into my mouth, and the sweet, chocolatey fudge nearly dissolves. It reminds me of my grandmother. Sitting out on her porch as she sneaks me a piece while we look out onto her vast yard. "So good."

"Mmm, that is good," Len says. I peer over to find her chewing and nodding. "Very good."

We sit and talk for a few more minutes until I give my dad the signal that we have to leave. They'll meet us at the game later, but I have to attend a team meeting and then get ready.

My mom does a quick clean up while we buckle ourselves in. "Len, we're going shopping if you want to come with us?"

"At the outlets nearby," Iz clarifies.

"I wouldn't take fashion advice from my sister," I warn, trying to give her an out, or at least something she could grip onto if she didn't want to spend the day with my family.

Instead, Len smiles. "Well, I should be working on something, but that sounds like fun."

My mom claps her hand once and then moves to sit and buckle herself in. "Excellent. We'll only drop Isaiah off, then." To my father, she yells out, "One for the bus stop!"

"Who's outnumbered now?" he shouts back.

I interlace my fingers with Len's, surprised she wants to go with them. She seems content, though, she and Izzy already talking about what they're shopping for. Izzy's telling her she needs a new pair of shoes and who knows what else.

Soon, Dad comes to a stop in front of Knightley, and I turn to give Len a kiss on the cheek. "See you there?"

She pulls at her shirt with my cartoon face on it. "Wouldn't miss it."

I wave to everyone else. "See you in a few!"

Dad meets me at the stairs, patting my back. "Good luck tonight. Remember, unicorn sparkling poop pucks, play well."

"You got it, Dad."

He locks the door behind me, and I turn to wave as he guides the big boat away from the curb. No one pays attention to me. With a shrug, I jog up the steps and head to our suite. It's quiet without Len. The absence of her presence hangs heavy while I throw my stuff into my gear bag and leave for the Warner arena.

This past week while Len was working on her super-secret article, I watched tape of our upcoming opponents. They're going to be a tough team to beat, but I'm jazzed about the game.

Halfway to the practice rink, I spot Adam, and we slap hands. "Haven't seen you around."

"Yeah, I locked shit down with Len."

"I knew it. Dude," he smiles, "I like her. How have things been?"

"Really good, actually. She's in the Swaggin' Wagon with the fam."

"The Swaggin' Wagon!"

I laugh, knowing he'd appreciate that. My teammates dubbed the RV with that moniker, and I'm pretty sure my dad secretly loves it. "You're not going to believe the shirts they have on today." When he looks at me expectantly, I shake my head. "You'll have to wait. You need to see it in person."

"How's your family so cool?"

"Luck of the draw."

We talk a bit more, but we're silenced when we walk into the practice rink and are greeted by the coaches and our teammates' loud banter.

Coach gives us a rundown lasting almost an hour, and then we're rushed to the bus for our skate time at the city arena. After practice drills, we're led into the home locker room that's not even ours, and today, it hits different. I stare at the other players' names on the cubbies, shaking my head. I'm better than this. Most guys on my team are better than this, and it pisses me off all over again that Warner hockey is a joke.

Before I can go down the rabbit hole, the PA system turns on, and the bass echoes even in here. Every game, the annoying noise is a subtle reminder of the pregame ticking down.

Coach stands from a lone metal folding chair. "It's almost go time."

He launches into his pregame speech, which always varies by opponent. He's fantastic at getting the juices flowing, pacing in front of us, clenching his fists, using his words like a battle cry.

Eventually, he ends with, "One, two, three!"

And we all scream, "'Dogs!"

My skin buzzes, electricity coursing through me while I walk through the tunnel. I smile when my right blade hits the ice. Crazy to think that the last time I was here was with Len.

I find my family in the stands. Once again, Len is all in with them, ringing the cowbell and jumping up and down. My heart leaps in my chest.

"James!" Coach yells as I skate to the opposite end of the rink, but I only have one thing on my mind.

My family gave her a shirt with *girlfriend* on it, but I can do better.

My teammates catcall.

Lenore sees me coming and tilts her head. I point at her, then down at the area where I can meet her. Izzy pushes her forward, and she starts walking, my parents hugging her as she passes them. She gets down to the ice level, and I skate next to the wall while she walks the perimeter until we meet where the Zamboni comes in.

She faces me. "Shouldn't you be with your team?"

Behind me, I can still hear them calling out incoherently. Everyone knows what this is. "I got something for you."

"What? You don't like my shirt?"

I grab her shirt and pull her forward, sealing my lips to hers. My team goes crazy, and she starts laughing so hard I have to end the kiss far sooner than I wanted.

I hold my blue jersey out to her. "Since you come from hockey royalty, I don't need to explain to you what this means."

"You like me?" she asks coyly.

"Understatement. You put this on, you're telling the whole world—or a couple hundred people," I say, peering around at the audience, "that you're mine."

I hold it out to her, heart thumping, suddenly so nervous my hands shake.

She takes it from me. "You know, I never really understood the jersey thing, but now that I'm standing on this side, I get it." She pulls it over her head, and behind us, the crowd applauds. In my ears, it's an eruption.

"You want to be mine?"

"I'm already yours, Isaiah James. I was from the moment I saw you outside my window."

I swallow. "We have some time to make up."

"We do."

Taking her chin, I guide her toward me, kissing her again. This time, a short, sweet brush of lips. I don't trust myself not to dive in and embarrass us both.

I tug the jersey as I skate backward. Seeing my number across her chest makes my stomach flip. "Looks good on you, Len."

Eventually, I run into a thick wall of muscle as my teammates celebrate behind me, patting my helmet, my shoulders, knocking sticks with mine.

I blow her a kiss, and Adam calls out, "Let's take this game for Z!"

"For Z!"

# CHAPTER TWENTY-TWO

Len

My stomach squeezes as I wait for Zaiah and his teammates at Richie's. The restaurant had a facelift when I was a freshman, so now it looks like a nostalgic diner from the 50s. Bright red-and-white striped booths and a black-and-white checkered floor are highlighted by neon everywhere. A throwback to a period when the owners weren't even alive.

My phone vibrates, and I stare down at a text from Zaiah:

Almost there.

I rub the back of my neck, wondering what the vibe will be when they arrive. The Bulldogs lost. Sixty minutes of sloppy play and missed opportunities. Plus, the other team performed better. The Bulldogs got beat off the puck and on the puck. It was a hard game to watch.

My dad used to take the losses home with him. He'd be miserable, and he wasn't even a player. The disappointment would bleed into our everyday lives. Hockey dictated everything.

I don't know if I can take more of that.

A peal of laughter makes me jump, and I peer over to the other side of the diner where the football players hang out, their tables packed with girls and teammates. I recognize the starting lineup because of all the research I did for the exposé I wrote. The tall one is the quarterback, and the big one—West, I think his name is —is touted as an All-American and expected to go pro shortly after he graduates.

They look like they have it all.

The bell over the door rings, and I look up to find Zaiah, Adam, and a few of their teammates walking in along with a lone girl. I scoot out of the booth to greet Zaiah, who's staring at the floor.

"Hey," I say.

"Hey, sweetie." He offers me a small smile before wrapping his arms around me, his fingers curling into my back.

"Tough loss," I murmur into his ear, echoing what the other men in the box used to say to my dad after a defeat. They would line up to give him placating pats on the back, and afterward, I would hug him like this, but he didn't squeeze me like Zaiah does.

"Thanks," he replies, sighing into my hair. He steps back, frowning when he takes me in. "No jersey?"

"I wouldn't want to wear your jersey either after you fumbled that puck in the corner," Adam teases.

Zaiah laughs it off, but the stress lines around his mouth deepen and a furrow in his brow starts.

I reach up onto my tiptoes and kiss his cheek. "I didn't want to get anything on it. It's right there. Do you want me to put it back on?"

He shakes his head quickly and then waves his hand in the direction of the booth, so I slide in again. "Did you order yet? Sorry we took so long."

"No, of course not. I was waiting."

The tension in the air hangs heavy. The teammate and his girlfriend are pushed all the way inside in the opposite booth, talking softly to one another while Adam sits next to them. Zaiah follows after me so we can fit another teammate on the end of our side. These booths are big when normal-sized people are sitting in them, but not stuffed with large hockey players.

No one talks when the waitress brings over the menus. Our sad party is such a contradiction to the ruckus that's happening on the other side of the room. Cade, the wide receiver for the football team, is telling a story animatedly, waving his hands in large gestures that has everyone in stitches.

Zaiah peeks over, and the tension on his face increases. He turns away, the vein in his neck protruding.

I lean into him, pretending to look at the menu. "What are you getting?"

"Not sure if I'm hungry," he states, shutting the menu and sliding it away from him.

"A big guy like you just expended all those calories. You have to eat, Zaiah." I place my hand on his thigh. "Don't make me call your mother."

A smile plays over his lips again. "What did they say?"

I shrug. He probably wants a play-by-play of what we thought during the game, but I'm not going there. The sooner he forgets the loss, the better. "They said they'd see me next game. I bought some clothes earlier. Your sister helped me pick them out."

"Oh Lord."

"Did you know she's into fashion? I had no idea."

"Yeah, she has a sketchbook."

"So cool. She put outfits together that I would've scoffed at on a hanger, but I was so impressed."

His grin stretches a little, even though it still looks fake and his eyes are hollow. "Can't wait to see them."

Acting like Positive Polly isn't getting to him, so there's nothing I can do to make it better. I sit back, order, and talk when I'm talked to, but the next hour goes by excruciatingly slowly with only Adam attempting to make this a social gathering.

With a stomach full of mac and cheese, I walk out hand in hand with Zaiah, his teammates in front of us. We all break apart, going to our respective vehicles, and I drive Zaiah back to Knightley in silence. At a stoplight, I peer over to find him drawing hockey pucks in the fog of the window.

I seal my lips shut, reminding myself that he's allowed to take the loss in whatever way he sees fit. What I don't understand is why he invited me out with his teammates if he was going to wallow in his own misery, bringing up what they could've done better in the game over and over. Adam seemed to be the only player who wasn't taking it like a knife to the chest.

After parking, I push the button to turn off the car and hesitate. Zaiah reaches to release his seat belt and gives me another distant smile. I return it, and we both get out and walk to the suite the same way we endured the ride—lips tight and unmoving.

Once we step into our suite, I head for my bedroom. It's late and I'm tired, and Zaiah obviously needs some time for himself. Hopefully, tomorrow will be better.

"Hey," he says when I'm in the doorway to my room. I stop, turning slowly.

"I'm sorry I'm no fun."

I shrug, not knowing what to say. All these new feelings and old feelings are mixing, and I'm not sure if the anger bubbling up inside me is directed at Zaiah or my dad. Or both. "You have every right to be sad."

"I'm not sad, I'm disappointed."

I sigh. I don't want my life—my emotions—to be dictated by hockey anymore. I don't want to have to walk on eggshells after a loss, wondering when the person I live with will return to normal. "It's fine, Zaiah."

My stomach tumbles over when my response sours like a lie inside me. I don't want to be the person who takes it anymore. I don't want to be the person who needs to write letters years after because they felt like they couldn't say what they wanted to, and I shouldn't feel that way around Zaiah. I take a deep breath. "Next time, please don't invite me to eat if you're going to stick me in the corner, barely talk, not introduce me to your teammates I haven't met before, then sulk the whole time."

He lifts his gaze, and for a few seconds, he isn't bleak anymore. A storm fires in his eyes. Like thunder, he glares my way. "You're mad at me?"

"A little, yeah."

He breathes through his nose, nostrils flaring. It's the same look he had on his face the whole game.

Old Len would've backtracked to keep the peace, but I can't. Not with him. He deserves the best of me. "It's not all you. My father would take losses hard, and it bothered me. I would get ignored or have to listen to tirades for hours—sometimes days—and I despised it, okay? I realize you're allowed to take the loss however you want, though, so I'll be in my room. If you want to talk about it, I'm here. I promise."

A shiver runs through me, the memories crashing like glass shards from the sky that splinter at my feet. No one knows what having to hide from your own family member is like unless you've been through it.

Or having to walk on eggshells so you don't poke the beast.

Immediately, his gaze softens. He moves toward me, grabbing my hands. "You're right. Adam wanted to go out and I didn't. I really only wanted to see you. Hold you. I'm sorry."

I lift my shoulders because I really don't know what to say. Zaiah isn't my dad. I know that. Closing my eyes, I lean my head on his chest. His heartbeat thumps, reverberating through me until it's all I can hear. "Losses happen in your line of work. We can figure something out. We have to."

"We'll make a new tradition. Something happier."

His hands filter through my hair, and I smile against his shirt. "I like that."

"You'll have to help me come up with one because everything that springs to mind revolves around me taking you to bed."

"Typical hockey player," I tease, leaning back to look at him.

He bands his arms around my body, not letting me get too far away. He traces the lines of my face with his stare like he's imprinting them to memory. "No, that's not it at all. I'm addicted to you, Len."

"Zaiah..."

"It's true. I played like shit because I kept thinking about you in the stands wearing my jersey. Sneaking glances at you in my number when I should've been listening to Coach. Imagining your thighs wrapped around my head while I tasted you. You don't under-

273

stand what it did to me seeing you wear my name across your back. I wanted to stop the game and take you in the locker room."

"And then?"

"No, *take* you, sweetie. Drive inside you until it felt as if we were the only two people in the world."

All thought leaves my body.

"You're blaming me for your poor play."

"I'm blaming you for this feral need inside me."

"No wonder you were slow off the puck."

He grins. "Keep talking hockey to me and see what happens."

He lowers his hand to my backside, pulling me to him while he rolls his hard cock into me.

The contact makes me shiver. This is all so surreal. That I could conjure up any of these feelings in Zaiah emboldens me. With his hand still pressed to my back, I wrap my legs around his hips. He lifts me effortlessly, as if I'm weightless, and carries me to the closest wall, positioning me on it as he once more proves how hard he is, his stiff length rubbing against my leggings.

"Penalty for high sticking," I eke out, my mind a complete mess while it's trying to process all of these emotions.

"God, I love your brain." He moves in, claiming my mouth. Somehow, his lips and his hips work in tandem until I'm flooded with heat, arousal lapping at me. My own body moves with him until he pins me to the wall, breaking the kiss. "You haven't seen anything yet."

He changes up the pace, using his fingers to circle

my clit while I gulp in breaths. Slowly, he lowers me to my feet, but continues dropping until he's on his knees. His hands inch upward, grabbing my waistband and pulling down.

Suddenly, Zaiah's between my legs, kissing a trail up my thigh. "*Oh.*"

"Is this okay?" he asks, eyes heavy. He pushes my thin panties aside, revealing more of my hip and kissing so close to the inside of my thigh where it meets the inferno currently firing.

I nod, my hips bucking into his mouth, and he moans deep, the sound near animalistic.

He hooks his fingers around my panties, tugging them out of the way. His hot breath hits my center. "Two minutes with this pretty pussy and I might die and go to heaven."

He dives between my folds, licking straight up the middle, then curling his tongue around my clit.

"Zaiah," I whisper, body moving of its own accord.

He tears himself away, staring at my center like a foodie drooling at a spread in front of him. I wiggle at his attention, and he pulls my leg and places it over his shoulder before surging forward once more.

I'm open to him. Bared. He takes his time, unlocking me like a puzzle, trying new things, but going back to the ones that curl my toes and the most unholy sounds leak out of my mouth.

"You taste so good, sweetie."

Every time I attempt to move my hips against his face, he pushes them back to the wall. "I want to make you come all on my own. I want to hear you scream my name."

I groan when he returns, working my body like he has the playbook in his back pocket. His lips, his tongue placed perfectly where I need them, molding me until I'm living for the moment.

"Zaiah," I whisper as he brings me higher and higher. It's like climbing a cliff in anticipation of the actual jump.

My limbs shake. I fist his hair while he flicks his tongue across my clit.

"Oh, baby. Come on my face."

*Holy shit.* He works me higher, my body barreling forward. "I'm going to—"

He sighs and moans, and my lungs return the favor. The pants coming out of me would make me die of embarrassment if it wasn't with him.

I pull his head closer until my nerve endings explode, and I shout, "Zaiah!" My scream echoes so loud it startles me, but the feeling is quickly replaced by undeniable pleasure.

His tongue slows as my body jerks into his mouth.

"Fuck, sweetie. I need you to wear my jersey every day."

I laugh, my body convulsing, and then he moves my panties back into place before getting to his feet, his arm sweeping underneath my knees and carrying me to my room.

He lays me out on the bed, and it takes a while for

my heart to return to normal. Zaiah's wrapped me in his arms again, holding me.

"You're beautiful," he murmurs.

"If you say so."

He kisses the top of my head. "It's a new law of physics. When Lenore Robertson orgasms, flowers within a hundred-mile radius bloom."

I chuckle. "You're delusional."

"Mmm," he muses. "At least we found a new tradition."

Lord help me, but I might've just wished he'd lose more often.

# CHAPTER TWENTY-THREE

### Zaiah

"And this!" Len exclaims, twirling into the room with another new outfit. The way she glows, not only lighting up the room but making my chest warm, should tell me everything I need to know about my feelings for her as she gives me an impromptu fashion show with the clothes Iz helped her buy.

"Oh, I like that."

She poses in the doorway, one leg up on the frame, arching her back with her hand outstretched. The thin material of the shirt tightens around her chest. I laugh while a thunderous need to claim ricochets inside.

She giggles, pushing away from the door, unaware of how transfixed I am. Of the feelings coursing through me. I could kick myself for letting my loss dim her light yesterday.

It'll never happen again.

She holds up a finger. "There's more."

"More?" She's already shown me a few. Iz must've talked her into buying a whole new wardrobe.

"Oh yes," she calls back from within the confines of her attached en suite. "I had to call Dad to tell him I was using the emergency credit card he gave me. I was worried he'd report it stolen."

"So, you made up with him, then?"

"I...spoke to him." Shopping bags rustle and then stop. "It was brief. We didn't talk about what happened, but he knows I barely ever use the card, so he was fine with it. In fact, he told me I should use it more often."

"But you don't?"

"I can do things myself. Without him."

I love how strong she is. Determined. Her dad is only misguided when it comes to her future. It's clear he loves her. "You should have a candid conversation with him—without yelling. Get your feelings out there."

She peeks her head out, her blonde hair cascading down like a waterfall. "I agree. Easier said than done, though. To catch time with him, I have to contend with the very thing that bugs me about him."

I move up the bed, my stomach flopping with her words. "Is it really about hockey, though? You don't mind me playing hockey."

I hold in a breath, worried about what she's going to say, especially with our argument yesterday.

When she doesn't say anything, I keep going.

"What I mean is...he could be a businessman in another field. Maybe a corporate hotshot for a big financing company, and I bet he'd still work a lot and try to get you set you up with his work..."

She steps out of the bathroom, a light tank top hugging her. It stops an inch above her shorts, and it's hard not to take her in like that, even though we're talking about such a serious topic.

"I know you're right," she says, brows furrowing. "I've had conversations with myself about how hating hockey is irrational. To be fair, I don't much like any sport. Remember the articles I wrote about the football team?"

"Yeah, but I don't care about football either."

A grin pulls her lips apart. "You're too cute. You don't want me to hate hockey."

"I already know you don't."

She crosses her arms over her chest. "Just because I go to the rink to cheer my man on? I could be dying inside. Slowly suffocating."

"You aren't," I challenge.

"Maybe I only enjoy hanging out with your family?"

"That ranks up there, but there's more. I can feel it."

She shrugs. "Too bad I'm stubborn and won't ever admit it."

Turning, she whisks away again, and I laugh to myself. It's so easy with her. There are no hidden meanings behind her words. No riddles or tests I have to figure out. She wears her heart on her sleeve. She says what she means, and the fact it's a breath of fresh air is ridiculous but worth its weight in gold.

She squeals, the sound sending my heart racing. I jump out of the bed. "Are you okay?"

I nearly fall on my ass trying to maneuver around the corner of the bed. I'm steps away from the bathroom when she appears in the doorway. Grabbing the doorframe, I have to put the brakes on so I don't accidentally slam into her.

She grins, and I breathe a sigh of relief. "You scared the crap out of me. I thought you were hurt."

"I have good news."

My brain winds down from alarm mode so I can finally take in my surroundings. She's standing in front of me in nothing but a black lace bra and shorts. I swallow. "Is it that you look amazing in this outfit? Not that I'd want you wearing it outside the apartment."

I step toward her, but she stops me with a hand to my chest. "It's bigger than that."

"Nothing is bigger than you." My mouth goes dry as soon as the words leave because I realize how true they really are. I'm falling for this girl, so fast, so freaking hard. She's...everything.

She also isn't looking at me, and instead, is staring at her phone.

My stomach squeezes. If she knew the thoughts racing through my head right now, she'd probably drop her phone in a heartbeat. I open my mouth to tell her, but she says, "Remember when we had that discussion about doing anything we could so you could live out your hockey dream?"

I nod.

"Shortly thereafter, I threw myself into research mode, and I found a few things out."

"Yeah?"

"Around that same time, I wrote your coach an email asking him for all your game tape, and..." she draws out the word, "he's given me access to the online files! Zaiah, do you know what this means?"

I blink at her, thoughts swirling through my head.

"We're going to make you a press package." She touches my nose with her fingertip. "We're going to gather your best plays, best attributes, I can even record you doing practice drills if that isn't in here, and then we're going to apply to AHL teams."

My legs bow underneath me, and I grip the doorframe for support. "You...did this? For me?"

She nods, her fingers wrapped around what she thinks is the gift. My game tape. But she doesn't understand it's more than that. It's the way she believes in me. It's the way she's gone out on a limb to show me that she thinks I'm more than what I am.

"Lenore, you're—" I break off, three words tumbling through my head, but I don't want to say them and freak her out. But the truth is, she's the trophy at the end of a long life. I could be playing hockey, I could be coaching it from the sidelines or owning a team like her father, or I could be plain old

Isaiah James, working for someone else, but if I have her, I'll be rich.

"Amazing? Smart? Talented?"

"All of those things."

She thrusts the phone in front of me. "You should see what your coach wrote."

I read his words, rubbing my chest.

---

*Dear Ms. Robertson,*

*I appreciate your email and am happy to share whatever the team has on Zaiah. He's a talented young man who hasn't been given a fair shot. If I'm honest, I should have kicked him off the team a few years ago so he could blossom. I'd be happy to make some connections myself and will start brainstorming.*

*Thank you for your support,*

*Coach*

---

A MOMENT of pure awe swallows me whole. "He sees it too?"

"He must've told you."

"I don't know. He's always trying to get the best out of me, but it's another thing altogether to have him on my side."

She squeals again, throwing herself around my torso until her legs are wrapped around my hips, her phone falling, forgotten, to the floor. "I got something else, too."

I cock my head, and she instructs me to take her to bed. My brows rise, but it becomes clear quickly that she didn't mean it like that. As soon as I sit on the bed, she leans over, reaching underneath. I grab her hips to steady her.

"This is heavier than I remembered," she grunts, but finally, she heaves a box up and holds it between us. "I checked and neither of our laptops were powerful enough for video editing software, so I bought this."

She nudges it toward me, and my brain finally clicks. "You bought a laptop?"

"She's a big one. She has sexy RAM, breathtaking graphics, and the screen is..." She makes an exaggerated kiss noise and smiles. "Big Bertha has everything we need to splice together a package for you."

"And you think you hate hockey."

I move the laptop to the bed, and she leans into me. "It's not about hockey. It's about you."

I hook my hands under her thighs to pull her close, tugging her down so I can kiss her. Her lips melt against mine, and I eat her up before rolling her onto the bed. "This means everything to me. Thank you."

She locks her legs behind my ass. "I have a good feeling." She works her fingertips through the hair above my ear. "The scouts won't come to you, but you can go to the scouts. We'll make people see."

I take a deep breath, and it shudders out of me like an exhausted engine. A heavy feeling remains, sitting on my chest.

"What?" she asks.

"I don't want to disappoint you."

"Zaiah, the only way you'll disappoint me is if you don't try. You can't tell me you want to make hockey your life, then sit back and not do anything about it. I do have my dad's genes in me. For better or for worse."

"I... What if I fail?"

"What's that meme? 'Oh, but darling, what if you don't?'"

*What if I don't?*

I lean down, capturing her lips with mine. I've hit the lottery with her. Someone who pushes me to be better. Someone who believes in me and supports me.

The kiss turns from sweet to insistent.

I rock my hard length into her, and she breaks the seal of our lips to moan. Reaching my hands between us, I make quick work of her shorts. First, unbuttoning, and then leaning back so I can slide them past her knees and off. I kiss a trail down her neck, licking her collarbone and then the swell of her breast. Her chest heaves. The lace leaves nothing to the imagination, her nipple poking against the detailed fabric. I wrap my mouth around it, flicking my tongue over the bud.

"Zaiah." Her hips move against mine and then she stops, nudging her panties down.

I shove my joggers down next, just enough to free my dick. I need her so fucking bad.

I arch into her. Her soft, yielding flesh giving way to me. She's wet already, and that only makes me harder, more fervent.

"I need you," I breathe, finding her entrance.

She opens her mouth to respond, but I cut her off by sliding inside her in one long stroke. Her unspoken words turn into a cry that whips through her entire body.

"Jesus," she sighs once I'm fully seated. Reaching down, she traces her fingertips across my backside before staring up at me. "Then you better take me."

I prop myself up, pistoning into her with a force we haven't tried before. Her eyes fly open, pleasure sizzling there, egging me on.

She meets my strokes with her hips until we're fucking. There's no other way to explain it. This isn't two people making love, this is two people trusting one another enough to let it all out, showing our raw wants and desire.

Luckily, we were adult enough to have had the birth control and the clean talk. I had myself tested after Trish, just in case, and Len hadn't been with anyone in a while, so coming together like this—skin on skin—is stress-free.

My breathing ratchets up. The force of my strokes jiggles her breasts, and I reach up to pull the cups down so I can watch them move uninhibited. "Tell me what you want," I grind out.

"This," she says, still meeting me, her fingertips digging into my skin. "Just like this."

"You like the feel of me?"

She moans, the sound drawn out, and then a short cry flies from her mouth like an exclamation point.

I keep my gaze on her, sweat dotting my brow. I could come inside her now. Lose myself in her.

"Babe..."

"I'm almost there," she pants, as if she can read my mind. "Please don't stop. God, don't stop."

*Fuck it. I'm never stopping.*

I lift up, pistoning my hips until her eyes widen again. "Zaiah!"

My name on her lips only encourages me. "You feel so fucking good."

"Mmm."

"So fucking good, sweetie. Will you come for me?"

"Oh."

We meet a few more times, and as soon as I feel her pussy squeeze my dick, I come too, the passion on her face and the noises escaping her fueling my orgasm. Her body grips me, and I rock into her until the convulsing stops.

Arms heavy, I drop my head next to her on the bed. "Shit, Len."

She wraps her arm around me, working her fingers up my neck and into my hairline. "That was hot."

Her pussy squeezes my dick again, and I groan. "Are you doing that?"

"You can feel it?"

I shudder again. "Oh, I fucking feel it."

Standing, I pull her with me, then dip down to scoop her up, carrying her into her bathroom. Clothes are everywhere, and I step around them to walk her into the shower. It isn't big by any means, but we make it work. She unclasps her bra and throws it out at the last second before the spray comes on.

"We should do that again."

I grin into her neck. "Quick? Hot?"

"I was going with passionate."

"That too."

She shivers in my arms. "Thanks for making me puckable."

I snicker into her neck, kissing her there. "Thank you for believing in me. For everything."

"Of course, Zaiah. You're going to do it."

# CHAPTER TWENTY-FOUR

### Len

Izzy plops down as the buzzer marking the end of the second period blares around us. She sighs. "Is it me or is my brother playing like shit?"

"I'm not walking into that one." I worry over my lip, watching Zaiah skate off the ice, head hung low. I want to chase after him. I want to shake him a bit, give him a pep talk, and smack his ass.

Though, I kind of just like his ass, so maybe that part's for personal reasons.

"He's having a tough game," Mrs. James says, standing. "Does anyone want anything?"

"I'll come with you," Zaiah's dad offers, and they walk off together.

"Seriously, though." Izzy groans, kicking at the chair in front of her.

I give the cowbell a slight ring-a-ling and then set it

down. Nothing seems to be helping him, anyway. "I think it's my fault."

"What? Did you guys fight before the game or something? The last two games? Please tell me you didn't break up. I'll cry. I swear I will."

I shake my head, laughing at her dramatics. "We didn't break up."

She hits me with her shoulder. "Well?"

"I don't know if I should say. Zaiah didn't want me to say anything."

"You're pregnant."

My mouth gapes open. "Pregnant? What the fuck is wrong with you? Do I *look* pregnant?"

"No!" she exclaims. "I'm sorry. Mom always says I watch too much TV, and this felt like the right part in the script for a bomb to drop."

I would laugh if I wasn't currently choking on my own air. "Oh my God, Izzy. I swear. Life isn't a script. If it was, everyone would have a happy ending."

"If you were pregnant, it would be a happy ending."

I give her the *are you crazy?* look. "I have goals and they aren't kids right now. Why are we talking about this?"

"I meant that if he did..." she waves her hand around the proximity of my lower half, "impregnate you, that would mean you'd be a permanent fixture in my life, and I like the sound of that."

"Aww." I move to hug her, and she gives me a squeeze. "That's really sweet, and we can be friends no matter what, but please don't put out that energy. I'm a senior in college, Iz."

She pats my back. "Noted." Sitting back, she frowns out at the ice. "But you still have to tell me the other thing."

My mind is torn. I do a quick pros and cons list, but I selfishly move forward because I don't have a lot of people to talk to about this. Plus, I never liked the idea of keeping it a secret from his family. They would want to know. "So, a couple weeks ago, Zaiah and I made this amazing video—a highlight reel of sorts. Then we sat down and emailed pretty much every AHL team, asking them to take a look."

"Really? Wow. Good for Zaiah."

"Yeah, except...I think it's put him in his head. Or at least the lack of response has. He checks the video all the time. We uploaded it to YouTube with a private link so you can see how many people have watched it, and he has absolutely zero views."

"Ahh." She sits back, dribbling her fingers on the armrest. "He's pouting."

I shrug. "Kind of, I guess? He's definitely in his head about it. Please don't say anything. He didn't want you guys to know. I keep reminding him that tryouts are still months away. The teams are winding down their current season, so they're probably not even looking at emails right now. The fact that there's no response yet doesn't mean anything."

"Coming to Warner killed Zaiah's confidence. He was the hotshot in his leagues. Warner promised him the world only to be overlooked, and now he's got nothing."

"Did he used to talk about playing professionally all the time?"

"All. The. Time."

My stomach flips. Regret courses through me as I think about the article I secretly wrote and sent out that's most likely now sitting in some magazine's slush pile.

For the best, probably, but when I was doing research for Zaiah on how to make it to the NHL without being drafted, I got carried away and kept digging. People who don't give up—people like my father—they're a special breed. They hear no and instead of walking away, they dig their heels in.

The article idea wouldn't leave me alone, and after Zaiah and I made the video, I started to work. Not the same piece I promised him for the college paper, but another one. "The Sport of Dreaming." I wrote about the highest of highs and the lowest of lows. I got quotes from current pro players in various sports. It all came together with shocking speed, and honestly, Zaiah going after his dreams motivated me. I sent it out to a bunch of magazines. My first piece, on an editor's desk.

I wished I'd let Zaiah read it first, but he hasn't wanted to talk about hockey or the video.

I rub my throbbing temples. I didn't want the "crushing defeat" scenario to play out in front of me. Zaiah's story should be different.

My eyes start to water, my throat closing.

"Hey." Izzy grabs my shoulder. "Whatever happens, it won't be your fault. Zaiah should try. I'm glad you had a hand in this. He's changed with you. Completely changed."

"Yeah, now he's losing games. Go me."

I wipe at an escaped tear and breathe out, hoping I can stop the waterworks before Zaiah's parents come back. The last thing I want to do is explain to them why I'm crying.

"That's on him," she explains. "Losing happens in sports. He knows that. He's been playing his whole life. Plus, he's not the only player out there. He doesn't have to carry his teammates on his back, and you don't have to carry him either."

I nod, taking a deep breath, willing the tears away. Several even breaths later, I have it under control.

She pats my arm. "Good?"

"Better."

Mr. and Mrs. James return, so I sit back in my seat, nerves still frayed. When the players come back out on the ice, I pick up the cowbell and stand with Zaiah's family because it doesn't matter how he plays, we'll be cheering him on no matter what.

Luckily, they eke out a win, and when the Swaggin' Wagon drops me off, I'm not as tense as I could be as I make my way into the suite to wait for him.

I dress in my pajamas and put on *The Secret Circle* TV show so I can get mad that they canceled it again. Luckily, I've read the books, so I know how it ends, but the show was so good. Jerks.

Time passes, and the next thing I know, I'm roused by hands sliding under my thighs. My eyes fly open, and Zaiah is there, lifting me from the couch. "What time is it?" I ask sleepily.

"Late. I went out to get something to eat with some of the guys. I texted you, but you didn't respond."

"I must've fallen asleep."

I wrap my arms around him, and when he goes to lay me on the bed, I hold on, giving him no choice but to follow after.

He scoots in, and I lay on my side. "Congratulations on the win."

He shrugs. "None of it was my doing."

I watch different emotions play over his face from the moonlight streaming in through the open curtains. "You're a team."

He rolls his eyes.

"Oh, so you take credit for the wins when you play well?"

"Of course not."

I give him a look, and he sighs and rolls onto his back. "I don't want to talk about it."

I chew on my lip, reminding myself that I wanted it this way. He can choose what to talk about when it comes to hockey. I'd rather this than sitting in a booth being ignored.

Scooting closer, I lift his arm and sneak underneath it so I can lay my head on his chest. He closes it after me, rubbing my arm.

294

We lie there in silence, a heavy tension filling the room. Pressure screams off Zaiah like a banshee. I don't know how long it takes me to fall asleep, but when I wake the next morning to an empty bed, my eyes itch and they're hard to open, like they're still clinging to sleep.

The sun streaming in through the open curtains doesn't help. I get up to shut them, but it's too late. Once I'm up, I'm up, and when I check the clock, I can see why. It's nearly eleven a.m.

Begrudgingly, I head to my en suite to get ready, and when I finally walk out into the common area, Zaiah's seated at the small kitchen table. "Morning."

"Morning," he says, distracted.

Instead of letting him stare at his orange juice some more, I pick his hand up, straddle his lap, and sit, smiling up at him.

He returns the grin, wrapping his arms around me. "Well, that is a good morning."

"You seemed out of it." I shrug. "What time did you wake up?"

"Didn't sleep well. I've been up for a couple of hours."

I trace my hands up his chest, then scoot forward to kiss him. These past months with Zaiah have been amazing. Worrying over living with someone I was dating was short-lived. We fell into a rhythm so easily. So much so that I've been anxious about what happens after we graduate. There hasn't been a good time to discuss it with him.

"Hey, I've been wanting to ask you something," he says.

I pull away, wondering if he can read my mind. It's not surprising he'd be thinking about it, too. Graduation feels like it's hurtling toward us at the speed of the asteroid in *Armageddon*... And now I remember why I stopped watching apocalyptic movies.

The stress.

My stomach squeezes. "Yeah?"

I try to calm down, reminding myself that these conversations are normal. Izzy thought I could've been pregnant yesterday, so this isn't weird. Zaiah and I are together.

"No one's watched the video yet. I checked again this morning."

Disappointment hits me hard and fast. I can't disguise the frustration in my voice. "Oh." I move off him, heading toward the Keurig to make my own coffee.

"I need to be realistic about my expectations."

I swallow, trying to kick back the negative thoughts pinging through my brain. "It's a great video, Zaiah. When someone has the time to look at it, they're going to respond. The teams are still in their regular seasons. We have time."

I'm a broken record at this point.

"If I don't get drafted, chances are slim."

"Fourteen percent of players in the NHL weren't drafted, including the GOAT." I smile to myself for that. Took that line right from my article, but it's also the truth. Wayne Gretzky, who's recognized as the greatest player of all time, was never drafted into the NHL.

Full stop.

"I think we should be realistic."

"We are. You're not giving it enough time."

He breathes out, and the heaviness in the air swirls around us again. "I know you want to be positive for me, and I appreciate it, but I...know. It's not going to happen, and I was wondering..."

He pauses, and I turn to look at him, waiting.

He wipes his hands down his face. "I was wondering if you could ask your dad for help. He has connections."

My stomach drops. Irritation thunders through me like a tornado as my mouth opens, then closes again without saying a word.

"I know it's asking a lot of him," he explains. "And it might not do anything."

My hand clenches. He's not even thinking about this from my perspective. My shoulders fall as disappointment hits me as well. I don't want my dad's help, so why would I ask for him? "No," I say tightly.

"What?"

"No, I'm not asking him."

"I know you guys don't have the best relationsh—"

"Then you don't know anything, Zaiah," I spit, anger whipping through me. "I can't believe you're asking me this. No. No, I'm not going to my dad."

His voice rises. "No one's going to look at the stupid video."

His words are like a blow to the gut. We spent so much time on that video, and he was so excited at first. I crafted the email myself, and it's compelling as hell. "Stupid video?"

The Keurig sputters behind me, and I nearly jump.

He sighs and stands, walking over to me. "What if I'm not good enough?"

"You are," I say, my voice catching.

"Maybe your dad could give us the next steps? What if we're going about it the wrong way?"

My hands clench into fists. "*I* did the research. *I* know. If you'd done the research, you'd know."

He backs away, eyes guarded. "You really won't reach out to him?"

"I said no." Why doesn't he realize that every word he says about this is tearing me up?

His lips thin. "If my dad had ties to the publishing world, I'd jump in for you."

Disbelief courses through me. "I wouldn't want you to. I want to make it on my own merits."

He takes a long time to respond, looking anywhere else but me. "Well, I guess that's that, then."

"I guess so."

"Bye-bye hockey dreams," he muses as he walks away.

"Oh, don't fucking put that shit on me," I snap, and Zaiah looks up, startled. "You're good. Okay? You're good enough to make it. I don't know why you don't listen. We'll keep emailing. We'll call the teams to make sure we've sent the emails to the right people. We'll ask them over the phone to watch your video, but this *woe is me* attitude isn't helping. I can't do the work for you. And you're letting it impact the way you play the game."

"Oh really?"

"When you finally get the call, you still have to ace the tryouts, so don't start playing like shit now, Zaiah. You're playing like you've already lost when you're only getting started. This is when you need to be at your absolute best. And the worst part is, you're great. You just don't see it. I don't know how many times and in how many ways I can say it so that you'll hear me."

He doesn't speak for a while. The smell of coffee lingers, but either I go nose blind to it or the aroma drifts away because by the time he responds, I can't smell it anymore. "You're right. I already feel defeated. I'm grasping at straws." He swallows. "I shouldn't have asked you that."

"No, you shouldn't have."

He closes his eyes, tilting his head toward the ceiling. He stays that way a few moments, like he's calling on some sort of higher power. When he looks at me again, his eyes are pleading. "Forgive me?"

"I want the best for you too, you know."

"I know." He walks forward, picking me up to hug me. I place my legs around him, and he lifts me onto the counter. "I know I've been miserable to live with lately."

I take a deep breath. "Maybe we can find a mindset coach?"

His eyes shutter closed. "I'll go to the gym. That always helps me think clearly."

"Yeah?"

"Yeah." He laces his fingers through my hair, bringing me close. "I'm really sorry, Lenore. Please forgive me. I won't say anything like that again, and I'll try to be positive."

*He's desperate,* I remind myself. *There's so much at stake here.* "You're forgiven. I believe in you, Zaiah. Wholeheartedly. But you also have to believe in yourself."

He gives me a squeeze, pulling me off the counter before dropping a kiss to my forehead. "At least I've got you."

*To do list,* I note in my head as I watch him gather his gym bag and leave. *Look up sports mindset coaching.*

# CHAPTER TWENTY-FIVE

Zaiah

"ONE MORE STEP."

Under the blindfold shielding her eyes, Lenore smiles. Her arms wander out aimlessly, a giggle falling from her lips.

"Okay, I lied." I can barely keep the excitement out of my voice. "It's more than one step. I only said what I've heard others say."

"What others say when they blindfold their girl-friends and walk them out of their dorms?"

She always has a way of saying things that puts a grin on my face. *Focus on the good things,* my mindset coach had said. *Feed the great. Starve the bad.* I've only met with him once so far, but I already feel better.

When I listed out the positive things in my life, Lenore was at the top. The past few months would've been a disaster without her. Aimless and miserable.

The best decision I ever had was asking if I could be her roommate, a fact I'm going to make sure she knows over the next couple of days.

She squeezes my hand, prompting me to talk. "There's going to be a step up in two, one…" Her foot moves up, searching. "Bring it down."

It lands on the first step, and I help guide her up the stairs of the Swaggin' Wagon. When it jostles back and forth, I assume she knows exactly where we are. Her head tilts, like she's trying to figure out what surprise this could be. She's been in my parents' RV before, but we haven't done this.

She makes it up the rest of the steps without being prompted, and then I pull her into the small foyer, pushing her blindfold up. She peers around, gaze narrowed. "Okay, what's up?"

"My dad drove The Wagon here for me. I told him I wanted to take you someplace special, just the two of us."

"Really?"

I nod.

"You can drive this thing?"

Shrugging, I play it off, but internally, my nerves rear up. Dad offered to set us up at our destination, but that wouldn't be very romantic, would it? "I got this."

"I'm loving the confidence."

"Then wait for what I have in store, Len. I'm about to blow your mind."

I lead her to the front of the RV, and she situates

herself in the passenger seat. "It's so scary up here," she squeals peeking over the hood.

I laugh, but I'm having the same thoughts. Dad took me to an abandoned parking lot nearby where I practiced. He gave me the good ol' James thumbs up, so I must be good. He wouldn't let his baby into my hands if he didn't think I was ready, that's for sure.

I start her up. She sounds like an angry dragon beneath us, vibrating with the need to take off. I ease off the curb, but instead of backing up like my father does, I take her around the whole campus to avoid reversing this hunk of steel.

"So, where are we going?"

"Someplace fun. Know that my dad is super jealous."

"Oh Lord, that could be good or...plain weird."

"It's good. I promise."

We get to the light at the end of campus, and I pull the rig out onto the road nice and steady. Len claps her hands and high-fives me. The next big test is maneuvering her onto the highway, which also goes as smooth as butter.

"You're good at this. You better tell your dad you'll be driving next time."

I chuckle, still white-knuckling the wheel. "That would break his heart."

The upscale RV resort we're going to is about an hour down the highway, so we settle in. Len tells me she turned in the article she's written about me. Or the team. Actually, I have no idea what it's about because she doesn't want me to read it until it comes out. That date draws nearer, so she's buzzing. Afterward, we talk about my parents and her dad, who we saw last week in a much smoother meeting. No comments whatsoever about my hockey career, and to be truthful, I'm sorry I ever mentioned that to Lenore. I'm desperate.

*Correction. I was desperate.*

Everything is an opportunity. Everything is a stepping-stone.

Our easy chatter makes the time fly by, along with the fact that driving this thing hasn't been an issue. Soon, we're nearing our exit, and I put my blinker on.

Lenore sits straight up. "Are we close?"

"Yep." My stomach squeezes. Partly in anticipation, partly because the narrower roads out here in the sticks freak me out, but I go slow, nearly crawling when we pass other vehicles. Within ten minutes, I'm pulling up to the main image I saw on their website. *Serenity Ranch and Spa.*

"What?" Lenore's forehead wrinkles.

"We're here."

I roll down the window as a male gate attendant walks toward us dressed in a polo and cowboy hat. "James party?"

"Yes, sir."

"Nice rig." He hands over some paperwork. "You got a premium spot, dinner, and hot springs reservations. Please let us know if there's anything else we can do for you."

I give him a nod. "Thank you, we will."

He taps the RV twice, and I take that as the signal to roll on through.

As soon as I let my foot off the brake, Len starts asking questions. "Zaiah, seriously. This is like a camping spa?"

"Yeah, kinda. My dad found it. He's been talking about taking Mom up here, but they haven't done it yet, so I stole his idea."

"This is so freaking cool." She squeals, pointing out the windshield on my side. "There are horses!"

"They have trail rides. I just have to make a reservation."

"Are you shitting me? This is the coolest place. I'm in love."

"It has everything. We can go on nature hikes around the lake. There's a pool, but Serenity's claim to fame is the natural hot springs. You've got to see it. The pictures on the website are amazing."

She gasps, and when I peer over to see what's grabbed her attention now, she's staring at her phone screen. I should've known she'd go straight to the website.

"That's it," I tell her. "Isn't it beautiful?"

"This is... Holy shit."

"This is what we've needed."

She reaches over to rub her hand up and down my arm. Ahead, I spot our site: number five. Luckily, it's a pull-through, so there's no reversing this baby, and we also have a prime location with a lake view. The sites are set up to give ample distance from one to the next, and each one has their own permanent stone structure that boasts a small kitchen, a fireplace, and a rooftop terrace, along with a working, plumbed bathroom.

Upscale.

Like I've done it a thousand times, I pull right in and park the rig in a good spot. When I get out to check, I'm amazed that it looks damn near perfect.

Climbing back in, I shut the engine off and push the auto-level button. I've seen my dad do this a thousand times, so I tell Len to go out and start enjoying the site while I hook up the electric and plumbing.

It's too bad we can only stay one night, but Lenore and I can't spend too much time away with our senior year dwindling down.

After I set everything up, I find Len standing at the front of our site, gazing out over the lake. I place my arm around her shoulders, and she immediately leans into me. "This is so pretty."

To the west, a stunning view of the acres of horse pastures greets us. Pressure releases from my shoulders nearly on cue. Here, I can't obsess over hockey. My mindset coach told me to set the intention and let it go, so that's what I'm doing. I'm freeing up space to enjoy life.

"You've changed," Len says, turning into me and reaching up to place her palm on my chest.

"I've changed a lot."

"I know we said it before, but this mindset coaching is going to do wonders for you. I can already tell."

Her gaze staring into mine anchors me in place. "I feel like a different person," I tell her honestly. I'd been living in so much negativity. *No one's watching my video. The scouts don't come to see me. I'm not playing well.* Those thoughts kept me prisoner, but when the coach told me to turn everything into an opportunity, my mind shifted.

I pull Len in for a hug. "Selfie for the fam? We need to take a lot of pictures to make them jealous."

She laughs. "I think even my dad would get a kick out of a place like this."

"You told me he wouldn't set foot in an RV."

"But look at this," she says, but before I can view the scenery once more, she jets off toward the stone structure.

She passes two wooden swings that face the lake and a circular stone fireplace. Inside the half-open structure is a gas fireplace with a cozy seating area. Then there's a small kitchenette with a sink, a fridge, and the door to the bathroom. I snap a couple of pictures until Lenore finds the staircase to the roof.

She peers over her shoulder. "You're kidding."

Before I can answer, she's running up the steps. I follow after and emerge to a breathtaking 360-degree view. Black handrails surround the space on all four sides, and the comfiest-looking half-moon chair sits smack in the middle. Len crawls right onto it, spreading out with the myriad of pillows.

"I'm in love."

"Oh, you're in love?" I tease.

She grins, then sits up to pull me down with her. "This is the sweetest thing anyone has ever done for me."

"That's my new middle name. It used to be pessimistic asshole, but I've had it legally changed."

She giggles, and the sound is like a tinkling bell. I lie next to her, peering out over the lake. "This is the perfect selfie." I pull out my phone and snap a picture of the two of us cozied up on the half-moon chair. I send it off to my family group chat along with another snap of the view before us.

*Dad's going to go ballistic.*

After a few minutes of contented silence, Len asks, "I heard mention of dinner and possibly spa reservations. When are we doing that?"

"Dinner reservation is tonight. We still have a couple of hours. Spa reservation is tomorrow. We can get tickets into the hot springs or a trail ride whenever we want. We just arrange it through this nifty app they had me download onto my phone."

She grimaces. "I'm kind of hungry."

"Then you'll love the room service feature." I pull out my phone again, tapping on the app. "They'll bring it right to us. We should order some snacks. Oh, and my mom made us some stuff, but I haven't had a chance to look yet."

We look at the options, settling on a fruit and cheese tray. It's delivered within fifteen minutes and brought right up to the rooftop terrace for us, splayed out onto the half-moon bed. I tip the delivery girl and watch her drive away in a golf cart.

Len's eating a piece of cheese when I turn. She talks around a mouthful. "I think your dad's got the right idea about this RV-life thing."

"You mean now that there are horses and room service involved?"

She shrugs. "I liked it before, the tranquility of it all, but you can't say horses and room service don't make everything better."

I sit next to her, eyeing up the tray before deciding on a few grapes.

Soon, we're cuddled up next to each other again, Lenore pulled into my lap while we watch a pink sunset over the lake. Len takes a few pictures, then sets her phone aside. Neither of us have much signal up here. I had to tie into the Wi-Fi to get the room service, but I disconnected right after.

It's perfect like this. Just the two of us.

My stomach flips as I hold her. I planned a lot of speeches for today. I've fucked up a lot recently, and for whatever reason, she understands, but I don't want to be like her father. I don't want to be someone who constantly disappoints her. Someone who she's guarded with. I want Len to be her whole self around me.

"I need to thank you, Lenore."

"Hmm?" she says, squeezing my forearms that are crossed in front of her.

"For believing in me. For sticking with me."

"Of course I believe in you, Zaiah."

I press a kiss to her temple. My stomach clenches. Nerves tightening. We've been together a few months, and there were so many times that these words almost sprang from my lips, but I held them back in fear. I don't want to live like that anymore.

"I love you," I tell her, my voice raspy, my words barely audible. For a second, I wonder if she's even heard me and if I should attempt to say it again.

Slowly, she turns in my arms. "I love you, too."

My heart takes off like a stampeding horse in one of the pastures. "You're everything I could've ever asked to be brought into my life when I needed it the most. You're my North Star. All I have to do is look to you, and I know what direction I should be going in."

She inches forward, making me spread my legs to accommodate her as she leans in to kiss me. I maneuver my palms to the side of her face and seal the kiss, infusing every bit of emotion that's been building up inside these last few months into this; into making sure she knows exactly how I feel.

I'm a flawed man. I don't deserve this. I don't deserve Len, but as long as she'll keep by my side, I'll try for her. I'll attempt to be everything she wants me to be and more.

# CHAPTER TWENTY-SIX

## Len

My honey-infused lemon coated skin buzzes as I step out of the hot tub, Zaiah's hand in mine. We've been at the spa all morning, and despite never being in one prior, I'm convinced. Pure relaxation from head to toe.

"You surprised me with this, you know that?" I say to Zaiah.

He squeezes my hand. "That was the plan."

"That's not what I meant." I grin. "I'm surprised by what you chose, and I really, really love it. Promise me we'll come back sometime."

He pulls me in to kiss my temple. "It's a deal."

He holds my hand for as long as he can until we have to separate to go into the individual locker rooms. My body feels like mush, and my brain is in a sort of zen state. The massage, rainfall shower, and hot tub dip were probably the longest I've gone without worrying about something. Especially recently.

I tug my clothes on, sniffing my forearm to see if I still have the aroma on me. It fills my nostrils with ease. *Delectable.*

Today, we still have the hot springs and a trail ride to try before we head back to campus, though the trail ride might have to wait for a different visit if we can't fit it in.

Being here has been so romantic, conjuring up all the swoon I have for this man. The way my stomach drops when he still looks at me. The way I want to be close to him because of how safe I feel. Comforted. Alive. It's as if there's a drawstring between our hearts, and the tether keeps tightening and tightening.

When I'm finished changing out of the plush robe and into my normal clothes, I walk out into the foyer. It's a far cry from the rustic modern look of the spa, mostly log cabin chic with everything in sight made from raw wood.

I sit in one of the log-hewn chairs facing out onto the lake and stare out. A few minutes pass, and Zaiah hasn't come out yet, so I grab my phone to let him know where I am in case he missed me and walked back to the RV.

The text goes into an unsent status, and when I look up at the top of my screen, I find the culprit. No signal. I go into my Wi-Fi settings and connect to their internet so I can send him a message. My phone dings repeatedly with notifications, which I ignore...until one catches my eye.

### RE: QUERY/THE SPORT OF DREAMING

My heart pounds. I pull down my notifications and press on it. A response from Athletics, Inc Magazine. Excitement burrows into me. It could be nothing. In fact, it probably is, but getting my first rejection is also a rite of passage. I'm well aware it'll be tough to sell my first article, and possibly even my tenth or more. The market is competitive and—

---

*Thank you for sending this to me. I really enjoyed it. It was thought-provoking and intriguing with a depth of story I don't often read from the slush pile. I'd love to talk more about this, but most importantly, I'm dying to know what happened to your friend. Did he make it?*

---

Phone in hand, I stand, shaking. The editor. The actual editor. He liked it.

My arm drops, and I peer toward the ceiling. I could burst right out of my skin. I can't believe it. Everything I've worked so hard for coming together like this. Hope springs in my chest.

"Hey, sweetie."

I nearly jump out of my shoes, but I turn to Zaiah with what I'm sure is a half-crazed look on my face.

"What is it? Are you okay?"

Tears slip down my cheek, and he brushes them away, his brow furrowing. "They're happy tears," I promise.

"What's going on?" The way his smooth voice wraps around me lulls me.

I grab his hand and pull him to a loveseat nearby. "Zaiah, I didn't tell you because I was sure it wasn't going to come to anything, but I wrote this piece on professional sports and up-and-coming athletes. You inspired me to do it with all the research about getting you a chance, and it's the first piece that I sent off to major magazines."

He blinks. "Oh."

"I've heard back from the editor of Athletics, Inc... He likes it! He wants to talk."

"That's great," Zaiah says, but his voice still sounds confused. "I thought you weren't interested in writing about hockey?"

"It's not about hockey, it's about individual athletes."

"Oh, so sports? I thought that was the sort of topic you would shy away from?"

The electricity zinging through me starts to fade. "It's more of a human-interest piece. Sports is the background, the goal—the need, in some people's case. Like yours." I clear my throat. "You're actually in the article. Your perseverance moved me, and I wanted to write about it."

"Wow." He sits back, staying silent. The longer it stretches, the worse I feel.

I should've let him read it, but I honestly thought nothing was going to come of this. It was a longshot. The kind of Hail Mary you take when the clock is winding down.

I sit back too, staring out over the lake. This is not how I expected to celebrate my first win. It's not an offer of publication per se, but it could be. Editors don't carve time out of their day for writers they're not interested in.

"I'll let you read the article," I state.

"I wish you'd told me. How did you find out about it?"

"What do you mean? I researched editors and sent off a query along with the article."

"No, here. How did you find out about it?"

"I got on the Wi-Fi to tell you where I was sitting and it popped up."

He nods his head slowly, still not looking at me.

I stand, agitation building. Doesn't he see how happy I am...*was*? I'm not going to sit here and let him dictate my mood. "You know, if you'd come running out of that locker room to tell me you had even one view on your YouTube video, I would've been jumping up and down with you."

Fierce eyes finally meet mine. "Thanks for reminding me there aren't any."

My mouth drops. He can't be serious. "You missed

my point. The point is, it's not the Zaiah show twenty-four fucking seven."

I turn on my heels and make for the exit. I have absolutely no place to go besides the RV, but I'm not going to let him ruin my moment. This is bullshit.

"Hey," he says, running up behind me. "I'm sorry. I—"

"Stop saying sorry and fix it," I fume without looking back.

"Woah," he grinds out, his sneakers crunching the gravel right behind me.

I stop with him, crossing my arms over my chest. It's possible that was a little harsh—maybe—but he needs a reality check. Turning, I stare him down. "Zaiah, I just had great news, and you made it about you. I have dreams too, you know. What's happening to me is the equivalent of you getting a call from a farm team. It's a shot."

His jaw clenches. Gaze stormy. "I don't know what you wrote about me, and I'm embarrassed."

"You think I would embarrass you? Really? Me?"

He runs his hands through his hair. "No, I guess not."

"I've been nothing but supportive. I've been doing so much research for you. I took the initiative with your coach and got the laptop for the video. I've done nothing but try to help you, and you think I would write something that painted you in a bad light? Maybe my next article should be about unsupportive boyfriends."

I turn, about to walk away again when he grabs my hand. "Lenore..." His voice cracks. "I had no idea I was coming across like that. Please. You have to believe me. You're so smart. So talented. I feel like second string next to you, and I allowed it to get to my head."

My shoulders deflate. Slowly facing him again, I see the regret in his eyes.

"I keep fucking this up, and I don't want to do that. Hockey is my first love, you know. It's all I've thought about for a long time, but none of that even matters right now because I'm supposed to be celebrating you. I'm only trying to tell you where my reaction came from."

"You're jealous."

He starts to shake his head but stops. "Maybe. Maybe it's that, and it's because I'm afraid you're finally going to figure out that you're better than me and helping me is a waste of time."

"Where did all those mindset prompts go? Just because I win doesn't mean you lose. It definitely doesn't mean *I* think you lose. When you read the article, you'll know exactly how I feel about what you're doing."

He wraps his arms around me. "I'm sorry. I'm really happy for you. So, so happy. You're going to be a writer extraordinaire. I knew you would."

His attempts bring a smile to my face because they're genuine, but I can't shake the feeling that I had to yell at him to get them. I had to point out that he was doing wrong.

"Hey, please don't give up on me," he states, voice quivering. "Hockey makes me crazy, and I'm stressed and feeling the weight of graduation coming soon, but that's no excuse. I was out of line, Len. Please, I'm ridiculously happy for you." He squeezes my hands and gives me a desperate smile.

I let out a breath. It bothers me that he's reacted this way because I know he's better than that. He's sweet and kind. Yes, hockey does make him crazy, but I understand the pressure. My dad's been on me since I was a sophomore. These are growing pains, right? Totally normal.

"We're going to celebrate, okay? I was actually late coming out because I bought us tickets to the hot springs. Let's order some wine and you can tell me all about the article."

I lean into him, grasping onto his promise that he'll make this right. "That sounds perfect."

His chest rises and falls with a breath of relief. "I love you."

Now that has me smiling. The butterflies come back with a frenzy that warms me from the inside out. "I love you."

He whispers in my ear. "I'll do better."

And he will because Zaiah can do anything he puts his mind to.

# CHAPTER TWENTY-SEVEN

Zaiah

WAITING FOR A GAME TO START FEELS LIKE molasses dripping in winter...

*And now I want cookies.*

I clock Lenore's shut door again. It's still closed like it has been most of the morning since my family didn't take us out for a getaway. "Lose Yourself" by Eminem blares through my headphones, and even though I should be meditating like my mindset coach said, I can't stop wondering why today feels off.

In half an hour, I have to leave to meet up with the team, and I've barely spoken to Len, even though we're always together on game days. Always.

The song switches in my ear, and I skip it on my phone when a sad melody starts playing. I don't need to double up the emotions coursing through me. Poor Len. What was supposed to be a trip that showed her what a great boyfriend I could be turned into a nightmare. I'm not sure she'll forgive me. That has to be why she's been distant for the last week. It's like I'm living with a roommate and not a girlfriend—and definitely not a girlfriend I professed my love to.

My leg bounces up and down as I try to talk myself out of going to see what she's doing. I don't like this. I'm usually calm and settled before a game. In fact, the last time I wasn't calm and settled before a game was when I was with Trish. She would guilt me into feeling bad that I had to take time out of our relationship to play a game I loved. That's not what Lenore is doing, but my gut clenches all the same. I want us to be good. I don't want to go into the game worried that there's something wrong.

Pulling out my phone, I text my sister.

> You guys still on the way?

No. We decided we didn't like you very much, so we turned around an hour ago. We were going to wait for you to find out when you looked up into the seats and didn't see us.

> Shut up.

Well, don't ask stupid questions.

My fingers hover over the screen. Iz and Len have gotten close. Would they talk about me? Would she know if something is up? The temptation is too much to keep quiet, so I send a text.

> Has Len said anything to you today?

Her response takes a little time.

No. What's up?

> Nothing. I was only wondering.

Well, obviously, there's something.
You don't write me random things, Z.

> She's been in her room all morning.

Maybe because you're an idiot

My heart pounds.

> Did she say something to you?

No, I just forgot the question mark.
Are you an idiot? What did you do?
You know she's the best girlfriend
you've ever had. Smart. Funny. Pretty.
The trifecta.

When I don't write anything, she texts again.

Why did you assume she said
something to me? I really hope you
didn't do anything to her.

> Geez, whose side would you be on?

Hers!

> Never mind. Forget it.

Ha. I'm sure nothing's wrong, big bro.
She's probably writing or something.
The whole world doesn't revolve
around you.

That last comment sucker punches me in the gut. Talking to Iz isn't helping at all. I put my phone away, sighing. I have to leave in ten. Iz is probably right. Maybe she's writing. Maybe she doesn't want to be disturbed this morning because she's working on another article.

The convo she had with the editor from that magazine went really well, and they're going to publish it. Not only that, but I also read it and it was phenomenal. She was right about it not being a hockey piece. It was a piece about goals and dreams and the determination of people to do those things with sports as a backdrop. The way she portrayed me was amazing. It was the kind of thing you would want people to write about you. She described me as driven and passionate, and not the loser I'd built up in my mind.

I turn the headphones off, the meditation clearly not working, then stretch a little before grabbing my bag. I can try again on the bus over to the rink.

Walking toward her room, I hear her voice. It's soft,

and I can't tell if it's muted because the door is closed or if she's intentionally trying to be quiet. Without thinking, I knock and walk in.

Her gaze flies up to meet me. "That's fantastic. Thank you so much," she says into the phone before hanging up. She beams at me. "Hey."

"Who was that?"

"Oh." She hesitates. "My dad."

My stomach drops. At least it's good to know that she's a terrible liar. "Yeah? What did he want?"

"To see how I was. You know, the usual."

She's collecting up stuff on her bed and putting them together, casually closing her laptop. On the comforter, her phone pings with a text, and I see the name *Clark* before she swipes the message away.

Okay, what? This is so not like her. Before I can ask her if everything is okay, she says, "I'm going to be a little late for the game. I have to meet with Clark about the, um, paper, but I'll be there."

My shoulders slump. If she looked at me at all, she'd see there's something wrong, but she doesn't. Instead, she gets up from the bed, making sure everything is tidy and put away, all the while avoiding my gaze.

"What about the paper?"

"Oh, there's some sort of emergency. You know how he is."

"I thought you weren't letting him walk all over you anymore?"

She finally peers up at me. "I'm not. This might

actually be an emergency. If it's not, I'll be at the game earlier."

She shrugs like everything is fine, but I'm sick to my stomach. She wouldn't cheat. Not with him. Not with anyone.

Right?

Distrust flows through my veins like a long, winding river going downstream. Despite telling myself not to go there, it picks up speed.

She walks by me, lifting to her tiptoes to give me a chaste kiss on the cheek. "Don't you have to go?"

My hands clench into fists. She doesn't care that she's going to be late to my game. She's acting like it's no big deal. This is what I get for ruining her announcement about her article, I guess. If she's trying to get back at me, I understand what she felt now. I didn't know she could be this petty, though. I apologized.

"Yeah, I do."

"Have a great game. How did the meditating go? Do you think it will work?"

I force a smile to my face, kind of wishing now that I did actually meditate. Maybe then I'd be able to navigate around these emotions bouncing through me. "Yeah," I lie. "It went awesome."

"That's great!"

The grin she's giving me looks authentic as hell. Either she's getting better at lying or... Or I don't know what.

She walks over and wraps her arms around me,

laying her head on my chest. "Have the best game, Zaiah. You're going to do great."

Those few words quiet the fear inside me. I squeeze her, kissing the top of her forehead. I'm being ridiculous. My regret about how I treated her is being mirrored back at me, I think.

Honestly, I have no idea. I'm new to this introspection shit.

However, my gut is telling me I'm worried she's doing something wrong because I did, and I'm scared I'll never be able to make it right.

That sounds legit, though. Like I could've been a damn therapist. Maybe I should do that instead of prolonging this hockey heartache. Still no views on the YouTube video, but I dismiss those thoughts. They don't serve me, or whatever the technical term is that my mindset coach uses. I can only control a few things, and whether anyone views my video isn't one of them.

"See you there," I tell her.

"I'll be the one wearing blue."

I smile at her, then grab my bag and head toward the practice rink to meet up with the team.

After a brief meeting with Coach, we load onto the bus. I try meditating again, putting on my headphones and closing my eyes. I visualize the game happening like my mindset coach instructed. How fast I want to skate. The feel of the stick in my hand. The scoring motion as the red light goes off when I sail more than one puck into the net. I make myself feel excited, ready, positive. We're going to win.

It's difficult to do when things haven't gone as planned this morning. No parents. No girlfriend. Just me, myself, and I. Much like the crowd that's going to be at the game.

Despite that last thought, I stay as positive as possible through our pregame routine. In warm-ups, my limbs buzz, and when I get my mind on the actual task at hand, anticipation builds.

However, the second I remember how abandoned I felt this morning, it all comes crashing down, and I have to build the confidence up again brick by brick.

*They'll be there.* She'll *be here, sitting in the stands.*

We go back in to dress and hear Coach's pregame speech. He's drawing out a couple plays on the whiteboard when the muted echoes of the announcer greets us. A few of us look at each other. I glance at the clock on the wall. He's talking earlier than normal. In fact, he barely talks at all.

Coach shrugs. "They're probably testing the system."

He goes back to drawing circles and arrows, but then other noises begin, too. It starts as a low buzz and grows.

Coach claps his hands to bring our attention back to him. "I want you guys to go out there and play your asses off." His chin is stone, solid. Tension radiates through his body. "Let's get this win for us!"

I've been on this team for four years, and I don't remember Coach saying that before. He usually has the same spiels. He might switch it up year to year, but this is something brand new.

"On three?"

We move close, putting our gloved hands into a circle. Coach yells, "One, two..."

Then we all chant, "Bulldogs."

We start our way through the tunnels, and something is definitely up. The announcer is still going, music echoing around us. The low buzz is still there, growing louder and louder the closer we are to stepping foot on the ice. We each give one another confused looks, and once we arrive at the mouth of the tunnel, my eyes blink in disbelief.

That sound isn't a buzz at all, it's people. It's the hum of a crowd talking all at once.

When we turn the corner, we see them. The seats...they have people sitting in them. "What the..."

Adam mirrors what I'm thinking. "The fuck is going on?"

"Let's go, gentlemen," Coach says as he leads us out, not stopping like the rest of us. The crowd starts to cheer, and when my blades hit the ice, I skate in a large circle, taking everything in. So many people sit in the stands. In fact, it takes me a second to find my family in the throng, but they're there, watching me, screaming their heads off. My mom wipes at her face, and I really would like to know what the hell is going on.

No one ever comes to see us. No one.

I search the seat next to Izzy where Lenore always

sits, but it's empty. I remind myself that it's okay. She said she'd be late, but I want her to witness this.

*Holy shit. People are here for us.*

A chorus of boos rise up, and I peer around, worried that people have realized they're here for a hockey game, but instead, I see the other team has skated out onto the ice.

A grin nearly takes over my entire face. Adam comes up and hammerfists me in the chest pads a few times. "Let's go! We better have the game of our fucking lives."

I do the same back. "Let's do it!"

We skate back to our bench. The announcer starts listing off the starting lineup for the players on the opposing team, but then the lights dim and blink out.

"Shit," I mutter. *Of course this has to happen. We're literally about to have the coolest game of our collegiate life, and the lights go out. What are the odds?*

A strobe light flickers. Then another. Sinister music follows.

My gut clenches.

"And now, your Warner Bulldogs!"

I nearly pass out. None of us know what to do when they start announcing our names, so Coach pulls us up one by one and shouts in our face, pushing us over the wall to skate onto the ice. I'm the fourth announced, and when he gets to me, he smiles, slapping my shoulder. "This is what you've deserved, Zaiah. All these years. Go out there and make them fucking wish their asses were sore for how long they

328

should've been planted in these seats. Do you understand?"

"Yes, sir."

He pushes me, and I skate out onto the ice, the applause nearly deafening. I skate in a circle, peering up at everyone. My mom is recording, and I'm so glad because Lenore needs to see this. That I matter. That I'm doing something with myself. What a shame that she had to miss the puck drop of the game of all games.

"What is going on?" Adam asks when I find my spot next to him.

"No fucking clue."

"There has to be a reason all these people are here. Look, there's hella students in that section." He points in their direction, and that section stands, screaming. "Oh, shit. Did you see what I did?"

I laugh, patting him on the shoulder. "You're like a wizard."

"I'm Harry Fucking Potter all of a sudden. Lumos Maximus." He points at the student section again, and as if on cue, they all go bananas. "I like this."

We stay out on the ice while they play "The Star-Spangled Banner," and then we skate to our bench again, waiting for puck drop.

All the guys are hyped, but there's a general consensus that no one knows what is happening. Why are there so many people here?

The lights dim again, and this time, I'm pretty sure it's not because the rink is about to lose power. It's because the game is about to start. The crowd screams louder.

This hype. This energy... It's addictive.

I skate to my starting position, body tingling. I spy the same excitement in my teammates' eyes. We're all on fire. When the puck drops, they skate like their asses have literal flames flickering out of them. They skate like there's no fucking way we're going to lose this game, and holy shit, who knew that all we needed was people to believe in us?

Throughout the game, more and more people fill the arena. Unbelievably, nearly all of the lower level is sold out, people sitting and cheering.

I'm on and off the rink with my line, trying not to listen to the chatter because I understand how important this game is. This single game could change the direction of Warner Bulldog hockey. If we win, if people like watching us, this could be our norm.

So far, we're completely wasting our opponent, seven to nothing. I have more than one goal. Two, I think. Maybe three. Truthfully, the game has been a haze.

I keep peering up, trying to spot Len, but she's still not in her seat. Sweat dots my forehead. I'm handed a bottle, and I swallow it down, handing it back over my head, wondering where she is. I thought she'd be here by now. It's the third period. She said late, not missing the whole damn thing.

Someone leans behind me and says, "Hey, I texted

my girlfriend to see what was up. Why didn't you tell anyone?"

"Tell anyone what?"

"About the article your girlfriend wrote."

I turn, finding one of the assistant coaches staring back at me. "What are you talking about?"

"Dude, it blew up." He turns his body to block out Coach, then shows me his phone. "People everywhere are reposting it."

I peer at the screen, expecting to see the headline I read a few days ago—the one she's publishing in the magazine—but that's not it at all. He's showing me the front page of today's Warner University paper. "If You're Not a Hockey Fan, You Need to Be" by Lenore Robertson.

I nearly pick the phone right out of his hand, but Coach shouts my name.

"You're shitting me," I say to him, and the assistant lifts his shoulders.

She did this.

I jump over the barrier and jump back onto the ice. I'm dying to look up into the stands to search for her again, but I keep my head in the game, stealing the puck and getting a breakaway. The opposing goalie is the only thing in the way of my puck and the net, and I deke him out, sailing one into the corner below the crossbar.

I throw my hands in the air, and the roar of the crowd coupled with the sirens gets my blood pumping.

My teammates skate over to celebrate with me, and then I sit back down on the bench.

With only a few minutes left, Coach calls for third string so we don't annihilate the team. Plus, he probably wants the lower classmen to experience this. Keep them sticking around year after year.

Again, I look up to where my parents are. Iz is staring at me, and she waves. I smile at her, but Coach would have my ass if he thinks I'm not paying attention to the game, so I don't wave back. I certainly don't ask where Len is, even though I'm dying to know. I also need to get my hands on that article. Front page and everything.

Our third string scores again, so by the time the game ends, it's nine to zero. Not a single person has left their seats when the final buzzer sounds. We skate onto the ice to shake our opponents' hands, and then we celebrate a little, raising our sticks in the air.

This is... Wow.

I slowly skate off the ice, peering around and taking the cheering crowd in. What a game. What a moment to remember. This is what life for me could be.

We're all hyped as we walk down the tunnel. Adam slaps my back. "Holy shit, dude. You got a hat trick! You'll be the talk of campus."

"I just want any talk," I joke.

The rest of my teammates laugh. Replays of the game begin immediately, players recounting their scores. We turn the last corner to head into the locker room, and a body runs up to me, throwing its arms around me.

I squeeze it back. For a split second, excitement builds. Len saw the game. I'm so—

But then it's all wrong. The hair color. The height. The squeak that's coming out of her voice. Plus, I'm not sure Len would throw herself at me in front of all my teammates. When I peel the person off me, my heart sinks.

It's Trish.

# CHAPTER TWENTY-EIGHT

Len

My heart thunders. After bribing a security guard with charm I don't actually possess, I walk-run my way through the arena tunnels.

I wait in the area where they all converge until I see him turn the corner. Around him, his teammates laugh and smile. The excitement on their faces makes me want to jump right out of my shoes.

*I* had a hand in that.

Zaiah knocks his helmet with another teammate's like they're toasting with wine glasses. His sweat-soaked hair—still dripping—a testament to how hard he played. He owned that rink with passion, with determination. The sound from the crowd was nearly deafening, and Zaiah certainly played up to the moment.

Coach and I arranged cameras everywhere, not only for Zaiah, but for his teammates, too. Hopefully, this is the start of a better future for Warner hockey. They can use the footage for promo on social media, the Warner athletics site, and of course, it would be nice to have highlight reels to wow the crowd with before games.

Zaiah gets closer, and I walk out of the shadows. A few players block my way, so I sidestep around them. I can barely contain my excitement...

But when the path to him clears, I stop.

Someone else has their arms around Zaiah. Nails painted bright pink. Wearing a myriad of bracelets. No matter how badly I want it to be Iz, it's not.

My stomach falls. It's Trish.

Years of memories collide inside me with the force of a Mack truck. I back up against the wall, breathing heavily. She tries to talk to him, but he shakes his head and turns. Soon, he's swallowed up by his teammates walking into the locker room.

As the tunnel empties out, she places her hands on her hips. Her gaze narrows, lip thinning.

*What is she doing here?*

I try to make myself walk away, but her presence freezes my feet to the cement as scene after scene of what I thought was our friendship plays out inside my head. What a farce. It turned out to be a master class in manipulation. Stringing me along like she did Zaiah. I've long suspected I meant nothing to her, only there for her amusement.

She turns, and my stomach clenches when she meets my gaze. I'm like a deer in the headlights. Fear ripples through me, but I force myself to stand up straighter.

*You are stronger now.*

*You're wise to her games.*

*You know who she really is.*

She strides toward me and despite all my positive self-talk, I want to throw up.

"Wow. Never thought I'd see you at a hockey game. Never thought you'd write about one either."

"I guess that's a hello?"

She smirks. "You're right. Hello, old friend." She looks me over. "You look...good."

It's that. The little hesitation that says everything about her. I used to make excuses for it, but now I know it's a way of elevating herself. The way I used to lie to myself and say she did it because she didn't want to hurt anyone's feelings. I was caught up in her web, and she was the master spinner.

Instead of shrinking down like I would have and asking for advice, I smile. "Thanks, I know."

Her brows rise almost imperceptibly, but you don't live with someone for years and not pick up cues. Sticking up for yourself only eggs her on, but I'm not the meek little friend anymore.

"So, I was in your apartment—"

"What the hell, Trish?"

She shrugs. "I figured you'd weasel your way into Knightley this year and told the front desk I'd forgotten something in our room. They gave me a key. I had to see it for myself, and I have to tell you, I didn't see you as the dating-my-leftovers type. Then I thought about it some more and wondered why I thought that way at all. All of that stuff you said to me before—about Zaiah —and what you really wanted was him to yourself. Kudos. Well played."

"I'm not playing a game. Only sad people like you play games."

A flash of something pings in her gaze. It's not that the truth hit her, Trish is more complex than that. Or maybe it's the other way around. Maybe she's simpler. She operates on her wants, kind of like a toddler. Superficial. Spoiled.

"I'm sure Zaiah will be interested to hear how you orchestrated all of this."

I laugh, and she tilts her head in confusion which amps me up. "Trust me, Zaiah's aware, and from what I saw when you desperately threw yourself at him, he wasn't having it. So, please, tell away. I'm more than interested to see him put you in your place for cheating on him. Or are you delusional enough to attempt to pull off the lie that I also orchestrated that? Did I put that other guy's dick inside you? I'm curious. Is that the lie you're going with?"

Her face turns red, and I imagine her simmering like a pan of water about to boil.

I take a step toward her. Part of me wants to tell her to stay away from Zaiah, but she would see that as a challenge. Besides, I'm not scared of anything happening between them and she needs to know it.

I pull out my phone. "Should I text him to meet you?"

"I can contact him myself."

"Pretty sure he has you blocked. Unless you're the kind of stalker that got a different phone number to contact him. It's cool. I'll send him something right now telling him you want to...what exactly? Get him back? Tell him lies about me to make me look like some sort of creeper?"

She shakes her head. "Wow. You finally grew a backbone. Congratulations."

"Yeah, turns out I had to because there are evil bitches like you in the world." I start to type on my phone. I don't message Zaiah. I want him to celebrate with his team, but I do text Iz and tell her SOS in the tunnels. If I can't talk Trish out of here, his family showing up will do the trick.

"You were always jealous of me."

I turn my head. "Actually, I think you're right. But then you showed your true colors, and now I don't think of you at all."

"Come on, Nor. This is stupid." Her eyes round, like the emoji with the sad, watering eyes, and she puts some whine into her voice. "I don't know why you're acting like this. We were such good friends."

The way her demeanor switches in an instant means she's a full-on psychopath. At the very least, she's an amazing actress.

Thankfully, I'm not malleable to her underhanded charms anymore. I have her clocked, and she knows it.

"Were we, though? I think I was just a pawn of yours, and now you're mad that you don't have it to play with."

"How can you be so mean? First, you tell Zaiah about me. We were best friends. Where's the loyalty? Then, you don't contact me when I leave, and when I come back, I find out you're fucking my boyfriend. And you're saying I'm the liar? The bad person?"

Her voice has risen a few octaves, drawing the attention of a few of the rink staff. I wave at everyone who's turned to look at us. "Hope you're enjoying the show. This is called *someone throwing a tantrum when they don't get what they want.*"

Trish's eyes flash again. Surprise this time. Disbelief that I didn't cave as soon as she turned the tables and pretended to be the victim.

"You don't affect me anymore," I say, stepping closer. "I have real friends. I have a great boyfriend. I certainly don't need your master manipulations in my life." I stare her down for a few seconds, my fingertips buzzing. I send up a silent *thank you* that I'm actually saying everything that I've dreamed of throwing in her face. "What made you show up, anyway? I'm sure you didn't happen to be in the area. Did another one of your unsuspecting victims figure you out, so you decided to prey on an old one?"

She swallows. "Turns out, I still follow all of Warner's socials. I saw your article and the social media about the team. It reminded me of what a good fuck Zaiah was, so I came back for some of that. When I went to his old room, some rando told me he was living with his girlfriend in Knightley. Of course, I never in a million years thought it was you."

*Ha.* So there's the truth. She didn't go to Knightley first. Zaiah was her object all along.

"To my surprise, the doormat at the desk told me his roommate's name."

"And you thought you'd make yourself comfortable in our apartment?"

"Oh, don't play the victim. You fucked me over, Nor."

"My name isn't Nor. You'd know that if you were ever my friend, so no, I didn't fuck my friend over. I fucked a lying, cheating, gaslighting bitch over. You were never my friend. You only used me."

"*Like a pawn.* Yeah, I heard you before." She shakes her head. "You're unbelievable, making up so many lies about me. You had to make me the bad guy, otherwise you would've felt horrible for taking my seconds."

"Don't you dare talk about Zaiah like that. He's no one's seconds. He's not someone you come back to because you remembered how good of a lay he was. Your pettiness is showing, and it isn't attractive."

"At least I start out attractive."

I swallow, unable to keep the flinch off my face. Always straight to the jugular with her. "Excuse me if I don't trust your eyesight. It leads you to terrible decisions like treating people like shit, cheating on people, using people—"

"—and in general, just being a horrible bitch," a voice snaps.

Trish spins, and I grin when I spot Iz a few paces behind her.

She looks Trish up and down. "Look at the trash. Don't they clean this place up?"

Mr. and Mrs. James wait near the exit. Thank God because if something awful comes out of my mouth, I don't want them to think badly of me.

"Aww, Iz," Trish says, opening her arms.

Iz ignores her and comes to stand next to me. I swear she takes after her brother because she appears taller, more grown up with her don't-fuck-with-me face. "It's Miss James to you."

"Excuse me?"

The evilest grin turns up the corners of Izzy's mouth. "I'm waiting for the day when you've completely talked yourself into a corner and everyone finds out who you truly are so you end up being a maid in my mansion where I sit back and eat popcorn while watching you clean up after me. Every once in a while, I make it interesting by tossing down kernels right in front of your stupid face, watching you get angrier and angrier. But that only makes me laugh louder."

Trish's face scrunches up, but I sputter out a laugh. "That was oddly specific."

"I've daydreamed about it for a long time." She throws her arms over my shoulder like her brother does. "Have you met Len? Take a good look because this is what a real girlfriend looks like."

Trish peers from me to Iz and back again. Her brain is turning. I can see it. Churning and churning. Imagine having to live your life looking for the next angle, the next move, because you couldn't be your authentic self. I'm starting to feel bad for her.

Not that bad. Maybe just a micro-feeling. The smallest of sads, definitely not something you can see with the naked eye.

When I realize she doesn't have anything to say to that, I wave to her. "Bye, Trish."

That's it. That's everything. That's what I can offer a so-called friend that I lived with for the better part of three years. The person I told my secrets to.

When she walks away, sadness creeps over me. It's like saying goodbye to something, even if it all ended up a lie. The only good thing I can say about Trish right now is that she showed me what I won't accept, and you know what? Maybe I should thank her for that.

Do I think she's all bad? No. I think somewhere, things went wrong in her brain. I think deep down, she's actually a very scared, insecure person, but she's not ready to see that yet, and it's not my responsibility to show her. I can cut that tether and be done with it, sending Trish to the barren desert of my brain where I keep everything else I'd rather not think about.

She sees Zaiah's parents, and for a second, she stops. However, she must think better of approaching them because she keeps walking.

Good.

"Duuuuuuuuude, what the puck?" Iz finally rants.

I turn toward her. "She just showed up. She threw her arms around Zaiah like they were still dating."

"Ew. Oh." Iz's eyes go wide. "You know he hates her, right?"

I wave her worries away. "He pushed her away. It's the audacity."

"Let me guess, she saw all the stuff you did and decided to come check it out?"

"Not exactly. She went into territory I'm sure you'd rather not hear."

The Jameses start walking toward us, so I wave.

"Like what?" Iz asks.

"You don't want to know."

"I'm dying to know, actually."

"Okay... She came because she remembered your brother was a good—"

"Don't say it."

"Told you."

"I swear, this friendship will only work if we never talk about your sex life with my brother. I will vomit."

I laugh. "Trust me, I'm good with that."

"Yikes," Mrs. James says. "I hope that awful girl didn't bother you." She exchanges a look with Zaiah's dad.

"Oh, her? I thought she was a street person. I gave her directions."

Iz can barely keep a straight face, and Zaiah's mom's eyes light up.

"Well..." She walks forward, giving me a gigantic

hug. "What you've done for Zaiah is incredible. I haven't seen him skate like that in a long time." Her words are muffled as she talks into my hair, but I close my eyes, soaking it in. "I'm sure he's so thrilled to have you in his life. I know I am."

When she backs away, tears well in her eyes. I swallow, keeping the emotion at bay that wants to bubble to the surface. Mr. James gives me a hug, too, patting me on the shoulder.

"Oh, I hope you two get married," Mrs. James says, clapping her hands.

"Woah, Mom," Iz says, giggling.

"What? You know you've thought about it, too."

Iz leans down. "We've already picked out your house in the neighborhood."

Nervous laughter bubbles over, a release of pent-up stress. Seeing Trish, the sheer panic I endured trying to get everything right tonight, keeping a secret from Zaiah—everything—it all washes away in a circus of laughter with Zaiah's family.

I grin, and we all move into a big hug. Mostly, it's a James family hug where I'm squished in the middle, but I'll take it.

# CHAPTER TWENTY-NINE

## Zaiah

FRESHLY SHOWERED, A STACCATO BASS OF exhilaration pumping through me, I emerge from the arena with Adam's fist hitting me in the chest. He hasn't stopped giving a play-by-play of our highlights. His rundown is a nice sort of chaos in my ears as I organize my own feelings. Happy. Excited. Exhilarated. Though, I wish Lenore had come, considering she set the whole thing up.

Plus, now I have to tell her that Trish showed up, and I'm really not looking forward to that. Despite those things, nothing could ruin this moment that's four years in the making.

Adam cuts himself off. "There she is!"

He takes off, running in my path to the bus so I have to stop short. I don't see who's caught his attention until she's hoisted in his arms and smiling down at him.

Red-hot jealousy pierces my skin with the velocity of a blow dart, and I kind of want to punch him in the face.

A round of applause rolls through my teammates. Adam hikes her onto his shoulder, and they all start to chant, "Len! Len! Len!" Her smiling, happy face quickly dissolves into discomfort, and she bows awkwardly with a flourish of her arm. This only eggs my teammates on, and they reach up to high five her. I stand back, in awe of her and what she's done. We have the momentum now like we've never had. Skills and gameplay were never the issue, it was the intangibles. It was getting eyes on us, and that's exactly what she did.

She peers around, gaze flitting this way and that. I decide to put her out of her introverted misery, so I walk forward, the crowd parting for me.

"Relinquish the writer," I tell Adam, reaching up for Len's hand. "We might need her again."

Adam drops her and then grabs her at the last second before her feet hit the ground. She blows out a breath, pulling her shirt down once she's on her feet. The moment she meets my gaze, all of her unease melts away. "Relinquish, huh?"

"I thought my dictionary girlfriend might enjoy that one."

"It was a bit Regency-era romance novel, too. 'Unhand the fair maiden.'" She grins. "I loved it."

My family moves in behind her as my teammates line up for the bus. My lips break into a smile. I hadn't realized they'd all stayed.

Win or lose, I always receive proud statements

from my parents, so it's no different from before other than a fresh tinge of excitement in their voices, like they're pleased to show off what they've always known. Or maybe those are my own thoughts cast onto them, but whatever it is, it feels amazing.

I squeeze all of them into a big hug, not letting go until my dad says they have to take off if they want to get home at a decent hour.

"Thank you for coming," I tell them. "Always."

Iz grins. "Just remember we were coming before it was cool."

I muss up her hair, and if she could set me on fire with one look, I'd be burning right now. It makes me want to do it again, especially when she casts a sheepish gaze at my teammates.

Before I can tease her, Len says, "See you at home?"

I pull back on her arm. "Ride with us."

She gives me a wary look. "Won't Coach veto that?"

"Not his star marketer."

She shrugs. "If you think it's okay, then your family can take off from here."

"Good, it's settled."

My parents hug Len, and it hits me how much they genuinely care for her. Their fondness has grown, my mom even tearing up and telling her how proud they are and how much what she did meant to them.

They've taken her in like one of their own, and for Len, who doesn't have a mother and has a strained relationship with her father, it makes my stomach clench. I always knew my parents were cool people, but this... the feelings I already had for her intensify.

They walk off, and I embrace Len from behind. "I wish you could've been there."

Her body freezes. "Excuse me, what?"

"At the game."

She turns in my arms, lashes fanning over her cheeks before smirking up at me. "Zaiah, I was there."

"You weren't with my parents."

"I was in the student seating along with everyone else from Warner. I figured if I was going to write it, I should do it."

My throat closes. "So you saw?"

"I saw."

She looks like she wants to say more, her fist wrapping in my shirt, but then Coach calls for me to get on the bus, so I walk her over. She peers sheepishly at the ground as we approach. I nod toward the entrance, then at her.

Coach gives me a look. "Just this once, James. Get on the bus."

She walks up the stairs ahead of me. "See, I told you he wouldn't like it."

"He'll get over it."

My teammates welcome Len with another string of high fives. Some of them yell out, calling her our "lucky charm." I wish I could see her face, but right now, I want to be in my seat so I can wrap her up in my arms.

"Right here," I whisper in her ear, pointing out my

usual spot. She scoots inside, settling in. It doesn't last long because as I sit, I lift her up, moving into the window seat while I place her on my lap.

She gives me a startled stare, and I grin. The bus fades away until it's only me and her. The urge to kiss her is strong, but there's one thing I have to take care of first. Reaching up, I cup her face in my palm. "I, um... I saw Trish today. She hugged me."

I swallow, waiting for her response. Len doesn't make big scenes—at least, I haven't seen one before—but there's a first time for everything. When she just stares, my stomach squeezes even more. I should've said something when we were alone and not on a bus filled with my teammates.

Finally, she sighs. "I know. I saw."

"You saw?"

She leans into me. "I was waiting for you in the tunnel."

"I pushed her away," I say immediately.

"I know." She touches the zipper of my coat. Her posture switches, though. She pulls away, not meeting my gaze.

"I don't care about her anymore."

"Oh, I know." She waves me off. "It's not that. We had words. She's the same old manipulative bitch. She only came because she saw Warner's socials. A couple of the posts went viral. She knows we're together, though. She was in our apartment."

"Wait, what?" My jaw clenches, my arms holding her tighter.

She nods slowly. "She conned the guy at the front desk. She said some pretty awful things…" She grins. "I got to tell her off. It was… I'm searching for the right word. Liberating. Amazing. She doesn't have an impact on me anymore, and now she freaking knows it."

I tug her toward me to kiss her cheek. "One thing she doesn't know is us. She's too petty. Too self-absorbed. She wouldn't understand a relationship like ours."

Len lays her head on my chest. Underneath us, the bus starts to shake when it maneuvers away from the curb. Adam moves down the aisle, looking like he's going to sit with us, but I shoot him a glare. He takes another seat.

I hold her to me, lazily caressing her arm. "So you lied about being late to the game?"

She brings up her fingers, holding them millimeters apart. "A white lie."

"You had me so confused. Not gonna lie, I was upset."

She tries and fails to retain a straight face. "I thought you were going to explode, especially when you saw Clark text me. But you know now Clark was writing me because of the article, right?"

I'd completely forgotten all about that. I shrug. "I was definitely jealous."

"Ooh," she teases, "big bad jock, jealous. All due to little ol' me?"

I nip at her earlobe. "When Adam raised you in the air, I wanted to rip his limbs from your body."

Pulling away, she gives me a surprised yet impressed look. "How caveman."

"I'm a bit possessive. I know what I got."

"And what's that, Isaiah James?"

I work my hand through her hair. "The kind of girl you don't let go of. The kind of girl you make sure knows how you feel every second of every day. And I am in love with you, Lenore Robertson."

She bites her lower lip. "Well, if you're a caveman, I might be a cavewoman. I had some pretty indecent thoughts earlier."

Brows furrowing, she peers away. I tip her chin up and make her look at me. "If no one else was here, I'd have you straddle my hips and slide down my cock. Over and over. But no one gets any piece of you but me. Not your quick breaths. Not the sexy noises that spill out of your mouth. They're all for me."

Heavy-lidded eyes stare back at me, but we're interrupted by Adam standing up. "Yo, we're all going out tonight. No excuses. We just played a kick-ass game in front of actual people."

Whoops of delight whip around the bus.

"Nice, Adam," Coach says. He stands at the front, rolling his eyes. "You will be gentlemen. If I hear any bad business, I will not hesitate to bench your asses. You will be on your best behavior, and for fuck's sake, no alcohol. Or worse." He points an accusing finger at us. "Maybe I'll do a surprise drug test on Monday."

Adam grins. "It's not a surprise if you tell us, Coach."

Coach points at him. "Think about what that means, son." He peers out over the bus, taking us all in. "I'm so proud of you kids. Way to show them what we're made of."

The answering cheer has Lenore putting her hands over her ears.

We enter Warner, and the guys stand, knocking on the windows and the roof of the bus. The driver honks his horn in long, loud spurts.

I slide Lenore off me to partake in the action. Then it's high fives all around again, my skin on fire. Viral videos, a damn near full crowd, a fucking hat trick, and a girl who supports me more than anything.

Everything is fucking amazing.

I pull Len up, sealing my lips to hers. The guys go nuts. Several of them hit me on the back as I pry her mouth open with my tongue. She gives in but cuts the kiss short, her chest rising and falling. A splotch of red creeps up her cheeks, and I cup her face in my palms. "Sorry."

She peeks at the floor with a grin. "It's okay. I'm glad you're happy."

We sway with the bus braking in front of our practice rink. One day, Warner will have an arena on campus. State-of-the-art everything like the football team has. I can see it now.

The driver honks again, and a wave of cries flies up. The guys and I all look around, and then we stare out the windows. We have a welcome party. A few dozen students wait outside the rink, cheering.

"Holy shit."

The guys start filing off the bus, so I grab my gear and turn, bending over to see everyone greet the guys as they step down the stairs. Pride swallows me whole.

Finally, we're being seen. A thrill shoots through me, and when I get off the bus, people call out my name. I give them a wave, not sure what else to do.

"Feel free to come to my place tonight, James!" a girl shouts. "I'll give you a special score."

I grin, shaking my head. Reaching out, I take Len's hand— *Since when is there hair on her knuckles?*

"Dude," Watt says with a laugh.

"Oh." I turn, searching for Len. I could've sworn she was right behind me, but she's not. I stay where I am, waiting for all the players to pass by when I see her on the sidewalk, blending in with the people who came to welcome us back. "What are you doing?" I ask, waving her toward me.

She doesn't move, her eyes widening a little. I go back and get her, putting my arm around her, but she shies away. "Letting you have your time in the spotlight."

"Hey." I squeeze her shoulders. Her lips thin. Why doesn't she look as happy as the words coming out of her mouth? "Isn't this awesome? I'm going to drop my bag in the locker room, then we'll figure out what we're doing, okay?"

She pulls me a few yards away. "I'm probably going to head back."

"To the arena? Did you forget something?"

"No, to the apartment."

I drop my head. "Seriously? You don't want to come out with us?"

She shrugs half-heartedly.

I step in close. "It won't be like last time. Promise."

She flits her gaze up to mine. Pressing her lips together, she just looks at me, eyes guarded. "Yeah, okay."

"You sure?"

She nods.

"This is going to be great," I tell her, pressing a kiss to her forehead.

"We're all going to Bubbles!" shouts the girl from out front. "Come join us, hockey hotties!"

I shake my head. "I think she's drunk, Len."

"Yeah, something like that."

"Bubbles it is!" I shout back.

Every breath I take is a hit of dopamine. People are still yelling things, so I wave, squeezing Len. "I'll be right back. Do you want to change?"

She doesn't answer, and when I finally look at her, she's staring at her feet. "Do I have to?"

"No, you look great."

"Okay."

"Everything's going to be awesome." I hug her again. "Be out in a couple minutes."

When I run back into the locker room, the guys are still celebrating and talking trash excitedly. "Bubbles, gentlemen. We're all going to Bubbles. A few of you might thank me later."

My teammates high-five each other, and then we go into a Bulldog chant. I can't even describe the feeling. It's a heady, exhilarating mix that makes me want to keep taking a hit off it.

I need more. I will get more.

# CHAPTER THIRTY

Len

*IT'S FINE. EVERYTHING'S FINE. HE DIDN'T MEAN NOT to appreciate me. He's excited. He's overwhelmed. He—*

*He's acting like a fucking jock.*

I wear a path into the sidewalk outside the arena. Minutes tick by like time doesn't exist. Sometimes it's fast, sometimes it's slow. How much time has passed out here waiting for him to come back is as elusive to me as trying to hold on to a cloud.

I should want to go out with him to celebrate, right? That's what a hockey girlfriend does. Or any girlfriend supporting their man. It *is* exciting. I *am* excited.

Actually, that's a lie. My enthusiasm died somewhere between seeing Trish throw herself at him to the women outside his bus screaming his name.

I can't compete with hockey. I never could.

The world tilts. I root myself in place, my hands splaying out as if trying to grasp something to keep me steady.

*I can't compete with hockey.*

Growing up under my father's roof taught me that. My mom couldn't either. That's why she left. Though, that's an assumption. She's never been around to ask, but I'm sure that's why. It became blatantly clear about the time I started to want my own life outside of hockey.

I've done nothing but try to get Zaiah here, to this point. With the video and the emails and the article I wrote. Now I feel like a complete ass. Heartache grips me. All I did was make sure hockey was his priority by helping give him everything he wanted.

I start biting my nails, a habit I thought I'd kicked that apparently rears its head in stressful situations. In the past, I'd bite my nails all the way down until my teeth gnashed against skin and bled. Only the first coppery taste would make me stop, then I'd move on to the next finger.

I force my hands to my side, gripping my leggings so I don't put my nails in my mouth. I should be happy for him. I am happy for him.

My stomach squeezes. Going round and round with this isn't helping. I wanted a simple thank you. Even an acknowledgment. The way he looked at me on the bus... I thought he was going to say something, but he didn't.

Am I being selfish? It's his time. He played the game. All I did was put people in seats.

The doors behind me open, and I spin to find Coach stepping out of the building, a cigarette hanging lazily from one hand. He blocks the calm wind to light it while taking a big drag, leaving nothing but a puff of smoke in its wake.

He sees me, and I don't need to be a nosy reporter to read him. Surprise hits first, then under the glow of the sidewalk lamps, his cheeks redden. "This is our little secret, okay? The way the boys would tease me."

I walk forward. Over the last week, ever since I knew everything was a go with the paper, Coach and I have spoken numerous times on the phone. I even went to his office a few times to coordinate things. Of course, he helped me with Zaiah's footage, too. He's a good man. "Your business is your business." I shrug.

He stares down at the cigarette. "I quit a few years ago, but every once in a while, I have to have one. Tonight was amazing and stressful at the same time. It was about the end of the first period when I was already picturing the pack I had in my desk. Don't ever get addicted to anything, Miss Robertson. It's terrible."

I squeeze my leggings again, the urge to bite my nails rearing up. Fear slices through me and it isn't because I'm hooked on gnawing on my fingers. It's that maybe I'm addicted to Zaiah.

Maybe I'm obsessed with helping him. With making him happy. I've set my own wants and needs aside to focus on other people before...twice. One I grew up with, and one I finally told off tonight. In every relationship I'm in, I end up being the afterthought.

Graduation is coming soon. I should be focused on my own future instead of his. Truthfully, I let people disappoint me time and time again. He's not the only one who's had a win since we've been together, yet when I got a response from the editor, he barely said congratulations. We didn't celebrate. I didn't say, *Hey, let's go out to Bubbles with the drunk dudes who want to hang out with me.*

I swallow the sudden dryness in my throat and give Coach a half-hearted grin. "I'll keep that in mind. Great game tonight."

He leans against the side of the building, smoking the cigarette like he's a teen and his parents are about to come outside and catch him. "You did more for them than I could. They needed butts in seats."

"Why do you think that is?"

Another trail of gray smoke clouds from his lips. "Someone to play for, or even show off in front of. Athletes aren't complicated. They play for themselves, but they also feed off energy. The amount of electricity in that rink tonight couldn't have been duplicated by my before-game speeches or any of their family members telling them to go out there and get 'em. Or Zaiah's family acting like crazy fans. Those all help at first, but then the novelty wears off."

"But won't a screaming crowd eventually become white noise, too?"

"Ahh," he says, pausing to take another drag. "But it's always different. Different opponent, different audience, different noise, different signs in the crowd, and it gets more addictive the higher you go."

I scruff my shoe against the sidewalk. "You think Zaiah can make it?"

"Oh yeah. He's got the goods. Did you see the way he played tonight when he had an audience? When he had the cheers? You did that."

*I almost wish I didn't.*

The moment I think it, I crumple the thought up and throw it away, but the echo of it is still there. The selfish thought bleeds through my body until I feel dead inside.

What if I do only want him to see me? The crowd didn't make the video for him. The people at the game tonight only supported him once. I've been by his side longer.

Maybe that's the difference between Zaiah and me. I want to be seen by one person, and he wants the whole world to see him.

Coach puts out his cigarette against the side of the building, smoking all of it right down in the short time we've been talking.

He winks at me, spraying a mist of cologne over himself and throwing a mint in his mouth before he walks back inside.

What we'll do to hide our defects from people when we should be throwing them out there and letting people choose. Take me or leave me. I am who I am, and I'm not changing.

So what if Coach wants to smoke from time to time? Or if I feel neglected? Right or wrong, it's who we are.

I turn to walk away, heading toward Knightley. Pulling out my phone, I start a text to Zaiah telling him to go without me. I only get two words in when I stop, my feet hitting the pavement reluctantly. Is it duty that makes me want to turn back? To be the good girlfriend? Or maybe I want to leave because subconsciously, I want to punish him because he never celebrated my win with me.

"Len!"

Zaiah runs the few hundred feet I'd crossed within seconds. My name on his lips makes my eyes itch. Anger and jealousy rear up, and it's not a good mix. Battling myself every step of the way twists my stomach, leaving me a confused mess.

"Hey." He reaches for me, moving his fingers up my forearm. "I thought you were waiting for me? I'm going to drive, but if you don't mind, can you drive back? I might want to drink."

"Coach said not to."

He shrugs. "I won't have a lot."

His business is his business. That's the same thing I said to Coach.

A small grin crosses Zaiah's face, and he moves a strand of my hair away from my cheek. When I don't react, he tilts his head. "Something wrong?"

So many things. So many complicated things. It would be near impossible and exhausting to tell him every little thing I'm thinking right now. I'm even annoyed with myself, but I'm right about this. I don't want to be anyone's afterthought. "You never said anything about the article."

Yes, he had a huge win tonight, but so did I. Is this how it's always going to be? I can't celebrate my wins because he's too in his own head about his?

It shouldn't be like that.

"The article was amazing. Look what it did!" He grabs my hands, face lighting up. "I think we made everyone hockey fans tonight."

"We?"

"The team."

I nod slowly. That they did. I got them there, but they pulled off an exciting one-sided win. Suddenly, I'm that little girl again, vying for my father's attention. My nemesis was always hockey. Always.

"What if I told you that one of my articles went viral?"

"That's amazing." The smile stays on his face, but he isn't buzzing like he is with hockey.

"Social media picked it up, and it's been reposted a few hundred times."

"Wow, Len. That's great."

"It's spawned so many reactions."

"Of course it did. Because you're awesome."

I bite my lip. "Zaiah, I'm talking about the article that came out tonight. You already knew it went viral."

He narrows his gaze. "I'm not following, sweetheart."

"I wrote an article that a lot of people read. It's getting a lot of attention. But you're only excited about the consequences of that." Before he can say anything, I keep going. "Which you should be. It's what you wanted to happen. It's what I wanted to happen. Lots of fans. Celebrating, I guess. Throw your name out there more. Right? We wanted all that."

"It could change Warner hockey going forward."

"Exactly!"

He shakes his head. "I'm sorry, I—" One of his teammates calls his name, and he looks behind him, waving and telling them to give him another minute. "They want to leave."

I stand my ground. "Zaiah, I'm not trying to take anything away from you. You played amazing. You always play amazing, and yeah, there was a different player out on the ice tonight with everyone watching, but... You never said anything to me about the article. Look what happened because of it. You're living it. It took a lot of time and effort to arrange everything so you could have this night. Did you read the article when you were in the locker room?"

"No, I was making plans." He pauses. "Are you mad at me?"

My hands turn to fists at my side, my fingernails digging into the skin. "Zaiah, I want to be celebrated. I want your support. I want you to call out my name and tell me how proud you are of me. The past two times

I've had good news, where I've inched closer to my goals, I've gotten nothing from you. Nothing."

He steps back, brow furrowing, scrunching up his face until he doesn't look like himself. "I'm sorry. I'm— I'm sure I said something."

"You didn't, and I don't want to have to tell you to do it. It should be something you just do, Zaiah. Look." I take out my phone, bring up my text thread with Flora, and scroll, showing him all the messages she's sent me with how many views my article has. How many reposts. Nearly every business in town has posted it, too.

"I didn't know. I was playing a game when all this happened. You didn't even tell me you were doing this."

"You've been out of the game for over an hour. You were too focused on puck bunnies waiting for you guys on campus. Why would you think I'd care where they wanted to celebrate? I'm not your wingman, Zaiah."

"Woah," he spits. "Don't insinuate that. I was surprised to see them. That doesn't happen to us."

"So surprised that they're more important than me?"

"You're it for me, Len. You're being jealous. And ridiculous."

His angry words sit like an anvil on my chest. I step back.

He shakes his head. "Not like that. I mean about the girls."

"Well, when you were so busy telling me they were

drunk and listening to where they were going out, you could've been thanking me for writing the article. You could have been reading the article. Without the article, you wouldn't have known you had groupies."

"Why are you doing this tonight? I want to go out and celebrate with everyone, and you're—" He waves in my general vicinity.

"Telling you about something that's hurting me? Sorry to be the issue on your grand night."

"That's not what I meant."

"Then what do you mean? Why do we only celebrate you, Zaiah? That's the problem I'm having. I've helped and helped. I got the footage. I wrote the emails. I did the research to even know that we should do that. I wrote the article that's bringing you and your team all of this tonight. You've been waiting for life to happen to you, and congratulations, I guess that's what happened tonight. All of this..." I throw my arms out wide. Even though the crowd is gone, their ghosts still mock me. "This just happened to you. No one helped you achieve it."

"Thank you," he yells. "You're right, okay? I don't need my incompetence thrown in my face. Fucking thank you. For everything."

"If you don't want it thrown in your face, do better."

His nostrils flare. It kills me to see him angry. He's a good person. I know it. Zaiah would do anything for others, but for some reason, this is his hiccup point.

It's mine, too.

My voice quiets to a whisper. "Why do you think I support you like this? Because I want the same in return. I can't live hockey all the time. I'm not a rink wife, Zaiah. I'll support you and support you and support you, but it can't be one-sided."

His teammates call his name again. He turns, but then stops himself. Swallowing, his Adam's apple moves at a glacial pace.

I don't know what I want him to say or do right now. I'm mad I'm ruining his night, but at the same time, I can't let this go unsaid.

"Look, I'm sorry, Len. I've been selfish. I guess. I don't know what to say to make this better."

"Me neither," I tell him. His teammates call again, and guilt rises up. "Look, you should go."

"Aren't you coming?"

I shake my head. "Not tonight, Zaiah. I'm proud of you, though." My voice catches. "I'm really proud of you."

"I'm proud of you," he echoes, eagerness lacing his voice, but I can't shake the thought that I had to wrangle the compliment out of him. It's as if I had to tie a rope around his focus and pull it toward me to draw it out of him.

"See you later," I tell him.

"Hey, Len. We're good, right?"

"I... I think so," I answer honestly. The area behind my eyes heats, and I have to get out of here before he sees me cry. I can't take him away from celebrating tonight. That wouldn't be cool. No matter how much I want him to come back and hold me all night, I can't keep him away from this moment. "Have fun, okay?"

Turning, I walk away. His teammates call again, angrier this time. The first tear falls, wetting my cheek in a trail that leads all the way past my chin, clinging to my throat.

It hits me how wrong this is. Everything about it. I had a win tonight, too. Instead of going out with my friends, though, I'll spend it crying into my pillow.

And the one person who could make it right went off to celebrate his win. A fact I can't even get mad about.

Maybe I need a real dating coach because this shit is confusing.

# CHAPTER THIRTY-ONE

Zaiah

THE BED SMELLS LIKE...ME.

I push my head deep into the pillow and sniff. No hint of Len's shampoo. Or her body spray. Her scents have disappeared over the last few days. Dejected, I flip to my back and stare at the ceiling.

I already know what I'll find when I walk out into the suite. If she's here, she'll be perfectly cordial. She might even kiss me on the cheek. When asked, she'll say nothing's wrong, but something is. She's checked out. The beginning stages of zombieism or something. There's none of the banter, or the laughs, or anything even close to a genuine smile.

She's going through the motions, and I did that to her.

I throw the covers off and pull on some gym clothes. The weight room has been my friend lately.

That smells awful, too, but at least it doesn't feel like this. Like I somehow broke her. If there was a button I could push, a switch to toggle, I'd make sure it was in the right position.

After realizing she was right, I tried to tell her I'd do better. The day after our infamous win, I tried to have a heart-to-heart, but it was one-sided. At least at the gym, when something weighs heavy, I get some resistance. Some push back.

The aroma of burnt toast greets me as I walk into the kitchen. "Hey."

"Hey," she says with a smile that doesn't reach her eyes.

I bite the inside of my cheek. The excuses she's given me for treating me like a roommate ring through my ears. She's tired. She's busy. She's a thousand other things, but what she never says again is how I let her down. How I took her trust in me—the person she thought I was—and ruined it.

"Did you get something to eat?" I ask, only for something to say.

"Toast. Are you going to the gym?"

"Mm-hmm."

She gets up and places her dirty dish in the sink. "I have some homework."

"It'll be nice when that's over."

"Yeah."

She waves before turning to head to her room. She freaking *waves*.

If she was another girl, I'd think she's giving me the

cold shoulder on purpose, maybe even sleeping around and feels guilty enough to avoid me. But with Len, that's not the case. I doubt she even realizes she's pulled away to where I can't reach her.

The truth is, I drove the wedge between us, and I wish more than anything that I could fix it. However, as she walks into the room and closes the door softly behind her, she's out of my reach again.

I grab a granola bar from the cupboard and a bottle of water before taking off. If I know Adam, he'll be at the gym already. Maybe even with a few other guys on the team who finally woke up when everyone showed to support us. They're suddenly motivated, realizing that what we're actually doing here is playing hockey.

Admittedly, I felt that way a few times, too. It's like that old riddle "If a tree falls in the forest and no one is around to hear it, does it make a noise?" For us, it's "If we get on the ice and no one cares, are we still playing?"

Do we actually care? Are we motivating ourselves internally?

I like to think I was. Though even now, the fire in my belly is at a different level. Flames that, if I keep on stoking, could make an inferno. For fuck's sake, if only I'd told her from the beginning that she reignited my desire. That when I saw how much she cared, the ashes turned to embers. The sparks molded like a phoenix, taking shape out of seemingly nowhere, but it started with her.

My mind is so filled with thoughts, I end up at the

gym in no time. I stand in front of the squat rack, blinking because I forgot my gear. I ate my granola bar on the way, so all I have for my gym session is a bottle of water save a few swallows and me. No back brace. No lifting gloves. No towel.

The familiar melody of banging plates rings in my ears. Spinning in a circle, I spot the bench, take a seat, and bring the bottle to my lips, taking swallow after swallow until I nearly finish the whole thing.

"James, you asshole. You beat me again."

Adam swats me on the back and drops his bag next to the rig. When I don't say anything, he peers over his shoulder. "You good, bro?"

I lift my shoulders, and as Adam does, he turns fully to face me with the look on his face that he's about to start spewing advice. I swear I'm going to start calling him doc. He acts like he's the team therapist.

"Can I ask you a question?"

I look away. I'm halfway to spilling my guts to him anyway, so I say, "Sure."

"You've been cagey about Len lately. Every time someone brings her up, you change the subject. I don't ever see her around either. When we went out, she wasn't there, and you were acting weird as fuck."

"Is there a question in there?"

"There is, but it's a manly question. You have to read between the lines to answer it."

I flip him off. But the truth is, I don't need much prodding. "I think I messed up."

He sighs before pulling another bench next to me

and taking a seat. "If you think you did, you probably did."

I tip my bottle back to take another drink, but it's empty. I drop it next to me, hearing the crackling of the plastic as it hits and rolls against a twenty-five pound plate.

"She's mad. Well, she's not acting mad now, but she called me out after the game, and she hasn't been the same since. I'm losing her," I confess, heart lodging in my throat. "When I ask her, she says we're okay, but I know we're not. She's drifted away, and I don't know how to bring her back. She's the best thing that's ever happened to me."

"Did you tell her?"

I nod. "Literally every day."

"Have you showed her?"

"Showed her?"

"Let's start from the beginning," he says. "What did Len call you out on?"

I shrug like I can't remember, but the truth is, her words have been swirling around me ever since. Every once in a while, they run through me like a cold wind. They're the only thing that has threatened to take out the inferno inside me. Everything flickers, and it feels like a sucker punch to the gut.

"Come on, dude. You want help, right? I can see it."

My shoulders slump. "Well, there were several things." Shuffling my feet, my guilt takes over, and I'm suddenly embarrassed to tell Adam what's going on. It makes me look like a terrible person and a coward. I blow out a breath. "One, I didn't thank her for writing the article. Two, I never celebrate her wins. Three, I've been...selfish."

"So, she's been extremely communicative, then?"

I nod. "It's a heavy list because I didn't know I was doing it, but you didn't let me say the last one. I think four is what broke her."

"Well?"

"I was so excited after we won the game, and I went out even after she told me all the things that were bothering her. I let her go back to the apartment by herself. I was mad."

"Mad?"

"I didn't understand it at the time, and dammit, I felt like it was unfair of her to bring all that up after we'd had such a great game. Literally, the best thing that could've happened to us in the history of Warner, and she wanted to get mad at me."

"So, you were on cloud nine and you didn't give her props for helping you get there?"

"She didn't just help." I kick at something invisible on the gym mats. "I think she did the whole damn thing. We would've stayed cruising along in mediocrity. Not even Coach did what she did.

"She's amazing, Adam. I've only been seeing her for a few months, and she's already done more for me than anyone else. With her, I actually feel like I could play in the minors and then the league. She sees something and does it. It's a fucking talent. No wonder she was mad. I just let things happen to me, and I was excited to celebrate with people who didn't even help me get there."

The air around us intensifies until it's stifling. Sweat dots my temples, and I peer around to see if there's a reason why it's so damn humid in here, or if this is my body's reaction to me fucking things up with Len.

"Maybe I'm not the person she thinks I am."

"Timeout." Adam moves his palms into a T position. "Let's not play the woe-is-me card because it sounds like that's why Len is upset, along with the fact that you haven't appreciated her. I'm not going to comment on what you should've done or hammer the nail down that you messed up, but do you want to save this?"

"Of course I fucking do."

"Then you need to fight for her. It's what she'd do."

I give him a strange look.

"Listen, you got everything you wanted, right? People came to the game. If you're anything like me, people have been coming up to you on campus. They joke about wanting an autograph, and they promise they're going to be there next week, and you might have even had some girls ask you to their rooms. Unless that's only because I'm better looking than you." He beams at me. "Those people? That recognition you wanted? Faceless. Nameless. They're good for a short thrill, but there's nothing like the way I saw Len look at you."

I glare at him, and he lifts his hands into the "don't kill the messenger" position.

"I'm just saying, the way she looked at you at Bubbles? I could tell there was no way that other news geek would last. She was a goner for you. If I saw her now, I'd probably see the same. She's waiting for you to step up. Man, what I wouldn't give to have someone fight at my side like that, and it sounds like she wants the same from you, along with some appreciation."

"What if I'm too late? You don't understand the way things are right now. She's retreating, I can feel it."

"Give her what she wants and see what happens. Don't stand idly by."

His words hit me like a Mack truck. She said something similar. I've been letting her move further and further away, lamenting that I messed up. I should've been fighting for her the entire time.

"I should do something big."

He stands, hitting me on the shoulder. "You should."

My mind starts whirring. I can't only tell her I'm sorry and that I'll do better. Those are mere words. As Adam said, I haven't shown her anything. I haven't proven to her that I mean it.

"But what should I do?"

He chuckles. "You realize I don't have a girlfriend, right?"

"Why am I listening to you, then?"

"I've been wondering that this whole time."

His snarky grin makes me shake my head. I have to

show her what she means to me and support her, all while managing my hockey emotions. Prove to her that I can be the man she thinks I am. In doing so, I might actually become that man.

Now, if a half-decent idea fell into my lap, I'd be happy.

I stand, encouraged that I have a way forward. I don't know why it took me so long to figure it out. I don't play hockey this way. I don't wait for the puck to come to me like it's a gift, I go out there and get it.

I'm going to go out there and get Len. No matter what.

# CHAPTER THIRTY-TWO

Len

CURLED UP IN MY SHEETS WITH THE TV ON, I hear the suite door open and close. Before, I'd run out there and ask Zaiah how his day was. Even before we started dating, I'd make some excuse to go out there to be next to him.

Instead, I stuff my head into my pillow and wonder when he's going to get sick of my bullshit and break it off with me. I said some horrible things. I basically said I didn't like hockey. Of course he would want to celebrate that day. Why did I have to bring it up at all?

This stupid thought stays with me, biting like a piranha, taking little chunks out of me each time with every misstep.

Maybe we aren't right for each other. Maybe the fact that I love him actually doesn't matter. I tried too hard. I wanted too much. I tried to force a puzzle piece into a slot that didn't fit.

In my gut, though, it doesn't feel that way. If that were true, why would I be lying in my bed, miserable, watching *The Mighty Ducks* over and over, trying to connect to anyone who plays hockey when I really only want one person who plays hockey?

With bated breath, I wait in agonized hope to see if he comes to my door.

I've had my heart broken before, but never by someone I gave it to so willingly. So completely. I don't even want to know what it will feel like. If he decides what I did was too much for him.

In the main suite, I hear him rummaging around. The worry—the guilt—sits heavy like a dark rain cloud on my shoulders.

A soft knock sounds on the door, and I gulp, sitting up in bed. The air charges around me, and I'm too paralyzed to move.

Whatever relationships are like, I know it's not this.

Gathering all my courage, I slide my feet to the floor and get up. Slowly, I walk to the door and put my hand on the knob. Another breath later, I'm twisting it open to...nothing.

It's dark. Zaiah isn't waiting on the other side for me, and I'm stuck wondering if I imagined the whole thing. Maybe I wanted him to come to me so badly that I conjured it up at the same time the Ducks were doing the flying V for the first time.

I start to shut the door when a tiny flicker flares to

life in the kitchen, a halo of light that has me swallowing. Zaiah moves the flame to a candle. It catches to life before shifting to another candle. Soon, the kitchen is alive in a soft glow.

Stepping forward, I hit something with my socked feet. Rounded dark spots litter the floor in a trail through the living room to the kitchen. I take one step, then another. It isn't until I'm closer to the kitchen that the red petals pop out in a subdued haze. I lightly walk over them, a few of them fluttering away from me, until it brings me right to him.

I stop short of his shoes, my stomach tightening. Then he reaches for me, putting his hand under my chin and lifting so that I meet his gaze.

"W-what's this?"

"You just walked a pathway to the new and improved Isaiah James." He swallows like he's nervous. His gaze is earnest as he stares right into my eyes until my insides flip. I peer away from the intensity of it all, and he nudges me back. "The trail led you here, and it always will. Every rose petal is a promise I'm making to you, Lenore Robertson. What I did wasn't right. I took you for granted without giving you any of the credit. I saw the world through the eyes of someone so driven I didn't take the time to look around and see what the determining factor was. *You.*"

"I think maybe I—"

He shakes his head, cutting me off. "There's nothing you said that wasn't true. I'm ashamed of myself for doing that to you. You did so many things for me, and I want to be that person for you. I think I got caught looking through a pinpoint, and all I saw was what I was going through.

"I need to make this up to you because you being indifferent to me is slowly killing me inside, sweetheart. I want your laughs and your smiles. Hell, I'll even take your anger and putting me in my place as long as you're not indifferent."

"I didn't mean to."

He takes my shoulders. "None of this is your fault. What you said to me was spot on. You deserve nothing less than the best, and what I gave you wasn't even worthy of a third stringer."

I nearly smile at that, glad that I understand what he's saying, hockey references and all.

"So," he says, stepping back, "I'm doing something I should've done a while ago." He waves his hand to the kitchen table where a spread is laid out. My favorite pizza from the place in town, including the rolls dripping with garlic sauce. "This is your celebration dinner for hearing back from that magazine editor."

Walking over, he pulls out a chair for me, and I sit. When he moves to the other side, the candlelight flickers, reaching toward him, and I understand how that flame feels. Zaiah's a magnet, and whatever it is he attracts, I think I'm made up of mostly that.

MONDAY

I walk out of my bedroom, my feet nudging against something on the floor, pushing it away. Peering down in the early morning light, I find the rose petals from last night gone, and in the very spot where Zaiah kissed me good night sits a small white box with a clear top.

In the box, a word is written in thick, creamy hard chocolate. *Dreams.*

I open the attached notecard.

My dearest Len,
    I'm not surprised the editor wanted to talk to you on the phone. Your talent jumped out at him from the thousands of articles he gets every day, and you'll continue to amaze other editors, too. Watch out, publishing industry, Len isn't messing around.

The backs of my eyes heat. I hold the box to my chest, acknowledgment ringing through me.

He gets it. He understands.

TUESDAY

The newsroom buzzes. Flora bought a clickety-clack keyboard, and at first, it drove me up the wall, but the sound is kind of soothing...as long as she's typing.

When she stops, its absence is deafening, and I find myself staring off, thinking of Zaiah.

Every day that passes, he's making the past up to me, adjusting our puzzle pieces to the perfect fit.

Sneakily, I pull open my bag and break off a piece of my *Dreams* candy bar. After looking around to see who's watching, I pop it into my mouth. Flora gets handsy with sweets. Like she has a sweet tooth sixth sense, she looks over at me. I stop chewing until she looks away, then I start chomping down again, the milk chocolate nearly melting in my mouth.

I'm still hiding behind my laptop screen, trying to keep out of her line of sight, when the newsroom door opens and closes. I hear several oohs and aahs from my fellow journalists, so I poke my head up.

A dozen red roses sit in the crook of a delivery man's arm. Clark comes out of his office, and then he points at me with a scowl. I can unpack that later, but when the man starts walking toward me, I tense. I've never had flowers delivered before.

"Lenore?"

"That's me," I croak out.

He sets the flowers on the long table, and I eke out a thank you while standing to admire them, but suddenly, a small radio clatters to the table, and the delivery man's coat flips out as he spins a 360 like a graceful ballerina. I nearly shriek until he lands in a pose, one hand stretched high to the ceiling, remaining still for some time before his hand shoots out to hit *play* on the radio.

A note rings out, and I take a step back, nudging my chair out of the way. The delivery man turned dancer flashes the inside of his coat again. With ease, he shrugs it off, turns it inside out, and pulls it on once more before zipping it up. He stands still, showing off the entire picture. A tux. Well, a sublimation print tux. Somehow, he has a hat in his hand now and poses with his head down, the bass on the radio ramping up.

A few feet away, Flora giggles. I shoot her a look, as if to say "What is happening?" When I peek over, though, I spot Zaiah above her head. Hands pressed against the glass, he stares in at me, the softest smile on his face.

A flurry of movement in front of me catches my attention again, as well as a shout from the dancer's mouth that has me jumping. A rendition of Michael Jackson's "Bad" starts playing, except he doesn't sing *bad*, he sings *rad*.

The dancer grabs his crotch and does another spin, dropping into a split before pushing back up again.

"Oh my God!"

He sings about the sky being the limit, but when he hits the chorus, he says, "You know, you're rad. You're rad. You know it."

I double over, laughing. Everyone in the newsroom starts clapping and cheering as the singer-slash-dancer-slash-delivery guy does his thing. At the end, he does another spin and grabs my hand. "Congratulations on the article, Lenore."

Then, with fluidity I thought only known to cats,

he turns his jacket back the other way, hides his hat, and walks out the same way he came in.

"What in the world..."

Flora runs over, as well as a few of my other coworkers. I try to see above their heads, but when I search the glass for Zaiah again, he's gone.


THE FOLLOWING *Tuesday*

Zaiah yawns next to me on the couch. For over a week, I've had surprises every day. Sometimes, it's a little thing like a card thanking me for getting the laptop so we could make the video. Other times, it's big things like the dinner or the delivery dancer. My roses from that day still sit on the table in a beautiful blue vase. He takes them out every morning to refresh the water before putting them back in and arranging them again.

"You ready for bed?" I ask, trying to dismiss the sudden tightening of my stomach.

He nods slowly, helping me from the couch and walking me to my bedroom door. It's as if he's dropping me off from a date, even though we only walked a few feet. He takes my head between his palms, his hold like a caress. "I love you, Lenore."

"I love you, too."

He presses his lips to me softly, like he's done for the last week, but this time, I hold back on his hand when he tries to leave. He raises his brows, his gaze dropping to where I hold on to him.

384

I press into his hand, needing it to ground me as nerves skate over my skin. "Zaiah, why haven't you... come to my bed?"

Fully facing me again, his fingers immediately intertwining with mine. "I'm trying to show you the man I can be."

"Does the man you can be involve lying next to me?"

My heart pounds, the fear of rejection coating my tongue. Worry that I've pushed him too far away hovers like a shroud.

He moves closer, winding his arms around my back. He's in my space, but not suffocatingly so, like the two of us are in our own cocoon. "You think I don't want to?"

I lick my lips, gaining myself some time. "I don't know what I think. I just miss you."

"I've been waiting for you to feel comfortable, sweetie." His hot breath hits my mouth.

My eyes flutter closed. The bond between us has only gotten more palpable. Without me realizing what the issue really was, Zaiah solved it. I wanted to feel seen, to be heard, to feel loved. And like he knew the sound of my next breath, he gave it to me. Everything that was a mess inside myself, he knew, untangling the myriad of feelings, smoothing them out, and breathing life into them with every note, flower, and caring word.

He treated me like the woman I wanted to be.

"You've been showing me the man you truly are. Not who you could be, Zaiah, who you are."

He threads his fingers through my hair, capturing my neck in his large palm. "I'm only catching up to you. How do you think I learned to be this way? I took note of what you did for me. The way you believed in me. The way you celebrated with me night after night on the ice, cheering me on.

"Lenore, I'm this way because you were this way first. My North Star. My guiding light. I haven't been the best boyfriend, too wrapped up in myself, but that's gone now. You showed me I can be a person who goes after their dreams while supporting someone else because that's what you've been for me since day one. Look at you. You're perfect."

I run my hand up his chest, stroking the length of his corded neck. The way I love him is breathless. It used to scare me, like maybe he'd slip out of my grasp and leave me broken.

But I'm not scared anymore.

"Zaiah." I swallow, my throat suddenly parched. I force my breaths out in even measures. "Sleep with me?"

"You sure?"

"One hundred pucking percent."

The intensity ratcheting between us overflows until he grins. "So we're clear, is there going to be more than sleeping?" he asks, leading me into my room, his touch never wavering.

I don't have to answer because I slip away to take my shirt off, leaving it nonchalantly on the floor behind me as I walk to the bed.

When I turn, Zaiah is feasting on me like a hungry shark, and that look, it's as good as any card he signed with love. The spark in his eyes ignites a heat inside me, and while he slowly takes his own shirt off, I move my way up the bed.

We needed the gut-wrenching honesty, the pain and worry. The absolute relief I feel to have gotten through that and still be looked at with that same ferocity in Zaiah's eyes says so much. In fact, it says everything.

There isn't anything that can tear us apart when we grow together. Two people who care enough to work with each other. Who want to see the other win in the best of ways. Who will be by the other's side while they do it and be the first to don the party hat.

Zaiah has left no doubt that he'll be that person for me.

My body flushes with desire. "I'm going to need you to hurry," I breathe, nearly out of my mind with want.

A ghost of a smile crosses his lips. "I think I'm going to need to take my time. Savor you. Love you."

He starts unbuttoning his pants, a tantalizing tease as he slides them down his hips in a slow, seductive caress.

"Zaiah James."

"Lenore Robertson..." He waits until I meet his eyes, then he crawls up the bed, whispering beautiful things into my skin, his lips like a feather, his touch like a flame.

And there, we remind each other of the rawness of our love. We come together even more completely than we have before. All the barriers stripped away. All our flaws showing in beautiful simplicity, and we take each other, faults and all.

# CHAPTER 33

Zaiah

LEN AND I WALK HAND IN HAND AWAY FROM THE main lobby of Serenity Ranch and Spa. The sun lingers in the sky longer now than it did when we were here before, clinging to the horizon. Next to me, my little writer is a million miles away, worrying over her lip. A sure sign she wants to break out the laptop when we get back to our spot.

We walk past the other sites, RVs parked with people eating late dinners or staring out over the lake. I was able to reserve us the same site as last time, so once she walks up to the perch above the stone building, she'll have the most beautiful sunset to write whatever her beautiful mind is conjuring.

Squeezing her hand, I tell her, "I'll bring up some popcorn."

Slowly, she gives me one of her heart-melting smiles. "You're the best."

I take her words to heart, letting them fill me. Giving myself a pat on the back sounds cliché and dumb, but it's more than that. Making her smile, making her feel loved, is one of the greatest accomplishments of my life.

The path in front of us curves and twists, like the contents of my stomach. I've been waiting for the perfect time to pull this moment off. I thought I wanted her at my game, in my jersey, screaming my name, but it was the moments between the highlights that stuck out the most. The little things that grew bigger and bigger with time.

We walk the rest of the way in silence, the lake insects singing us their songs. Every once in a while, it's punctuated by the deep bellow of a toad or the swoop of a bird's wings as it glides to a stop on the surface of the lake.

When we return to the site, Lenore immediately moves into the RV to grab her laptop while I head to the outdoor kitchen. I take out the little popcorn packets I stored in there earlier and ready my cell phone to play.

I can't keep a smile off my face when her footsteps sound behind me. Spinning on my heels, I'm greeted with another grin. She reaches up on her toes to kiss my cheek, and when she turns, I discreetly push play on the audio file.

"And now, your starting player. The formidable,

the creative, the incredible..." The announcer from the rink draws the word out for more than a few seconds. Lenore stops, her foot already on the first step of the stairs, and she turns to peer over her shoulder as the announcer says: "The most talented writer in the world, Lenore Robertson." He finishes her name with the same flourish he uses when he announces the starting lineup at my games.

Her gaze morphs from confusion to excitement to bliss, and I'm brought back to when she did this for me, using her own voice in the hallway of our suite. Such an insignificant moment to some, but to me, it meant everything. In that one exchange, she told me she was proud of me, she told me she was thinking of me, and she told me that she thought what I did mattered.

She saunters toward me. "You got RC to say that?"

I nod, pausing the audio file. In the time I look away, she's already on me, throwing her arms around my shoulders. "Do you really think I'm the most talented writer in the world?"

"Who else would it be?"

"Oh, I don't know. There's about a few hundred thousand writers in the world."

"I like your chances."

"You're biased," she says, moving impossibly closer.

"So?"

She peers at my lips before moving forward. A bubble encapsulates us as I work my mouth over hers, savoring the caress, the feel, the emotion. It's not just a kiss. It's a promise.

Too early, she pulls away, but she's still smiling. "Do you want to know why I was a hundred miles away?"

"Because you have a story idea in your head, and if you don't write it down, you'll forget, and no matter what you come up with next, you'll think it's not as good as the idea that slipped through your fingers."

"Poetic."

"I've been living with you for months. It's bound to rub off."

She shuffles her feet. "Actually, I caught a glimpse of a notification I received when we were in the lobby, and I wanted to look at it to see if it was something worth telling you about."

I give her a look. "Okay…"

"Let me ask you a question. When was the last time you checked the views on the YouTube video?"

I side-eye her. "In forever." If it happens, it happens. I don't need to agitate myself to death over it, choosing instead to focus on the things I can control.

"You should check it," she says, shrugging like it's no big deal.

My brain worries I might obsess again. Falling into old patterns might be easy, I don't know. But when Len gives me a nod, I know I should.

Pulling out my phone, I connect to the Wi-Fi. I don't even have the video open in my tabs anymore, so I have to go searching for it. My brain conjures up a few possible numbers since she must be telling me this because people have viewed it, right? She wouldn't have me open the video to a big, fat goose egg.

The page loads, and my eyes bug out of my head. *Surely this isn't right.* I refresh the page. When the number goes up by two instead of decreasing by tens of thousands, I check the video title to make sure I have the right one. But there it is. Me, in my hockey gear, smiling at the camera.

My stomach flips. "This can't be right."

Her smile has already stretched wide. "When my article came out in the magazine, people were salivating over seeing the video." She moves next to me. "Look, there's a few hundred comments, Z."

"But—"

"I made the video public because your story wasn't just yours anymore. It was so many others', too. Past hockey players, young kids, they all wanted to see you, to know you."

I peer at her, and she's blinking rapidly. The moment she locks gazes with me, a single tear falls. "There's something else, too."

Pulling out her phone with shaking hands, she brings up her email. She taps the most recent one, then hands the phone over to me.

I read her screen, my heart beating like a drummer on crack.

I read it again to be certain I read it correctly. "It's—"

Glancing up, I spot Lenore with her fists on her face, knuckles obscuring her mouth like she's trying not to say anything, but then she bursts. "We started that email account when we signed up for YouTube, and it automatically added it to my phone. The comments started pouring in yesterday."

"The day your article released."

"This came in just now. Look, Zaiah, the Rochester Renegades. A farm team. A—"

"They want me to try out." My voice isn't even recognizable to me. It's so filled with wonder and awe. "You did this."

She shakes her head. "No, you did this. The little boy who didn't want to get off the ice. The teenager who signed with Warner. The man who never stopped trying. You did this, Zaiah."

I wipe my hand down my face. I don't even know what to think. Scooping her up, I spin with Len in my arms. "*We* did this," I whisper in her ear, overwhelmed with every feeling I thought this moment would be.

When I let her down, I shout into the air, pumping my arm. Birds fly off the lake, and I'm pretty sure I violated quiet hours, but *holy shit*. My hockey career isn't over.

I have a lifeline.

"I guess we make a pretty good team."

Spinning, I eye her up as she leans against the countertop. "Are you kidding me? We make the best pucking team."

"He seems pretty impressed," she says, pocketing her phone again.

A balloon inflates inside me. "I'm going to do it," I

tell her. "If not in that city, then another. I'm going to be on the winning side of the statistic you wrote about. I know it for sure."

The look on her face couldn't be prouder. It might have taken me a hell of a long time to get here, but I'm finally here. I'm not talking hockey either. I'm talking determination and belief. "I hope you're ready to stay a hockey girlfriend, sweetheart."

For a split second, worry overtakes me. What would this mean for her? What—

She walks forward, sealing her lips to mine. It's short and sweet and infused with so much meaning. "All I need is a laptop...and you."

I have to catch my breath. "You're serious?"

"Would I joke about hockey?"

"But—"

"But you, Zaiah," she says, placing a finger over my lips. "It's you."

A million thoughts swirl around me in a tornado of emotion. I know what it means to her to say those words. She's gone all in with me, and I take that realization with a steadfast protectiveness. "I won't let you down."

"I know you won't."

Her phone buzzes in her pocket as I lift her from the ground. Her feet slide around me easily, and I kiss her. I kiss her until my lips strain, until I want to take her back inside the RV, until she knows that I'll do everything in my power to be the man she deserves.

She breaks away, her breaths coming out in pants. "My phone is going crazy."

"I thought you were just happy to see me."

"It could be more teams."

The thought excites me, but not as much as sharing this moment with Len. I slip her phone out of her pocket and set it on the counter, then I carry her upstairs, her legs still wrapped around me, until we get to the half-moon bed.

We crawl up it, situating ourselves with the best view of the lake I've ever seen. The burnt orange of the horizon plays over the glassy water below. It looks like a postcard.

"I used to sit up at night, watching the stars, dreaming about this," I tell her.

She snuggles in closer. "You deserve it."

We sit in silence until the pretty colors recede and the stars are the brightest thing in the sky. If I knew then what I know now, I would've asked for this. For someone to share the good moments and the not-so-good moments. That's what life is. A mixture of both.

"I should've wished for you."

"You don't have to," she says sleepily. "I'm right here."

# AUTHOR NOTE

I am always overwhelmed to think that anyone is reading what I write. If you've gotten this far, it means you have, and for that, I can't thank you enough.

Zaiah and Len were such a ball to write. Their banter, Zaiah's family, the love they shared—it made it a breeze and a joy to sit down every day to get their story out of my head and onto something tangible.

If you also enjoyed their story, please consider writing a review to share your thoughts with others. It would mean everything to me to get their story out there.

Also, virtual high-fives to anyone who could hear the *Pride and Prejudice* quote in their head because they, too, have watched the 1995 BBC version so many times. So. Many. Times. You're my people.

# ABOUT THE AUTHOR

E. M. Moore is a USA Today Bestselling author of Contemporary and Paranormal Romance. She's drawn to write within the teen and college-aged years where her characters get knocked on their asses, torn inside out, and put back together again by their first loves. Whether it's in a fantastical setting where human guards protect the creatures of the night or a realistic high school backdrop where social cliques rule the halls, the emotions are the same. Dark. Twisty. Angsty. Raw.

When Erin's not writing, you can find her dreaming up vacations for her family, watching murder mystery shows, or dancing in her kitchen while she pretends to cook.

76537506R00238